I'm dedicating this to my sister Sonia Cook, whose patience in proof reading my work knows no bounds.

HOW WE CAME TO BE HERE

A novella triple

Sarah Burchett-Cook

OGGW Publishing

ISBN-13: 9781068747953

CONTENTS

HOW WE CAME TO BE HERE

A Novella Triple

1) **The Reluctant Vampire**
   (I'm dead – what the hell…)

2) **Sasquatch on Holiday**
   (I'm a great hairy lummox – what the hell…)

3) **Grey Witch**
   (I'm a witch – what the hell…)

Narrator:

An Englishman, a Scotsman and an Irishman walk into a bar... Hold on a moment – NO WAY. So okay, I know, that's all a bit predicable. In which case, how about this instead:

A vampire a witch and a sasquatch walk into a bar – better? I hope so, and now let's picture the scene.

It's night – it has to be, otherwise – vampire – poof! But no one's looking at him anyway. After all why would they? There's an eight-foot sasquatch walking in next to him for goodness sake. All heads turn to the big, hairy guy. What's he doing in an English bar? How did he get here? Didn't someone notice him at immigration? Perhaps they thought he was an extra from the latest Sci-Fi film or something.

Of course, we want to hear about the others too. It's not every day a vampire orders a Guinness. I have to say, he's looking a bit pale, perhaps he needs the iron – wait a minute, what am I saying? Of course he's pale, he's a vampire – he's dead!

And what's a self-respecting witch doing in such company? Maybe she's done mixing with a load of 'hippy-go-lucky', (no I didn't mis-spell that – I meant hippy), coven members with all their herbs and crystals and chanting. Yep, I think I'd rather spend my time with a vamp and a squatch too.

*****

The night moves along and the unlikely group of companions sit around a table telling their respective stories. Nobody's watching them any more. So typically British, the rest of the clientele shrug the matter away with that 'seen it all before' approach, and bend their thoughts to their drinks and nibbles.

Talking of 'nibbles' the vampire is about to begin his story...

BOB THE VAMPIRE:

The pub was full of people. Walking in with Kobbi, in full-on sasquatch mode, beside me caused a bit of a stir, but not for long. I scanned the main bar as we walked to our table. A group of seven witches sat at the long table with four warlocks. There were a couple of vampires huddled up close in a corner nook, three fae at a table by the big bay window – you don't see many of those around, and a pair of, what I thought might be werewolves, perched on stools at the bar. I couldn't tell for sure. The moon was waning at the moment, so they seemed very human. The rest of the clientele were, as far as I knew, all human – but I wouldn't stake (no pun intended) my unlife on it.

Kitha was already waiting for us at a small table in the middle of the room nursing a glass of something long and cool.

"Top up?" I asked her.

She downed what was left in the glass and handed it to me, never taking her eyes off Kobbi.

I went to the bar and ordered something called a spritzer for Kitha, three pints of beer for Kobbi, and a bottle of Guinness for myself, then joined the others.

Introductions done, we all decided to tell our respective stories, and I volunteered to go first – get it out of the way. Anyway, here we go…

THE RELUCTANT VAMPIRE

What happens when your life abruptly ends,
yet somehow it's NOT the end?

A Bit of Preamble:

I have to admit, I was the very embodiment of everyone's idea of Mr Average. Average height, average weight, average to look at, doing an average job with an average salary. My career as an insurance assessor didn't thrill me, but it paid the bills at my average semi-detached house. I was married to an average woman (sorry love!), no kids, but after eight years, it wasn't working out for me – or the missus. I suspected her of having someone else 'on the side', so when I followed her one night on one of her 'outings', I was more than a little shocked when some crazy guy grabbed me, pulled me into a back street – and wait for it – the psycho actually bit me on the neck – how weird is that? I'll fill you in on the details of course, but in reality, that was the day everything changed. My name is Robert – Bob for short – and this is my story...

CHAPTER 1 – MORTAL COIL

I'm Dead – What the Hell!

October 1979: I'd always taken the bus to work. It was cheaper and easier than driving. The buses and taxis in the bus lane moved along when the main lanes suffered the usual morning jams heading into the city – why they call it 'rush hour' when absolutely nobody can 'rush' anywhere I'll never understand? Parking in the city cost and arm and a leg too – so the bus it had to be. It also meant I could sit and read on the hour and a half long journey.

Oh, sorry I'm being boring – typical! I just wanted to tell you about the last day I was bound by my mortal coil, so to speak.

Anna, that's the missus, stopped doing my packed lunches about two years before. It was just another thing about my married life that had ended. Relations in the bedroom had long since ceased. I can't even remember the last time we made love. I guess that's indicative of how dull even that had become – for both of us.

I'd had my suspicions about Anna's 'outings', as she called her nights on the town, for quite some time. She'd stopped telling which of her girlfriends she was going to the club with, and several times I walked in on telephone conversations – that she cut off abruptly in my presence.

That day, as I sat in the bus heading into work, I pondered my dysfunctional marriage. Typically I was quite stoic about it, but it was our eighth wedding anniversary, and memories of happier days came to me in a series of painful blows. I wasn't normally one to get worked up over things, but by the time I'd got into the office that day, I was hyped up and determined to find out for sure if I was right about Anna's nocturnal activities. I forged a plan to follow her.

The day went by in a blur. I performed my work duties in a kind of autopilot mode. For once, I couldn't wait for the day to end so that I could put my plan into action.

"I'll be off now then Bob. Don't wait up," said Anna – all dolled-up, and on her way out the door.

"Okay sweetie." *Why did I still call her that?*

As soon as she was out the door, I grabbed my coat, slid my shoes on, and headed out behind her. I half expected a car to be waiting, not sure what I'd have done then, but no. She walked down into our local town centre. I ducked into a shop doorway as Anna headed for the curb to cross the road – perhaps I was getting a bit too close, but I don't think she saw me. I waited, and crossed over once she was well on her way up the street on the other side. It started to rain. She put up her brolly; I pulled my coat collar up higher – all the better to hide my face without seeming too suspicious to passers-by.

Someone was walking towards her, a man in a light mac. *Huh! She's screwing around with Columbo*. They greeted each other and embraced.

The man looked in my direction as he suddenly seemed to notice the creep who'd got a little too close, so I paused and pretended to be looking at something on a piece of paper from my pocket. My heart was thumping – had I been seen? Why was I in a panic? I was the one being cheated on after all.

I couldn't look in their direction as it might seem a bit too obvious, so I quickly turned back the way I'd come, with a plan to rush home and get settled before Anna got home – whenever that would be.

But too late for a quick getaway. Out of the blue, an arm reached for me, and the next thing I knew I was being dragged into the darkness of a side street. If my heart had been beating fast before, it was nothing to the way it was racing now. My chest hurt and my breathing came in great gasps. I shouted, but there was no one to hear me, or if they did, they weren't about to get involved. I struggled in an attempt to dislodge the arm-lock, but to no avail, the owner of the offending arm was unnaturally strong, I couldn't budge, not even a little bit. My feet tried to find purchase on the pavement, but I was being dragged much too fast to get them under me. *I remember that feeling of sheer terror as if it was yesterday*. Then suddenly we stopped. A man in a black coat, black hat and black gloves, yet whiter than white face, had thrust me around and was now staring at me with a toothy grin. I say 'toothy' because, no kidding, his teeth were like fangs. But it was his eyes that drew my gaze. I couldn't resist gawping into them. Black holes in a ring of fire, was the best way to describe them. I was paralysed by fear, a trickle of sweat dripped into my eye.

The strange man held me tight by the tops of my arms. I couldn't move and, mesmerised, I couldn't look away. Slowly but surely he opened his mouth, just a little too wide to be normal. Almost gently he moved a hand from my arm, and used it to tip my head to one side, then, with a sharp prick of those unnatural fangs he bit down. I could feel hot blood dripping down my neck, my body a rag doll. My mind filled with images of the past, they say that about the dying, don't they? Slowly the images faded until blackness took over.

CHAPTER 2 – NEW AWAKENING

I awoke the next morning in an unfamiliar place. I was on the floor of what appeared to be a shop. It clearly wasn't in use as the abandoned shelving was all but empty – just a couple of old rusty cans, a rag and a filthy dustpan and brush.

I put my hand to my neck. No wounds – how could that be?

I stood. It was dark, though somehow I could see everything clearly, as if I wore night-vision glasses. The windows were boarded up, and remnants of post, mostly junk mail by the looks of it, sat untidily under the front door. I had to get out of here. Heading for the front door, I heard a rustling, and a pattering. My head swung to the skirting board by the side wall, where a pair of mice scurried about. Before I knew what I was doing, I was on them. They were a squishy, bloody mess in my hands. I was about to lift them to my mouth – *can you believe that?* Then revulsion took over. Throwing the little corpses down, I rubbed my hands down my trousers. How could I possibly have considered eating the mice – no, not eating, I just wanted to suck out their blood – Yuk! What was the matter with me? I needed a shower, that much was certain.

Back to the front of the shop, and just about to pull open the door, a deep voice drifted over. "I wouldn't do that if I were you."

A ripple ran down my spine and I stopped dead in my tracks, turning slowly towards the sound. One of the shadows moved. It manifested into the weirdo that abducted and bit me the previous night. My emotions tripped over themselves, from surprise, to fear, then curiosity and finally settling on anger.

"Who the hell are you? What did you do to me? Why? Why did you bring me here? Why shouldn't I leave? I certainly don't want to stay here – with you!"

He moved a little closer.

I took an involuntary step back, shaking like the wimp I was.

There were a few moments of silence before he spoke again. Then, "I have a question for you. Why didn't you suck the mice dry? You clearly wanted to."

Incredulity was the next emotion on the agenda. "What? No. Of course I didn't. That's disgusting." I definitely needed to get out of here, so I turned back to the door.

"If you open that door, you'll die a painful, fiery death."

"What?" I said again.

"You are not the man you were."

"What the hell is that supposed to mean?"

Again he responded with questions not answers. "How do you feel?"

That's normally one of those questions people ask out of politeness, but don't really want you to answer with anything but a brief 'fine thanks how are you?' but this time I had the feeling he meant it, and I stopped moving as I gave it serious thought.

"Actually, I feel kind of weird. There's no pain from what you did to me last night, or in fact, from my usual bad back and dodgy knee, which is all a bit odd, but at the same time, I'm ravenously hungry and so thirsty I could drink a river."

"And the mice?"

I scanned about the room for them suddenly wanting to suck their tiny bodies of what little blood they had. I was desperate to do that.

The man just laughed.

For a moment I had forgotten he was even there as the

desire to find the mice took over. His empty mirth shocked me back to the moment, and I stared at him as he edged closer. I could make out his features now. His face wasn't as white as I remembered, nor were his eyes so creepy, in fact they looked blue now. I could hardly believe what I found myself thinking, so I said it aloud to consolidate the thought.

"You're a vampire. You fed on me, and now I'm a vampire."

"Bravo," he said, clapping his hands in what seemed like genuine delight.

Then another thought struck me. "That's why I can't go outside. It's daylight and… and I can never see daylight again." Of all the implications of my predicament, this was the one that crashed in on me at that moment. My anger flared again. I tried to speak, "you…you.. agh!" Was all I could manage. An uncharacteristic flare of crazed violence pulsed through me and I rushed him.

He grabbed my arms, just as he had the previous night, and held me fast. He was taller than me, so my feet dangled in the air.

"You are weak. You will be until you feed, and you must feed soon."

My head turned back to where the dead mice lay mangled on the floor.

"They would make a nice little snack to tide you over, but tonight you must feed. The first blood-drinking for a vampire is the most critical. You body is still largely human, and will not survive if you don't consolidate your vampiric body. Tonight, you feed or truly, and permanently die.

CHAPTER 3 – FIRST BLOOD

His name was Gordon. Can you believe that? 'Gordon the Vampire' – like something from a horror-comedy show. I asked him why he'd 'sired' me, he said it was because he wanted company. He was bored – well thanks a bunch! And hey, I hate to tell you this, but you dipped out. You've turned the dullest person in the neighbourhood into a vampire. Surely you could have picked on someone more interesting.

I glared at Gordon the vamp. "So what's with all the black clothes, bit of a Dracula cliché isn't it?"

"Not really. Vampires live in the shadows. Dark clothing makes us nigh invisible until it's too late for the human cattle to run."

My anger flared again. "Human cattle – is that how you see your victims?"

"It's what they are. A cow had to be slaughtered to satisfy your desire for a Sunday roast, now a human has to be slaughtered to satisfy your need for blood. It's all the same."

I folded my arms and raised myself to my best height – that was still several inches shorter than Gordon. "Well, I'm not doing it."

A throaty laugh and a half-smile came back at me. "Oh, you'll do it."

A little while later, as I paced the old shop floor, I quite suddenly felt chilled to the bone. I couldn't feel my legs from the knees down, my head swam, and my throat was dry – so very dry. I tried to speak, but it was like someone had torn my throat and mouth out.

Gordon came over and peered at me, frowning. Then helped me to the floor. "It's getting dark. Soon you will need to taste your first human blood."

"No. I can't do it."

"You will. I'll bring someone for you. Don't worry. Once you've had *first blood*, you can go weeks without more, especially if you supplement with animal blood, but even then, only human blood will sustain you long-term."

I glanced back to where I'd discarded the mice. My eyes were almost closed. I felt so weak, I couldn't even have reached for them if I wanted to. *No, no, no, this can't be happening.*

"Too late for a mouse-blood fix now my friend. I'll be back shortly." With that Gordon swept out the door.

I figured, now it was dark, if I could just get myself home, I could call a doctor or something, fix this – stupid I know, but my mind wasn't working well. Anyway, I crawled to the door and just about managed to reach up to the handle. Easing my way across the threshold, I dropped from all fours to my belly, and began wriggling along the alleyway.

About half way to the high street, a pair of strong arms grabbed me and propped me against a wall. My eyes opened in my lolling head.

"Hey mate. What's up with you? You on drugs or something? I'm calling an ambulance. There's a phone-box just round the corner. I'll be as quick as I can."

The man's face barely penetrated the haze before my eyes when he returned from making the call. I tried to speak, but just a kind of gurgle exuded from my arid mouth. Opening my eyes, I saw a young man, concern wrinkling his brow. He pushed the lower layer of his seventies-style feather-cut hair back behind his ear, then all I could focus on was the vein running tantalisingly down his neck. I moved my lips again, though no sound came out this time.

He bent down, I suppose to hear what I was trying to say, all the while explaining that help would be here soon. But that vein throbbed louder and louder as I stared.

He got just a tiny bit closer. A pain erupted in my jaw, like someone had planted a left hook on me. I tasted a little of my own blood as my canines elongated and stabbed my bottom lip. Opening my mouth to prevent further damage, my teeth, quite suddenly were buried in the lad's neck. I hadn't planned it, it just happened in a split second.

Heat rushed down my throat and reanimated my whole body. I was instantly strong again. It felt so good. I felt so alive. I gulped and gulped, but later, as my teeth retracted, I saw the light go out in the young man's eyes.

"Sorry, I'm so sorry." I shook him, but it was no good, He was dead. A young life snuffed out. Guilt was almost my undoing, but no, this was all Gordon's fault and I would make him pay for what he'd done to me.

I went to get up, and almost fell again. The energy in my rejuvenated body was so great, I could barely manage to contain it. I was practically bouncing around in the alley when I heard the ambulance siren coming my way. Of course, the lad had called for help – for me. Another wave of guilt assaulted me, and my anger grew.

CHAPTER 4 – MY LIFE IN A NUTSHELL

I hid in the doorway of the shop I'd woken up in that morning, and watched as the paramedics tried in vain to revive my victim, before finally taking him on board the ambulance. One of the paramedics glanced around the alley. Of course, they'd expected to find an older man on drugs, or having some kind of seizure or something. Now here they were dealing with a youngster. He'll be a mystery to them. Oh, they'll see the puncture marks, and note he'd lost a lot of blood, but no one really believed in vampires, so they'll be looking, unsuccessfully, for some other explanation.

I wept, yes, I actually wept, for this lad, and for his mum, and anyone else who cared for him. For their sakes, I would have my revenge on the monster that turned me into one of his kind. Instead of heading home, I waited.

Gordon arrived back at the shop a little while later, with a semi-conscious man slung over his shoulder. As he dumped the man in front of me, he went into a rage. "I've had to hide out with this stinking drunk for the last hour because of you. Isn't it obvious you need to be discrete? We'll have to find another lair, and quickly. The police will be all over this place any time now."

Well, as you can imagine, I was incredulous, but more importantly I was even more angry than my pallid maker. "This is your fault. *All* your fault. You could have just let me be last night, and that poor lad would still be alive. Now I'll have his death on my conscience for the rest of my life, because clearly he won't be on yours."

"The 'rest of your life' can you hear yourself? You don't have a life. And quite frankly, you didn't have much of one before. We've got to go, now. Come on, we'll talk about this later."

Leaving the drunk behind, well I suppose we didn't need him now, we headed back out the door, and just managed to leap clear of the back-street buildings, and into the next row of shop back-entrances, before two siren-toting police cars came to an abrupt halt nearby. Did I say 'leapt'? Well, yes I did actually. We *leapt* – right over a garage roof, and landed comfortably the other side. I had to admit, that was pretty cool, but at the same time, I wasn't about to let go of the indignation or the remorse I was feeling right at that moment – in fact I was determined not to.

Something else occurred to me then. "What do you mean, I didn't have much of a life before? How do you know what kind of life I was leading?"

Gordon burst out laughing. "Do you imagine I picked you at random? You just happened to wander by, so I grabbed you? Is that what you think? No. Vampires pick their victims carefully, and after much study."

"Huh! Like the drunk you mean?"

"Oh, he was just food, and the alcohol in his bloodstream might have calmed you down a bit too. No, I'm talking about the people we pick to sire. We watch them closely to see if they're a match."

My rage had cooled a bit, but my incredulity just took a leap forward. "And you carefully selected ME?"

"Of course. For a start, no one's going to come looking for you. Here's your miserable life in a nutshell. Your wife was about to leave you for 'Johnny Upstart meets Columbo' there, you've got no kids to wonder where in the world Dad's got to, and as for your job, you're one of several that look, sound and behave in exactly the same way. Who'll even notice?"

"Well, thanks for trashing everything about me. You certainly know how to win a guy over. Wait a minute, you said my wife was going to leave me?"

"Don't look so glum. This un-life you're starting out on, will be much more exciting. As for the missus, she's been cheating on you for at least a year. I'm surprised she hung around as long as she did."

"If I'm so uninteresting, how is you want my company so bad?" Huh, I had him there – or so I thought.

Gordon laughed again, "Silly little man. When a sire makes a new vampire, firstly he doesn't want to be, how shall I put it? – outshone. Secondly, being a vampire will actually go some way to making you more interesting, and finally, if and when I decide I don't want you around any more, I can simply sell you to another vampire."

"What? – sell? – what?"

"Some vampires prefer just to feed, and have no taste for siring, so they buy their minions from others. I've managed to secure myself a rather splendid basement flat in the city, partly from the proceeds of my previous sales. We'll be moving there tomorrow night.

"Just how many vampires have you sired? And for that matter, how many are there?"

"Oh, I've sired maybe forty or so. As for how many there are altogether, who knows? Could be hundreds, could be thousands, maybe even tens of thousands. There's a community of about eighty in the city."

"And no one knows?"

"No one wants to know."

CHAPTER 5 – PARTY TIME

How to go from 'boring insurance assessor' to 'minion for the undead' in one easy step…

"A motorbike? Seriously?"

"Not just any motorbike. A Harley Davidson Hydra-Glide. Just like the one Peter Fonda rode in Easy Rider, but without the outlandish customising. Now, stop whining and put your helmet on."

"Peter Fonda didn't wear one." I pointed out, as I slid the helmet over my head.

"Peter Fonda was quite happy to draw attention to himself. Get on."

I'd never been on a motorbike before. I was convinced I was going to fall off on one of the sharp bends Gordon didn't slow down for.

"For goodness sake, when we take a bend, just relax and go with it. Don't try to counterbalance back the other way. You're making the ride unstable, and we have a long journey. We need to get there before the sun comes up don't forget."

We arrived Gordon's flat in the city just as the hazy pre-dawn light glimmered on the horizon.

"Smoking can kill," he said laughing as he ducked under the canopy to park the bike.

Small tendrils of white smoke wisped into the air. I followed their upward journey with mild curiosity, wondering at the origin until… "Agh! I'm on fire," I yelled, whilst turning in a circle, and shaking my billowing hands.

Gordon could hardly contain his mirth. "Get in here, idiot."

Still trembling, I followed him through a door at the back, and down a flight of stairs. The door to the flat was heavy and black with large, filigreed, metal fittings. Gordon produced an over-sized key from somewhere about his person, and we went in. I could hardly believe my eyes. Luxurious ebony furnishings, draped in deep red velvets and silks filled the main room. Huge silver candlesticks decorated the sideboard, and an elaborate chandelier dominated the ceiling. No two ways about it. This guy was a walking cliché. A small kitchenette in the corner sported only a sink and a fridge-freezer – its pale colour stood in stark contrast to everything else in the room.

He saw me looking. "I keep a supply for emergencies."

"A supply of what?"

"Mostly O Positive, but there's a few packs of other blood groups too."

I stared at him. Yep, he was being serious.

"Oh, don't look so shocked. There's a difference in blood groups you know. It's subtle, as you'll find out over time. Each kill hones your knowledge of what you want from your meals."

A small flicker of hope flared in me. "I don't think so. If I can live on blood from packs, I won't need to kill anyone."

The bastard was laughing at me again. "Do you really think you have an option? When you killed that boy in the alley, did you have any choice in the matter?"

I went to speak, but he held up his hand.

"That was a rhetorical question."

"Two."

"What?"

"Two rhetorical questions."

His eyebrow went up as he gazed at me. At least this was a reaction that didn't involve him laughing at me. Perhaps I should think of other ways to correct him – just to piss him off.

"Enough. We're going to a party tonight, and we need

to find you something to wear. But first we'll rest up for the daylight hours. At least the days aren't too long at this time of year."

I crossed my arms over my chest. "Huh! If you think you're dressing me up like some Halloween freak, forget it."

There it was, the laughing again. I was getting sick of hearing it. He scanned me up and down. "You look about the same size as a companion I had a few years back." With that he went to another room and came back with a black suit, dark red shirt – with a ruff down the front, can you believe that? and – wait for it – a black cape, silk lined in the same red as the shirt. "What shoe size are you?"

"Nine. But if you think I'm going anywhere dressed like that, you've got another think coming."

Gordon seemed to expand, not really taking up more space, so much as growing in demeanour. His voice changed, deep and echoey, penetrating my whole body and giving me the mother of all headaches. "Get dressed."

I tried to resist, but before I knew what I was doing, I stripped off and donned my new clothes. I was helpless, utterly compelled to do as Gordon commanded.

"There now don't we look dashing?" he said as he shoved me in front of a huge mirror.

Well there's a thing. And I thought vampires had no reflection.

I shook from the futile effort of trying to defy my maker. Still attempting to show the pretence of free will and defiance, I said, "You realise we'll look ridiculous on that motorbike of yours with these capes flapping about. For someone that doesn't want to draw attention to..."

Gordon raised his forefinger. I could no longer speak, even as my lips moved trying to form words.

"Isn't it clear to you yet, silly little man, I am you maker. What that actually means is that I am your master. It's preferable you do as you're told without my using control methods, but I will as and when I need to. You will find it quite painful. Best avoided eh?"

We rested on couches as the full weight of my situation came crashing down on me – at least he didn't expect me to sleep in a coffin – what with the mirror thing, that was another pre-conception out the window. My mind reeled. I was his pet, newbie vampire. I do what he says, or he forces me – painfully. Already my mind was racing to think of ways out this crazy situation – to break the thrall he had over me. But it was like he could hear my thoughts.

"You are now considering means of escape. There are none. All of your predecessors had similar ideas. All are now sold or truly dead." His tone lightened. "Now, party time, and by the way, I have a car as well as a bike."

I hadn't even noticed the Jag when we arrived, even though I must have squeezed past it sideways to get to the door – such was my mental state at the time. But we headed out and joined the dual carriageway that bypassed the city. I had no idea where we were going, but decided not to ask. Speaking out loud may reveal just how broken I was feeling. We entered some kind of estate through large iron gates, headed up a long drive and stopped outside a mansion. A man, dressed in what appeared to be livery, opened the car doors for us to get out, took the keys from Gordon and proceeded to drive the car away, presumably to some out-of-sight parking area, just as the next car arrived at the entrance. Another flunky opened the doors to the new car and out came a pair of long stockinged legs that ended in red stilettos. The legs manifested into tall beauty. Adorned in a black pencil-skirted dress, covered with some kind of decoration that glittered in the moonlight, a fur stole – a dead animal perhaps, and an elaborate red hat, with a net covering the woman's face – she glided from the car and approached us.

"Gordon. What a pleasure. I see you have a new toy." She scanned me up and down as I squirmed under her scrutiny. "Hmm, not a cute as the last one. Is he for sale?"

"Angelica...

Angelica – seriously?

"...a joy to see you too, as always." He glanced back at me. "He's still in training – very new you understand – so I'm hanging on to him, at least for a while. I'll never understand why you don't just make your own – you can pick and choose then."

Angelica tittered. "A messy business – not an activity for the genteel amongst us." With that, she swept up the wide steps and entered the building.

Music intruded my galloping thoughts, as the front door appeared to open of its own accord. Then something she said filtered through. "What does she mean by 'a messy business'.

"Don't you remember Bob? I had to force some of my own blood down your throat." He thought about that for a moment or two. "No perhaps you don't remember. You were barely conscious."

I was horrified. "I swallowed your blood?"

"Of course. Why do you think I have such a hold over you?"

"So wait a minute. What happens when you sell one of your..."

"Minions?"

I scowled. "...whatever. Would that mean your power over me is gone?"

"Ooh! Quicker than most to make it to that particular thought process – however, it doesn't work like that. I'll always be your master. But if I sell you, the buyer just has to let a tiny bit of blood, and I make you drink it – it's what seals the sale. You'll see."

Ugh. He was laughing again. How I'd love to wipe the smug grin from his face. *I wonder what he means by 'I'll see'.*

The door opened once more as we topped the steps. Some piece by Handel, I forget the name, welcomed us into the main hall, where people – were they people? – danced and chatted. I glanced over to a table by the window. There was no food laid out, just crystal wine glasses filled with dark red liquid. I realised with a shock that everyone here was probably a vampire, and there must have been more than a hundred of them, so some must have come from other areas if the local community only comprised eighty vamps.

Gordon went over to the table and picked up two glasses, handing one to me. He sniffed. “AB I think. Oh well.”

I glared at the glass in my hand with distaste. I was about to put it back on the table, when I caught a whiff of the blood within. Before I knew what I was doing, I’d downed the lot. The warming fluid a comfort as it coursed its way through my body. The near lust I’d briefly felt, when I drained that poor boy in the ally, returned, and I almost swooned.

Gordon grabbed my arm. “It’s been concentrated and enhanced with added blood protein. Pace yourself when drinking it. You probably shouldn’t have more than two this evening, as you’re not used to it, and take the next glass more slowly.” With that he went off and mingled with the other guests, those that weren’t dancing, greeting them affably and chatting, while I followed him around like a scared puppy on a leash. None of these people addressed me directly, though a few asked him about me, and he responded as he had with Angelica.

It wasn’t until he decided to have a dance that he told me to stand quietly in the corner. I cursed myself for my instinctive obedience. I watched as they lined up and began some sort of 18th century line dance – lots of swirling, partner swapping, males bowing, females curtsying – it was like something out of a costume drama on the TV. I leant against the wall watching, mesmerised, until a shout went up, and all hell broke loose. I stared in horror as a man was literally torn to shreds by about a half dozen vampires. After the hullaballoo, someone came to clear up the mess, and the vampires involved started chatting as if nothing had happened. It was all over so quickly, I may have thought I’d imagined it were it not for the blood-soaked clothes, and the way Angelica – the only one whose face I could see from my position – peeled a bit of flesh from her extended canine, then casually licked her fingers.

At this point I knew for certain. I wanted out. It didn’t matter that no one had got away from Gordon before. I would.

Somehow, I would. If there turns out to be no other way, I'd stand outside as the sun came up and finish this nightmare once and for all.

CHAPTER 6 – MEANS OF ESCAPE

"What the hell was that all about?" I asked as we headed back to the flat.

"Vampires like to catch up, just like everyone else. Some of them are many hundreds of years old you know."

"Not the party, the savage attack on one of the guests."

"Oh that. Not a guest in fact. He started sweating – from fear probably."

I struggled to make sense of what he was saying. "Sweating?"

"Vampires don't sweat. He was an infiltrator. We have to keep secret, so if anyone discovers that we exist, they have to be dispatched." He went all conspiratorial on me then. "Actually we secretly hope a live human finds his or her way into one of our gatherings. It makes for an entertaining bit of sport."

"That man would have family – a life!"

Gordon frowned. "Then he should have attended to them and let us be," he snapped.

We got back to the flat shortly before dawn and headed for our couches. But I wasn't about to sleep until I had an escape to plan.

*****

I had a few ideas, but of course, Gordon was awake whenever it was night time, and that was the only time I could leave here. My first opportunity came when Angelica came to visit. Gordon told me to 'make myself scarce' while he *entertained* her. I went to my room, just about managed to squeeze out the window unheard – largely due to the amount of noisy grunting coming from the two of them – and made my escape. I'd already secured, well stolen actually, a few pounds from Gordon. A little at a time, so that he didn't notice – or so I thought. I went to get the bus from down the road, in order to head back to the little town I'd always called home, but when it pulled up to the bus stop, I couldn't move.

"Are you getting on mate?" asked the driver.

Staring wildly at him, I couldn't even answer. Each time I went to speak, my mouth opened and nothing coherent came out. With each attempt to step onto the bus, and to answer the driver, I got more desperate. I tried to force my foot forward, putting so much effort into it, that when I let go, I fell backwards against the bus shelter's back wall.

The bus driver called over, "Are you okay?"

Again I tried to speak, my mouth opening and closing, but only a strangled sound emerged from my throat.

The driver's eyes narrowed as he muttered, "Must be drugs."

The doors hissed to a close and the bus pulled out. A young couple came by about then. I reached my hand towards them, still with no luck on the whole speaking business. They giggled nervously, and walked on, giving me a wide berth. Trying to imagine how I must appear to anyone who saw me, I realised if I didn't get myself back to the flat, I'd probably get arrested for loitering or something. With heavy heart, I plodded back, scrambled back through the window and waited for my master to summon me.

Gordon knew, of course. His amused expression said it all.

I wasn't quite sure if he'd exerted his influence to stop me, or if my inability to get away from him was an automatic, unconscious thing – my tie to him being what prevented me from breaking our connection. So I decided I had to try again, but this time, he had to be distracted enough that he wouldn't know. Mind you, I'd have thought having it off with the luscious Angelica should have been distraction enough. So it would need to be something big – but what?

*****

I made the decision to act the perfect minion in the hope Gordon would learn to trust me. I made a big show of hanging on his every word, behaving respectfully, carrying out chores around the flat, ironing clothes, serving his guests and so on. During this time, he taught me a lot about the vampire world. All the who's who, the best places to hunt – not that I took another life during that time – I kept my thirst at bay with the blood packs. He showed me all his haunts in various towns near the city, as well as those actually in the city. We went to many parties, where I came to realise there must be thousands of vampires in this county alone, goodness knows how many exist in the world.

It was another two years or so before my big break came. Gordon decided to withhold the blood packs, insisting it was about time I had a dose of fresh life to feed on. By the time we headed back to my home town for the first time since I was *made*, I was weak and desperate for blood. Memories of that poor lad I'd killed that first night had haunted me ever since then.

"You see," said Gordon, "this is why you must feed regularly. Once you killed a few more humans, they'll all start blending together in your mind, and you'll no longer be mithering over any one victim. You have to remember, they're just fodder to us. The more you kill, the easier it gets."

I didn't argue with him, after all what would be the point? But I knew I would never get used to killing people, and honestly, I didn't want to be that blasé about it.

It was busy in town. It was December 1981, so the nights were long, and the stores were open late for the Christmas shoppers. Though Gordon and I were dressed mainly in black, with dark shirts, our attire was normal, allowing us to blend in with the crowds. What wasn't normal were some of the youngsters walking about. Brightly coloured hair, sticking up like cockscombs, torn jeans, and more safety pins attached to both clothes and skin than you could shake a stick at. What was it with these people? Some even sported huge music machines on their shoulders, with horrendous shouting and noises coming from them.

"Punk Rock," Gordon informed me.

How did he always know things? Even new things, when I was with him all the time and didn't have a clue? "It's horrible."

"I kind of like it."

"Really?"

He shrugged. "The punk movement started even before I made you, you know. You were just wandering about in your own little world, oblivious to what was going on around you. See, I changed all that for you. You should be grateful."

"Yeah, thanks." I could hear the sarcasm dripping from my own voice, but it just made him laugh – again. One day, yes one day, I won't have to listen to that laugh ever again.

Just then, one of the punk rockers bumped into Gordon, clearly a deliberate move. "Hey, watch yerself granddad," said the offending oik.

Gordon scanned the lad up and down, affecting his most condescending expression. "I believe you are at fault, both in your assumption that we are in some way related, but also in the assertion that you did not bump into me deliberately."

The lad carefully placed his music machine – and I use the word music advisedly – on the ground and faced up to Gordon, almost nose to nose. "Are you trynabee funny granddad?"

"Not in the least. Now, step aside."

"Why? Whatchoo gonna do about it?"

"Really, I think you'll be wanting to move along now?"

By now, a number of other punks, girls as well as boys, had come to watch, sniggering, and swaggering in a small circle around Gordon and the offending young man.

"Do you hear that lads? He want's me to move along. Do yer think he's scared or summat?"

Shaking fists and laughing, the crowd edged closer.

Gordon didn't look at all worried, but there had to be a least a dozen of them. I knew he was strong, but wasn't sure he could take on so many.

"I don't want to make a fuss, but this is your last chance to move out of my way before I start to get a little vexed."

The lad scanned the faces of his friends. I could sense a kind of rising of his blood as his daring, fuelled by the others watching, increased. It made my teeth itch. My canines elongated, so I kept my mouth closed in case anyone saw. There was nothing I could do about my eyes though. They would be dark and ringed by fire, just like Gordon's were that first night. The best I could do was look down at the ground and hope no one noticed. But the spectacle of Gordon and the punks was probably distracting enough that no one would pay any attention to me anyway. A quick glance at Gordon indicated he wasn't reacting in the same way. Either he'd fed recently, or he had more control than me. Probably the latter.

I edged backwards, and was now several feet from the unfortunate activity, when suddenly Gordon was on the ground, being repeatedly kicked by the crowd of punks. My first instinct was to wade in and help him – that, of course was a vampire instinct. I was never brave as a human. It was also my duty as Gordon's minion to protect him. But just as I was about to move in for the kill, the sight of my wife and her Columbo boyfriend coming out of WH Smith's pulled my thoughts away. It was such a powerful tug, I physically felt the snap as my link to Gordon broke. It was a jolt that nearly knocked me off my feet. I glanced once at Gordon, and felt no remorse at leaving him to his fate. After all, he took my life away, such as it was, and made me his slave. After more than two years of pandering to his every need, let them hurt him, that's what I say. Oh, they won't kill him, he's too tough for that. In fact they'll probably come off worse in the end.

Now, back to my beloved wife. I headed in her direction. I wanted to know if she'd even bothered to try to find me. If she cried when she believed me gone forever, quite frankly, if she gave a shit at all.

"Hello Anna," I said. Almost immediately I realised my voice came out with it's own little hiss, like my words were being uttered by some kind of reptile.

Anna jumped back. The terror on her face was almost my undoing.

"Get back," it was Columbo said that – still with the dodgy mac then!

"Anna, it's me, Bob."

The horror on her face eased, but only a little. "Bob?"

"Yes, yes it's me."

"But how? Where have you been? What have you done to yourself?"

She leaned forward a little and peered more closely at my eyes. I knew how they must look. No wonder she was frightened.

"Look at him Anna, he's obviously on drugs," said Columbo, who then addressed me directly, "Get away from us. You were no good for her even before, and now look at you."

"John, please, can't you see he's ill?"

Humph! John, so that's Columbo's name is it?

"If he's ill, he should see a doctor, there's nothing you can do for him."

I was gratified to at least see a modicum of compassion on Anna's face, but this John bloke was getting on my nerves. I spun my head towards him. It must have been really fast, as it was his turn to jump back. I was going to say something to him, not really sure what, but my anger invoked a different reaction altogether. I roared. Yes, that's right, I said roared – literally. It was a truly predator sound that reverberated throughout my body.

Anna screamed.

Columbo grabbed her arm, and the two of them high-tailed it down the road.

For some reason, which eludes me even now, I found it funny. All the nearby shoppers stared at me as my roaring turned into hysterical laughter, and slowly but surely everyone backed away from me. I felt more powerful in that moment than at any other time in my miserable existence. The other effect was that my thirst grew beyond anything I could bare. I had to feed, and I had to do it soon. I wasn't far from the alley where I was made. It would be nice and dark down there, no jolly Christmas lights. I'll do what Gordon did and grab someone from the street. But I won't kill them, I'll quench my immediate need, then leave them alive for someone to find and help.

It was simple. I only had to hang out in the alley for a few minutes before a lone walker with a little dog went by, a middle-aged woman. I grabbed her quickly and bit down before she even had time to scream. But I was the one doing the screaming. The pesky little mutt buried its teeth in my left calf muscle. I dropped the woman, having at least got a mouthful of blood – it would have to do – and shook my leg. The dog clung on for dear life, snarling ferociously. I had to prise its teeth from my leg, and I honestly think I was bleeding even more than the woman, at least at first. The wound closed up and healed over in minutes – one of the few advantages of being a vampire. I limped to the back of the shop, the same one as I woke up in that first day as a vamp. The storeroom was in darkness but the premises had been bought up by a book retailer, and I could see lights under the door. The shop was open for business. The shelves in the back room were full of boxes of books that hadn't found their way to the shop floor yet. The new owners had also installed a loo with a little sink, so I was able to go some way towards getting cleaned up.

"Who's there?"

Shit, someone had heard me. Well, I couldn't stay there, so I walked out, bold as brass and pretended to be a customer. "Hi, sorry, just using your loo. Hope you don't mind," I said to the man.

"It's not meant for customers. How did you get in here? I didn't see you come into the shop."

Quite suddenly my instincts took over once more. Clearly

the one mouthful of blood from the woman wasn't enough to get me through after all. My elongated teeth sunk into the shopkeeper's jugular before I knew it. I could feel the wonderful, warm blood infusing my body, making me strong, satisfying my need as I ignored his little whimpers. By the time I was done, the man fell lifeless to the floor.

The remorse I'd felt that first night, when I killed that young man who was trying to help me, came flooding back. Gordon was wrong. My self-hate at this heinous act wasn't any easier this time around. I stretched my body, I felt amazing, physically at least. And maybe Anna was right – this was like a drug, and it was a much greater high than any blood pack could be.

I couldn't stay there. Not now the shop was occupied. I had to find somewhere to go. Being free of Gordon's influence, I could go pretty much anywhere.

"Aghhhhh!" The loud scream resounded off the walls.

Light suddenly flooded the back room. A girl – the shop assistant had come looking for the boss and found him white, and dead on the floor, with blood soaking the shoulder of his shirt. I always was a messy eater according to Anna. The girl crouched beside him as she slowly lifted her head to me, her eyes wide with shock. I stared back, a little horrified myself.

I backed up to the wall, as appalled as the shop assistant at my total lack of control. After more than two years on blood packs, I thought I was passed this gross behaviour.

What I hadn't realised, was the shop assistant had heard her boss's weak protests, and the thud he made as he slumped to the floor, and she'd already called the police. The blues and twos screeched to a halt outside. I went to escape by the back entrance, but they were there waiting for me. With my vampire strength I could have easily fought off two officers, perhaps even three, but they'd come mob-handed, having already found my first victim in the alley. They had been looking for me, and the girl's call had them arriving in force.

Before I knew it I was shoved into the back of a van

and chained to the seat. Two officers sat opposite staring in revulsion at the blood on my clothes, around my mouth and in my hair.

"What kind of friggin' weirdo are you? What, you eat people?" One said.

Thinking back to that night Gordon made me. I thought he was some kind of psycho – I was probably right – but now I'm one too. For some unearthly reason I felt the need to explain – I was, in fact, desperate to explain. Shaking wildly, my voice emerged sounding pathetic, even to me. It probably didn't help that there was a bit of flesh stuck in my teeth, but I tried anyway. "The thirst...I couldn't stop...it's my nature... well no, not really... I don't want to... he made me...he..."

"What's the nasty little shit babbling on about?" asked the other policeman.

"Search me. He's just a crazy guy. Ignore him. We'll be away from here and his stench in a few minutes, said the first officer.

Stench? What stench? Do I smell bad? For some reason, this bothered me as much as killing an innocent man.

It dawned on me then – no pun intended – but yes, dawn would come, and I'd be in a cell down town. Light will come in. *What will they find in the morning I wonder? A burnt body, or just a pile of ash? No. That won't do at all. I had to get away. I couldn't be there in the morning, and just die. Not after all I've been through to gain my freedom. Damn, I'd wanted to escape Gordon, but talk about 'out of the frying pan and into the fire.' How am I going to get myself out of this untidy mess?*

We reached the police station, and I was led to a reception area where a bored, fat, older officer gazed at me in contempt as he tapped his biro repeatedly on the desk in front of him. I wanted to snatch the pen out of his hand. That kind of repetitive behaviour has always got my dander up. I was just about angry enough to stand straight and stare him right back in the eye. His response was to raise one eyebrow in an automatic reflex so like Gordon's, it made me even more cross.

It seemed ages, but was probably only moments, before he spoke.

"Name?"

I didn't want to answer. Even this was an awkward question under my somewhat unusual circumstances.

He chewed his bottom lip, then more loudly, "Name?"

"Bob... Robert."

He sighed. "Robert who?

"Robert...Smith." Well, I know it's not exactly original, but I didn't think it a good idea to give him my real name, and 'Smith' just popped out of my mouth. Oop, there went the eyebrow again, as he scribbled that down.

"Address?"

Now what? I had to say something. "No fixed abode," I announced.

He wrote NFA on his sheet of paper.

"Date of Birth?"

"I...I don't remember."

The policeman looked up at me from where he slouched forward to write, just as a snigger came from the officers that had brought me in.

"You don't remember your birthday." He didn't phrase that as a question as he sighed once more. Then he turned to the others. "Stick him in number three and read him his rights. Let someone else deal with him."

Before I knew it I was locked in a cell gazing at the beam from the streetlight outside my window. In a few hours, that will be daylight, and I'll be dust.

CHAPTER 7 – RESCUE

I'd been pacing the police cell for what seemed like hours, turning a surreptitious glance at the window from time to time to look for signs of the daylight I didn't want to see. Picture the scene: Police officer takes me to an interrogation room to grill me – again no pun intended – daylight floods through the window. Imagine his surprise when I burst into flames right there in front of him. Would he try to use an extinguisher to put me out, or maybe throw a fire blanket over me? For some reason I found the image in my head highly amusing. It began as light raising and falling of the shoulders, which got faster and faster. I tried to hold back, snorting out my hilarity, but I was busting a gut in my feeble attempts, until finally I could barely stand, I was laughing so much.

Footsteps. Then a slot in the door popped open and a pair eyes shone through. "You'll be laughing on the other side of your face when the Super gets here. 'Ee's got no truck with killers, especially the weird ones. Now shut it." The cover went back over the slot.

I stopped laughing as I pondered what the man had said. Oh, not the threat of his Superintendent – I'll probably be a pile of ash before he gets here anyway – no, the 'laughing on the other side of my face' bit. What did that actually mean? It was such a strange thing to say. I sat on the bed with my pointless ponderings. The upper part of my shirt was now stiff with dried blood. I tried rubbing handfuls of it to loosen the material and make it more comfortable. Dark red dust fell slowly to the floor, but if possible, it made my shirt even more messed up.

A new, more powerful light caught my eye. Daytime. *Well*

this is it Bob. Time's up. How do I make peace with myself after what I've done? I was never a religious man, but if there is a heaven and a hell, I guess I knew which one would be laying out the welcome mat for me.

"Back up to the other side of the room," came a call from outside. Was that Gordon's voice?

I did what he said. There was a spark and a huge boom, and concrete blocks folded into the cell amidst a cloud of choking dust. I ducked and slung my arm over my face as I cowered in the corner, anticipating my imminent demise as the dust settled. I didn't want to see my death coming, so shivering in the corner I kept my eyes shut tight.

"For heaven's sake Bob, you're so pathetic. Now get you're scrawny backside out here. We need to get going quick."

Trying to make sense of the chaos, I peered up at my rescuer. "Gordon?"

"Who else would give a shit?"

"But..."

"I know, you were trying to escape, and you left me to take a beating from a bunch of thugs. You really don't deserve a master like me, yet here I am. Now move it."

I scrambled to my feet and followed him through the jagged hole in the wall just as the cell door was flung open to the sound of running feet and shouting. Before I knew it we were heading down the road on Gordon's motorbike.

We got back to the flat. My mind reeled from the recent events. I'd abandoned Gordon the one time he actually needed me. Somehow, the link between us was broken, and I was free of his controlling influence, I hated him, or at least I hated what he'd done to me – and he knew it. And yet, he risked everything and came for me.

"Getting out from under my protective wing wasn't all it's cracked up to be, was it?" That eyebrow was up again. I thought his irritating laughter would follow, but it didn't.

"I...er..."

"You realise I haven't really pressed the whole 'being your

master' thing? I could be entertaining my friends by making you do little jigs for them at parties. Or I could have you cleaning my bathroom floor with your tongue – well all sorts of nonsense really, but I don't. I made you so that I'd have a companion. Someone I could trust and rely on."

There was the guilt trip I was expecting.

"I've had many companions over the...years."

Hmm, hesitation on the 'years'. I wonder just how many years. One day I'll ask, but no today.

"Most I've sold on, a few I've had to dispatch,"

That made me twitch.

"But I have high hopes for you."

"Why me? I'm just so...average."

"Would it surprise you to hear that I wasn't always this suave and sophisticated? Once I was just like you. No one noticed me, I went about my dull life having no impact or influence on anybody. Being made a vampire was the best thing that ever happened to me."

Something I'd never considered before. "So who made you? Where are they now?"

Gordon turned away. It was the first time his expression had held anything other than bombastic self-confidence. "That's a story for another time."

Another burning question had been on the tip of my tongue. "What happened, you know, the lads that were kicking the shit out of you?"

He swivelled back towards me, and plonked down in a chair.

I sat opposite.

"I let them get away with it until you were out of sight. Then I simply stood up and shoved them away."

I was confused. "Shoved them away?"

Gordon sighed, as if having to explain a simple concept for the umpteenth time to a poor student. What am I saying? That's exactly what he was doing I suppose.

"You get the whole 'vampire' – lots of strength thing,

yes? It was quite satisfying actually. Each flew almost gracefully through the air, but landed in an dignified heap on the ground – oh," he chuckled, "one landed in a tree and couldn't get down."

I tried and failed to picture the scene as yet another question pressed to the front. "Do I have that kind of strength?"

"Well, not as much as me. It's something that builds over time, but you are at least twice as strong as you were when you were alive."

That gave me a jolt. I kept forgetting I was dead.

"Did they all survive? Those boys I mean."

"Don't know, don't care. And why should you care?"

I shrugged, I had no answer to that, only that what was left of my humanity still held a vestige of compassion.

"Okay, so the next thing is to re-establish our connection." He chomped down on his wrist and indicated I should do the same.

I wanted to spend some time thinking about that. About whether this was what I wanted, and what I could do about it if I didn't. But there was no time for that. Before I knew it, the thirst at the rich perfume of B negative got to me, and we were sucking down at each other's wrists. I was once more enthralled to my master.

CHAPTER 8 – VISITING ANNA

Spring 1982: I'd read in the paper some while back about a vicious gang fight in town amidst the busy backdrop of Christmas shoppers. How one young man was dead from a broken neck, seven others suffered minor injuries, and another had to be rescued from a tree, and is now undergoing psychological therapy, having claimed he was attacked by a vampire. It amazed me, that despite how many vampires there were, how much evidence had to be available, how many unexplained disappearances and deaths where blood was drained from the victims in unsolved murders, still no one believed in, or at least acknowledged, our existence.

I pondered many times Gordon's exertion that being made a vampire was the best thing that ever happened to him. It made me wonder about his life. Since he'd told me he was much like me back then, it gave me a new insight into my maker. Would I become like him? Partying through the night, having frantic, almost violent sex with stunning vampiresses, riding a fast motorbike, or driving muscle cars? It seemed unlikely. Despite the dull life I'd had before, I still mourned those days. And I still missed Anna even though our marriage was all but over even when we still lived in the same house.

That little bit of compassion I'd seen on Anna's face stirred up old feelings, and I couldn't stop thinking about her. Maybe we could have got some counselling or something, found a way to work things out and move forward. These thoughts got to be more and more consuming, until I was obsessing over her – and over the twillip she'd got herself involved with. It was now two and a half years since I'd become a vampire. I was more settled in the day to day – or rather night to night – routine, and Gordon trusted me more and more, so I got to go out on my own sometimes.

Cherry blossom and spring bulbs bloomed in gardens and road verges. I'd always loved spring the most out of the seasons, though now it meant shorter nights to be out and about, and more time hanging about in Gordon's flat reading, watching the telly, playing cards, chess and trivial pursuits, and generally lazing about, getting bored. Gordon had just beaten me at backgammon, again, when I made up my mind to do something about Anna. I opted not to tell Gordon, he would only instruct me not to go, and I wouldn't be able to defy him. So one day I 'borrowed' the car, without telling him of course, and headed off to my old home town.

I'd seen on the news about the conflict in the South Atlantic, and it transpired that John was a naval man. He was away doing his bit in the Falkland's, so Anna was alone. I slid in the back way – I'd always admonished her for not locking the back door but this night it came in handy. I could hear the telly blaring out Kenny Everett's voice and the canned laughter of his pretend audience. The room was dimly lit, just as she liked it during the evenings. Her pallid arm reached for the glass of wine on the table beside her chair, but I got there first, picked up the glass to hand it to her.

"Agh! Who...Bob? Is that you?"

"Hi sweetie."

Anna gripped the arms of her chair, her body stiff as she tried to push herself further back in the seat, and her eyes wilder than even his own probably appeared. "How...what are you doing here? Where have you been all this time?" she squinted as she peered a little more closely at my face. "Why do you look so, I dunno, weird? Even the shape of your face seems to have changed."

I put the glass back on the table. "May I sit?"

She waved her arm to indicate the chair opposite.

I perched on the edge and leaned towards her. It was only then I realised she was pregnant – either that or she'd been eating copious amounts of jam doughnuts. The thought made me titter.

Hand shaking, she lit a cigarette. "I fail to see what's funny."

"Sorry." Now that I was here, I wasn't sure what I wanted to say, so I started with our last encounter. "Last Christmas, you and…him. You looked so scared of me."

She shook her head, a bit of her old, familiar exasperation at him creeping back in. "Have you any idea how you look? Your eyes – once they were blue, they're kind of dark red now, and your face is as white as a sheet. What the hell have you been up to? What have you been taking? I thought you had more sense than that." Her voice trembled and quietened. "Is it me? Did I drive you to this?"

I still didn't know where to start. I began to get angry when she was berating me, but then she'd blamed herself and I calmed a bit. "I knew you were having an affair. I followed you one night and saw you with him," I spat that last word. "I was heading home when I was attacked."

Anna sucked in a sharp intake of breath. "What happened?"

"I'm dead Anna, that's what happened to me."

"No Bob. Don't talk like that. You can find a new life. I'm sorry we weren't right together, but you must know I still care about what happens to you. There's someone out there that's made for you. You just need to get off the drugs and sort yourself out."

I bit my lip. A mistake as my fangs hadn't quite retreated from my earlier anger, and blood leaked from the wound.

"Just look at the mess you are. Your skin must be so thin to bleed so easily." She passed a box of tissues over.

"You don't understand. I'm dead. I mean, I'm actually

dead. I'm a walking, talking dead man. I was killed in that attack."

"You're not making any sense."

Oh well, here goes. "I was killed by a vampire, and now I'm a vampire."

She stared at me for more moments than was comfortable. "It's the drugs Bob. They're making you delusional. You need to get help. Look, John's away at the moment, you can sleep in the spare room tonight and tomorrow, then on Monday I'll call the doctor and see what he can do to, I don't know, get you in somewhere. Somewhere they can treat you. Now, can I get you a cuppa, or a beer or something?"

"Vampires don't drink tea or beer, only blood."

"Bob, listen to me. There are no such things as vampires. You're ill, and I'm going to help you get better."

I gazed at my wife – well, I suppose my ex-wife now, I'd made her a widow. That thought hurt. Then another thought occurred to me. "Are you married to this John bloke now then?"

"Yes. You were missing without a trace for so long, I was able to get our marriage nullified. John and I married last year. I'm expecting a baby in October."

I nodded, rather jealous, as we'd never been able to have kids together. He'd been able to give her what I clearly could not. "I can't stay," was all I said as I headed out the door.

"Bob wait," Anna called.

But I didn't wait. I ran back to the car and drove back to the city.

CHAPTER 9 – SHIPPING OUT

When there's not a thing in the world you need, but even that is not enough, where do you go from there?

"What exactly did you hope to achieve by visiting your ex?" asked Gordon when I told him where I'd been.

"I don't know. I just wanted to see her, to find out if she still had any feelings for me I suppose."

"And if she had. Then what?"

I sighed. "I guess I hadn't really thought it through."

Was that sympathy I saw on his face – surely not?

"Well, now that you've got that out of your system we can move on."

"What do you mean?"

"I've decided I'm tired, and really quite bored of the short nights we get here during, well, so much of the year. I've booked passage on a cargo ship. We will spend half the year in the southern hemisphere, whilst there are long days here, and come back in the autumn."

I'd never been abroad. In fact I hadn't travelled much even in Britain. The idea of all that foreign food... no wait what was I thinking? I won't be eating that anyway. I tried to think of reasons not to go. "What about the heat in those foreign countries?"

"Don't be ridiculous, I'm not talking about the tropics, I'm thinking of South America, I've always fancied travelling there, maybe get a cabin in the Andes. If that doesn't suit us, we can try the south island of New Zealand next year. The world is our oyster, as they say."

"But we have everything we need right here," I pleaded.

"But there's no excitement. What's the point of our long unlives if we don't use the time to explore the world and find new and exciting things to do?"

I so didn't want this, but knew I couldn't resist his wishes. Then another thought occurred to me. "What about feeding? Where will we get blood in the middle of the mountains?" I thought I had him there.

"Don't worry about that. We can stock up on blood packs before we take up residence, there'll be enough locals in the mountains if we need some real food, and we can always keep a few goats for emergencies."

Now I was incredulous. "Goats?"

"Okay, goat blood's an acquired taste, but we'll muddle through you'll see."

It seemed to take forever. The crew of the cargo ship thought we were strange, sleeping during the day, and only coming up on deck in the dark. We also had all meals brought to our little cabin, which we discarded when no one could see. I also learned something new. It turned out we could actually enjoy a beer or a glass of wine, in moderation – *how had I not known that before?* The alcohol wouldn't affect us directly – only if we drank from someone with alcohol in their bloodstream, but it meant that we could socialise a little without noticeably abstaining. So a few times we had drinks with some of the crew, though I couldn't help but notice they were wary around us. I asked Gordon why he hadn't told me we could drink before, and he just shrugged and said it hadn't come up. I was a little peeved, I could have sat and had a glass of wine with Anna when I went to see her. Still, that's all behind me now I suppose.

Despite Gordon's assertions about not going to hot countries, to get to the southern hemisphere we still had to travel through the heat of the tropics. I had trouble sleeping most days in the stifling cabin, though it didn't seem to affect him at all. However, once we'd crossed from the Atlantic, then the Caribbean to the Pacific through the Panama Canal, we took a left turn ready to make our way south to Chile, past Columbia, Ecuador and Peru.

We'd fed well before we left, but this was a long journey, and I was beginning to get a bit cranky with hunger.

"What are we going to do? We can't make it all the way without feeding."

Gordon frowned, "Mmm, I keep forgetting just how young you are."

I studied his pale face. He hardly seemed affected.

"The older you get, the longer you can go without feeding. We'll have to bring one of the crew in for you I think."

"What! We can't start killing the crew. Don't you think someone might notice?"

"Oh, don't worry about that. I'll stop you before you take enough to kill him."

"And then?"

"And then I'll simply glamour him to forget it ever happened."

"He'll have holes in his neck."

"He won't know where they came from. Stop panicking."

"So this glamouring business. That's another thing you neglected to mention before."

He grinned widely. "Yes, I suppose it is. Wait here."

I sat on my bunk shaking a little, then stood and paced, then sat again, tapping my feet alternately on the floor, paced again, and sat once more before Gordon returned with a young crewman following behind in a trance.

"Sit," said Gordon.

The crewman sat.

"Okay, he's all yours."

In all the time I'd been a vampire, I'd never just fed from someone in a premeditated way. It had just been an instinctive attack before. I glanced at Gordon.

"This is always the best way to feed. It's difficult to master at first, this is why I've not gone over it with you before, but your humanity is almost depleted, and the time has come for you to learn. You'll only be able to do this with my help at first. I'll have to stop you, and I'll have to do the glamouring – that can take years to get right."

I remembered the woman with the dog in the alley. "I stopped myself once before. I told you about that."

Gordon smiled patiently. "You stopped because the dog bit you. You then killed the shopkeeper because you'd not had enough to satisfy your requirements. Trust me when I tell you – it will take time, but I think you are ready to start. Now feed so we can get this chap out of here before he's missed."

I clamped down on the lad's neck, almost reverently at first, but as the thirst took me, I became desperate to fulfil my need. He was like a rag doll in my embrace. My body responded – yes it was like a drug to me. I couldn't stop. I didn't want to stop. But way too soon, Gordon was pulling me away. I tried to resist, but he was far stronger than me, and he efficiently separated us.

The crewman flopped onto the bunk, and Gordon gently licked his neck to stop the blood from getting onto the sheets. He wiped his reddened lips before proceeding with the next stage.

It was fascinating to watch Gordon carry out a glamouring, and amazing that in two and a half years of living with him and practically shadowing his every movement, this was not only the first time I'd seen the process, but I hadn't even heard of it before.

Gordon sat the crewman back up, took his face gently between his hands and stared into the lad's eyes. His own eyes took on that same appearance as they did when he made me – deep, dark pools with a fiery ring around them. Even I squirmed at the sight.

Gordon proceeded to create a new set of memories for the past half hour or so. "You were on your way to the hold to get some supplies for the kitchen – just like you do every other evening – when you slipped on some spilled oil. As you went down, you caught the side of your face and neck on a couple of nails protruding from the wall. They caught a vein and you lost some blood. Those kind English passengers cleaned the wound, and mopped up the oil and the spilled blood. You'll have to be more careful in future, but to be safe, you knocked the nails back into place so no one else hurts themselves on them." He then produced a hammer from somewhere, I don't know where he found it, and put it in the lad's hand before shooing him out into the corridor.

Later that evening, the bosun knocked on the door and thanked us for helping the crewman. The events that evening set a pattern for the rest of the journey.

Gordon had already purchased a 4x4 that we picked up on arrival in the Chilean port and a medium-sized property in the Andes. A local agent had arranged for total blackout blinds for all the windows, and a small flock of goats in a tract of pastureland next to the house.

I found it odd that I'd been so affected by the heat as we traversed the tropics on the freighter, yet the cold of the mountains was, if anything, pleasurable. Gordon pointed out that another term for vampires was *the cold ones*. We had no capacity to generate heat such as a living human had, so we were naturally adapted to the cold. I'd tried to argue that there was nothing natural about our existence, but it was just another thing that made him laugh at me. I was so sick of that.

However, life, if I can even use that term, here was actually quite agreeable. We passed the nights walking the hills – our extraordinary night-sight allowing us to enjoy the mountain vistas. We even bathed in small pools where they were fed by springs so weren't frozen, and I discovered the feel of the cold water on my skin was quite invigorating. In life, it would never have occurred to me to travel to such a place, but I loved it there. The only downside – goat blood tasted bloody awful, and the goats were terrified of us. Gordon didn't bother to glamour them, but he did encourage me to practice on them. It never worked, largely because they didn't understand me when I talked to them, and I began to suspect this was just another joke of Gordon's – anything to take the piss out of me.

The winter in the southern hemisphere passed quickly, and it seemed like no time at all before we were heading back to England. I was sad to leave.

CHAPTER 10 – TRAVELLING VAMPIRES

Winter 1984/5: Gordon studied his black nails intently – like they were remotely interesting. "I'm bored. What do you say to a bit of skiing?"

"You're kidding," I said.

"Not at all. You enjoyed the mountains a couple of years back didn't you? And as we'll only be out at night, we'll have the slopes mostly to ourselves."

"Mostly?"

"Well, skiing's quite popular amongst vampires."

I was incredulous, but also a little excited, and before I knew it, we were on an overnight flight to Canada.

"Isn't this a bit dodgy? Didn't you say yourself that any delays could have us out in the daylight?"

Gordon shrugged. "It's Air Canada – extremely unlikely."

"But possible."

"Of course, but some things are worth a little risk."

I hunkered down, grateful our flight left on time.

"Are you sure I can't get you gentlemen something to eat?" asked the stewardess.

"Thank you. You are too kind, but we had a slap up meal just before we left, and we're meeting friends for breakfast as soon as we arrive – I wouldn't want to spoil my appetite."

He wasn't kidding. We'd fed on the driver Gordon had

arranged, then on some poor unfortunate chap in the loos at the airport – we almost slipped up and killed that one – he was definitely looking a bit peaky after Gordon glamoured him, but we sent him on his way. We saw him afterwards in the waiting area being torn off a strip by the missus for taking so long.

"A glass of red wine each would be most welcome though," Gordon continued.

She gazed at me as if she wanted to ask if that's what I wanted too, and why couldn't I speak for myself.

I nodded, keeping my mouth shut. Even after all this time, it took me a while to retract my teeth after feeding. Gordon just seemed to snap his back into place almost immediately – I guess I'll get the hang of that one day. As vampires go, I was still a bit of a newbie.

The downside of a night flight was that everyone else was sleeping, or trying to at least, so we only got one movie before the lights went off. It was ET. It seemed a bit ridiculous, but then I'd thought the same about vampire movies until a few years ago. I started to wonder if aliens were real too, but was reluctant to ask Gordon, as he'd probably just start laughing at me – again. So I thought of a different tactic to get my answers.

"Gordon, you know I didn't used to believe in vampires, right?"

He turned and peered at me, waiting to hear what I was getting at. "Yes, of course."

"Well, what else is there? You know, other creatures, mythical beings and so on."

He glanced briefly back at the screen and grinned. "As far as I know there are no aliens, not that I'd be one to rule them out. I even tried to sneak into Area 51 once, but security was too tight even for one of our kind." He cocked his head, thinking. "So what else is there, let me see. Witches – there's lots of them and some are friends of mine – wizards and warlocks, fae – though they're rare nowadays, I've heard rumours of werewolves and a few other shapeshifters – oh, and of course, that reminds me, yetis, and sasquatches." He became more animated. "I'd forgotten about the sasquatches. I used to know a family of them, ooo, maybe a hundred years or so ago, when I last went travelling. I wonder if they're still there." He made up his mind. "We'll look them up as we'll be heading close to their territory."

I was staggered to find seven other vampires on the piste that first night. Gordon knew them all, though I'd never seen any of them before despite all the parties he'd dragged me along to. One woman vampire, Melinda, seemed perfectly happy just operating the chair lift. She had no interest in skiing, and had only come as her master demanded it.

I took to skiing quite well. The knowledge I couldn't really get hurt boosted my confidence somewhat, and before long I was doing some pretty good runs, though I say so myself, with a few small jumps thrown in for good measure.

It transpired Melinda and I were the only minions in the group. Aside from us, Gordon and her master Jeremy, the other vampires were 'independents', as Gordon labelled them. Melinda and I spent quite a bit of time together bemoaning our lot. To be fair, she had it a great deal worse than me as Jeremy expected a lot more from her than just serving drinks to his buddies. He apparently had 'unusual tastes' for their bedroom activities. It made me think back to the early days with Anna, and I realised that I'd not given such things a single thought since I was changed – apart from knowing to keep out of the way during Angelica's infrequent visits.

After a couple of weeks, and an investigation by the local operators as to why and how the lift and the slopes were showing signs of use in the morning after overnight snowfall, we all left and went our separate ways. Gordon, by this time, had made arrangements to head for the forest, and a cabin near to where the descendants of his sasquatch acquaintances lived. *How did he do that?* I didn't know – we had no means of communication that I could see. It's something that remains a mystery to me to this day. Either way, I was both curious and a little nervous to be meeting such creatures.

We'd been driving for hours in a hired 4x4 with snow chains on the wheels. Fortunately the nights were long this time of year and we made it to the cabin just as the pre-dawn light glimmered on the horizon. Inside the cabin a fire burned in readiness for our arrival. We didn't need it of course, but it made the cabin seem cosy and welcoming. We took to our plump, comfy beds straight away to see out the day time.

I awoke to a light tapping coming from outside. Donning my robe, I headed for the front door, hiding behind it to avoid the daylight. In bustled an elderly woman with a basket of goodies – milk, biscuits, bread, butter, eggs and bacon, and a few apples.

"That's very kind, but there's really no need," I said, though at the same time remembering how much I used to enjoy such foods – especially bacon. The thought drove me to a high pitch of hunger, and my fangs sprang forth.

I slapped my hand over my mouth, but it was okay, the woman wasn't looking my way fortunately. I'm Margaret. I'm sorry to disturb you. You must be exhausted after your long journey. Just thought I'd drop off a few essentials," she handed me a piece of paper, "that's my number, just give me a call if you need anything during your stay."

I was salivating.

Margaret just kept babbling as she put the food away in the fridge and opened cupboards to show me where things were for when we needed breakfast. "There's a little fat for frying the eggs, but you'll need to get some more when you go to the store. We expect you to keep the place tidy and..."

I wasn't listening. Somehow the thought of frying bacon awoke my thirst. I hadn't fed for a while. I was still young as vampires go, and couldn't last long without blood, not like Gordon.

"She was still chuntering on. "I'll be back with fresh sheets and towels on Wednesday..."

My deprived heart was thumping in my chest as I stalked around behind her.

"The bins are emptied only on Fridays…"

My face had elongated, and my cheeks had hollowed out since I was turned. My hair had grown too. I caught my reflection in the mirror. I *looked* like a vampire now, not just the weakling insurance assessor in a cardy and corduroy trousers I'd been before. I hardly recognised myself.

"I've brought you some leaflets about what's to see in the local area…"

Would this bloody woman never shut up? What did I care, all I could focus on was the carotid artery in her neck with its delicious, warm blood. It called to me, and I answered.

Margaret only screamed for a second or two, then whimpered for a moment longer before her eyes fluttered and closed. She was a puppet in my arms.

The blood pumped gloriously down my throat, hit the mark and invigorated me. But just as I vaguely thought that maybe I should stop before I killed the poor wretch, Gordon was there snatching her away.

"Dammit Bob, you idiot. What were you thinking?"

My swimming mind came back into focus, and I realised what I'd done. "Shit. Is she…"

"She alive, just about. No thanks to you. We'll have to keep her here until she recovers a bit. Then I can glamour her – or did you think you could do that?"

I cringed. I couldn't believe what I'd done. "It was the bacon. I…"

Gordon calmed a bit, and even grinned. "Bacon huh. They always say that's the one thing vampires miss the most in the early days." He changed tack. "Look, you were lucky this time. If you'd killed her, we'd have to move on again, and I have a mind to stay here a while."

I stared at Margaret while a little of the colour returned to her cheeks, and Gordon's saliva went some small way to closing up her wound, at least a little.

By the time Margaret left, she believed she fainted, and banged the side of her face and neck on the corner of a cupboard.

Gordon was the very soul of a concerned citizen as he helped her from the old, wooden kitchen chair. “Are you sure you’ll be alright now?”

Margaret frowned, disorientated. Looking about the large kitchen as if seeing it for the first time, she wobbled as she stood. As she briefly turned to me, her frown deepened.

Guilt warred with the satisfaction of a good feeding as I stepped towards her. She leaned back away from me, edging closer to Gordon. *Was there some residual memory of the harm I’d caused her?*

“Probably best if I walk you home,” said Gordon.

Margaret gazed at him gratefully and in adoration.

How did he do that? Must be part of the glamour I suppose.

CHAPTER 11 – CATCHING UP WITH THE JONES'S

The people we visited that day couldn't contain their amusement as Gordon graphically described my loss of control. I was the only one not laughing raucously. I couldn't figure out what we were doing here. We sat in the front room of a huge wooden lodge – the home of Jedd and Helen Jones and their nine kids of various ages from about two up to maybe twenty years old. It was a large family of, what seemed to me to be very ordinary people – definitely not vampires.

I kept glancing at Gordon, trying to question with my eyes what the hell we were doing here. At first I thought he'd targeted them as potential food, but no. He chatted away with them like old buddies, talking about Jedd's parents and grandparents several generations back. He'd clearly known these peoples' ancestors for hundreds of years. Again I found myself wondering just how old Gordon actually was. When I asked him once, he said he was thirty-eight, because that was his age when he was made. He wouldn't tell me when exactly that was.

Gordon's animated description of my indiscretion with Margaret reached a crescendo, and everyone fell apart with tears rolling down their cheeks, even the two year old, who couldn't possibly know what he was talking about, giggled happily. Once again I was the butt of his jokes. I sighed.

"Oh don't look so glum Bob. Relax, enjoy the company..."

I glanced once again at out hosts, and found nothing remarkable about them.

Gordon continued. "It's not every day you get to meet a family of sasquatches."

That totally threw me. "What? What do you mean? These are just people." Oops that sounded a little rude. I scanned around the shocked, and suddenly stilled faces. "Very nice people of course," I turned to Helen, "and I thank you for your generous hospitality, but..."

Out of the blue, they all started laughing again.

I didn't get the joke – as usual.

But then Jedd stood.

I watched in fascination as he expanded before my eyes. Pulling off his tee-shirt, hair sprouted all over his body as he roared. Almost as if it were a signal, his two oldest sons began to change too. Nails hardened, faces elongated, as did their arms and legs. I heard the ripping as their trousers split at the seams and fell from their bodies. My hands gripped the seat of my chair as I instinctively leaned back away from the eight-foot tall apparitions before me.

The grin on Jedd's hirsute face seemed incongruous on such a mean-looking beast. I simply could not stop staring.

Gordon piped up. "It's been a long time since I've witnessed this spectacle, but I never tire of it.

Helen tutted as she gathered up the discarded trousers. "How many times do I have to tell you lot to take your clothes off first?" She passed me a frustrated look as she explained, "I can't think how often I've had to sew these pants back together, like I've nothing better to do."

I turned my attention to Helen, amazed at her casual demeanour in the face of such a remarkable sight, but then I guess this happened a lot – it was 'old hat' to her.

Looking around the room, no one but myself, Gordon and Helen paid a blind bit of notice to what just happened. I gazed at Helen once again. "Are you all...?"

"Are we all sasquatches? Yes, of course we are, though little Jimbo there, " she indicated the youngest kid, "hasn't had his first change yet –another few years before that happens. Naturally us girls have the sense to strip first. It saves a lot of work, you understand."

I nodded, only because it seemed the right response, not because I understood anything at all at the moment.

Gordon poured himself a top up of wine. "That's why the rest of the family didn't change just now. Wouldn't do for the ladies to strip naked in front of us, now would it?"

My words barely came out in a faltering stutter. "Well no, I suppose not."

Just as I was catching the musky aroma emanating from three huge sasquatches, there was a slight shimmer in the air, and they shrunk back down to size, their fur disappearing like it had never existed. One naked man and two naked teenagers grabbed hold of their crotches and hurriedly skedaddled out of the room, to return a few minutes later dressed once more from the waist down. They grabbed their tee-shirts from the floor and pulled them on too.

I was still staring minutes later as I tried and failed to superimpose in my head how they'd appeared only minutes earlier.

"So," said Jedd, "Now you know why sasquatch sightings are so rare."

I frowned as my brain began to focus once more. "I do? Oh, I do. You're shapeshifters."

"Exactly that. All these numpties that come out here year after year trying to catch sight of us have no idea. We've even had them come to the door, asking if we've seen bigfoot – that's another name for our kind by the way. We tell them it's just a silly legend, and there's no such thing, but still they come. The crazy thing is, if any of them actually do get to see one of us, no one believes them anyway."

Everyone started laughing again. This time I joined in. It was good not to be the source of hilarity for once.

We visited the Jones several more times after that, and I have to say, they were great company, and we all decided to keep in touch. I really hoped we'd come back out here more often in the future.

CHAPTER 12 – GLAMOURING

Winter 1987/8: Of all the new things I had to learn about as a vampire, glamouring was the hardest. My abortive attempts with the Andean goats was, as I'd thought, just one of Gordon's jokes. Nonetheless, this was a skill I needed to achieve if I was to survive in my unlife. This was something I was apparently never going to be able do effectively and completely until all traces of my humanity had left me, and I was one hundred per cent vampire. Eight years since I'd been turned, and this only happened now.

I awoke one evening with a start. My fangs had elongated in my sleep – that had never happened before! I was almost choking, and pain wracked my body. I squealed like a little kid, and Gordon came running.

His voice was gentler than I'd ever heard it. "Okay okay, don't panic."

"What the hell is happening?" I breathed.

"You've come of age."

"What?"

"The moment we've been waiting for. You are now fully vampire. You have just shed the last of the human in you."

Still struggling to speak from the pain coursing through my whole body, I managed to croak out, "I wasn't waiting for this moment. I had no idea."

"Well no, I suppose not. The final transition is more painful in some than others. Actually, you seem to be getting off quite lightly."

I couldn't imagine greater pain than this, but slowly it dissipated.

Gordon clapped his hands. "Wonderful. Once you've recovered it'll be time to start your glamour training."

He'd clearly been waiting for this. Just another thing he'd neglected to mention. It took around three days to get back to feeling normal again – if normal was the right word for anything in my unlife that is.

"It's all in the eyes," said Gordon.

"The eyes," I stated, like it was a new concept. I'd watched him many times as he glamoured our victims, so I already knew that.

"Indeed. You remember when I sired you? You were pretty much paralysed as you gazed into my eyes."

The memory still made me shudder. "Well yes, but that's the point, I remember."

He sighed as he explained as if to a child. "That's because I wasn't glamouring you. I was changing you. There was no need to take your memories away."

I shuddered again. "I wish you had. That moment still haunts me."

"Really? How strange." He shrugged. "Anyway, if all we want to do is feed, then let the victim go, which we have to do a lot, particularly when travelling and access to blood packs can be problematic, then you must learn two things. One, how to stop feeding at the right moment – and that's not at the last moment of course..."

He was referring to my lack of control when the thirst got to me.

I winced at the thought of my various indiscretions over the years.

Gordon waved his finger at me in admonition. "It needs to be after only a few mouthfuls. This way the victim remains healthy and doesn't go rushing off to their doctor."

I frowned, wondering why that mattered to him.

He read my mind and sighed again at my ignorance. “If you want to stay in once place for a while, an outbreak of anaemia kind of draws attention.”

“Oh, of course.” I still wasn’t convinced it mattered that much. When no one even acknowledged our existence, why would anyone consider us to blame? Actually, I agreed we needed to restrain ourselves from harming our victims, but that, in my case, had more to do with caring for people. The whole feeding thing still made me feel guilty. I didn’t mention this was how I felt though. He wouldn’t understand, and he’d just laugh at me yet again. So I kept shtum.

Gordon continued. “The second thing, of course, is the glamouring itself.

Over the next few weeks, Gordon brought one victim after another to the flat in the dead of night – mostly poor souls sleeping rough in doorways, and a few late night revellers on their way home from a drunken night out. At first my efforts seemed to traumatise them more than glamour them, and Gordon had to finish the job before returning them to the streets. He was uncharacteristically patient with me during this time. After a while, however, I slowly began to have more success, and by the time our summer trip was in the offing, I’d got the process down.

CHAPTER 13 – MINIONS

As the years rolled by we travelled to many places, met all kinds of folk, human and – otherwise, fed on many of them, well the humans that is. We even met various groups of humans that knew about us, and got some kind of kick out of having their blood sucked out – I never did understand that, and I never did feel comfortable with it, but it saved the bother of glamouring.

I was glad Gordon taught me the whole glamouring thing – well it's easy when you know how – it gave me significant independence, particularly during our travels when blood packs weren't readily available. I also learned how he always seemed to have plenty of funds. He was quite the businessman, having global investments that had kept him buoyant for centuries – I still didn't know just how many centuries.

I changed a lot too. After the eight years, once the last of my humanity was gone, I converted, physically into a true undead being. I didn't age at all after my death of course, my white face elongated, my lower jaw more pronounced, my now long hair, remained black, I even grew quite a bit taller – not sure how that works, but hey, who am I to complain. Honestly, after a while, I looked, for all the world, like a movie vamp. All I needed was the cape – which Gordon was always happy to furnish me with!

I was pleased Gordon never sold me. We seemed to suit each other as companions, because that's what we became over time. He no longer treated me as a minion. In fact he sired a number of other vampires, kept them for a while in servitude, then sold them on. But I remained. I never followed suit. I had no desire to bear the burden of responsibility that goes with siring newbies.

The first new vampire Gordon brought back to the flat, after me that is, was a beautiful woman of about twenty-two or so. Long, straight brown hair, a stunning figure, and green eyes you could drown in.

"A bit of female company for you," Gordon announced.

Her name was Lynne, and honestly, I did feel the stirrings of desire when I looked at her, but truth to tell, I still held a candle for Anna, even though I knew that ship had sailed. Lynne had no interest in me anyway. For that matter, she had no liking for Gordon either. I remember that feeling. I hated him when he first made me.

"I could compel her if you like," said Gordon, matter-of-factly.

I was so shocked, I just stared at him, making him laugh at me – again.

"I would never..."

"No, of course you wouldn't."

"Neither of you are touching me, you freaks. That crazy bastard already bit me," spat Lynne as she reached to touch the spot, frowning when there was no wound to be found.

Gordon grinned. "Bit of a live-wire this one."

I was still staring at him, somewhere between incredulity and anger. "Whatever possessed you to kill this poor child?"

Gordon was about to answer, when Lynne went ballistic. "No one's killing me. I can defend myself you know, I have a black-belt," she shouted.

I glared even harder at Gordon. "She doesn't know?"

He stayed quiet, studying his black nails intently and leaving it to me to explain.

Ducking just in time as a lamp flew towards my head, I could see Lynne was searching for the next thing to throw.

"Please calm down," I said.

"Ooch," exclaimed Gordon with a sharp intake of breath. "Never tell a woman to calm down – no wonder your marriage didn't work."

I passed him a quick, scowling glance before turning back to Lynne and deftly catching a paperweight mid-air. "Please, sit down and let me explain."

"You threaten to kill me, then you want me to sit calmly while you tell me everything's okay, is that it?"

I cringed. "Well, no one's actually *threatening* to kill you. You see, you're already dead." I glanced at Gordon who was still expressing pretence at disinterest. "It looks like I'm the one to break this to you. Gordon's a vampire, well so am I, and now, so are you too."

I dodged a book.

"Are you all nuts? There's no such thing as vampires," she scanned me up and down, "even if you sad gits dress like Dracula."

I sighed, batting away another book that came my way. "Please stop throwing things."

Lynne redoubled her efforts and threw more books now that she sidled her way to stand by the bookshelf.

"I'm out of here. You'd better let me get to the door."

I appealed to Gordon.

He shrugged and commanded, in that weird, echoey voice of his, "Stop, remain still."

The book she'd been holding fell from her hand.

The strain of effort on her face gave away her struggle to move.

I felt sorry for Lynne, but at least there were no further projectiles heading my way. "Listen very carefully," I said, "you can't leave right now. It'll be dawn soon and you can't be outside in daylight. Vampires exist and you are now one of us. The reason you can't move right now is because Gordon commanded it. He is your maker, and therefore, now your master. You will have to accept your fate, because there is nothing you can do to change it.

Lynne was with us for just a few weeks. During that time, the hatred never left her eyes, and in the end, Gordon sold her. He'd commanded her to be quiet and respectful during the transaction, but his influence waned somewhat once she and her buyer were at a distance from him. The last we heard, she'd bolted for the door in fear of her new owner, and ended up running and screaming down the road in flames. She was such a new vampire, that her human body was still largely intact. The city's medical examiner couldn't give a reason why the woman, who'd been reported missing a couple of months earlier, had apparently spontaneously combusted on the street. The whole incident left me sad, not to mention really angry with Gordon, especially when he pointed out what a lousy minion she'd been.

It was month's later that Gordon brought home another newbie. A man this time, about the same age as me – or as I was when I was made. Christopher was a quiet one. Gordon told me that after the disaster with Lynne, he'd actually discussed with this one giving him eternal life. He said his existence would be so much better, and Christopher believed him. Once I'd heard the sad story of his life – one wracked with sickness and loss – I could understand why. He was with us for about seven months. During that time he only tried to get away once, on his mother's birthday. Gordon managed to stop him just in time before he almost went the same way as Lynne. After that he just remained subservient, but cheerless. Fed up with having Christopher moping about the place, Gordon sold him on. We found out later he slowly came round to accepting his fate, and actually making the most of it. His new mistress knew how to make him happy apparently – I'll say no more about that!

1996: It was years before Gordon decided he wanted to make yet another vampire. This time he took me out with him in order to let me help him decide whom to take.

"Why do you want to create another vampire anyway? Look what happened with the last two," I pointed out.

"Well, you turned out okay. Anyway, that's why I brought you along. After all, we'll both have to live with them."

"But we get on just fine without having a minion at our beck and call."

"Do I detect a note of jealousy?"

"Don't be ridiculous. I just don't see the point."

"Well, you know I've been doing this for hundreds of years..."

My head snapped up and my eyes narrowed. A little tingle shivered down my spine. Was I finally going to find out just how old Gordon was?

"How many vampires have you made did you say? And how many hundreds of years are we talking about?"

"Oh, never mind that. The simple fact is, I've sired an awful lot of vamps over the years. You, my friend – against all odds – have turned out to be the best of them. The others make a good diversion, and when I've had enough of them, I can just pass them on. There are so many of our kind that won't sire vampires, so it's a good source of income and adds a bit of diversity to our unlives.

We headed out to a late night bar. It was my idea. I thought it would give us a chance to really watch and study potential victims – and yes, I still call them victims, even now. What I didn't know was that Gordon planned that I should be the one to make our next minion.

We sat in a dark corner – well dark to everyone else that was. Our enhanced night sight allowed us to view everyone in detail, but we would have been virtually invisible to the people there. Just as well really.

While many were obliviously dancing the Macarena, we ticked off the stragglers sitting or standing alone.

"What about her?" Gordon pointed to a scrawny teenager sullenly nursing her beer bottle.

"No thanks! She looks a right misery."

"Hmm, you're probably right." He swung his eyes across the room. That one, with the blond hair at the corner of the bar."

"He doesn't look any cheerier than that girl."

Gordon shook his head in frustration. "Well, they're alone. That's the point. They'd look like proper plonkers if they were laughing or smiling when they're alone. It'll be fine."

It was late and the music changed to a slow dance piece to wind up the night. Those that were with someone smooched on the dance floor, the rest either stood and watched, maybe enviably, maybe not – who knows?

"Quick, he's leaving. Let's go," said Gordon, his eyes on the blonde guy.

We pulled our black cloaks around our shoulders and headed out the door. Blondie sauntered up the road, and we followed.

"You don't have to do this you know, we could just go home," I said.

Gordon passed me a sideling glance, but said nothing. He just upped his pace.

There was no indication the man saw us, or was in anyway aware he was being stalked. We were close now. My doubts heightened with every step as we closed the gap. I could hear blondie's breathing and heartbeat getting faster. Perhaps he'd made us after all. I wanted to stop, to pull Gordon back and forget the whole thing, but too late.

Just as we passed a darkened side-alley, he pulled the struggling man in.

I watched in disgust as Gordon held him just off the ground, feet trying to gain purchase. I knew what came next as my own turning replayed in my mind in graphic detail. But Gordon just held him there, not biting down as he should.

"All yours Bob," said Gordon.

"What?"

"This one's for you. Come on."

"No!"

"Why do you think I brought you along? It's time you tried this. If you find it's not for you, then you don't have to do it again. I promise."

"I don't have to even this time."

A tingling sensation ran through me. A feeling I hadn't had in seventeen years, and didn't expect to experience again. Gordon had pressed his influence on me as my master. I stared at him. It felt like betrayal after all these years. My legs moved, and in moments I was sucking at the blond man's neck. That in itself wasn't unfamiliar, after all, I fed without killing regularly, but this time it was different. This time I caught my own wrist with one of my sharp, black nails. I tried desperately to keep my bleeding hand away from the man's mouth until it healed – usually only minutes, but my master compelled me, and my blood dripped past his lips.

Gordon rubbed the guy's neck to induce swallowing, but in a move that shocked us both, he spat it out and freed himself from Gordon's hold.

A sharp pain lanced into my belly. Blondie had a knife. I staggered back, totally aghast. This was the last thing I expected.

But Gordon, even though he'd lost his grip, was still far stronger than any human. In a split second he'd snatched the knife away, and drawn it across the man's throat.

Blondie dropped to the ground.

My wound took several hours to heal, and was surprisingly painful.

Gordon stomped around the flat like a bear with a sore head, until finally I had to know, to get him to explain.

"What the hell happened? How did he release himself from your thrall."

At first he wouldn't answer. For three days and nights he wouldn't speak, until finally it all came out.

"Sit down Bob, I need to tell you something."

Finally.

I sat and waited patiently.

He poured two whiskies. We rarely drank spirits, though like the beer and wine, it had no significant effect, though it was somehow comforting as the flavours burst across the inside of my mouth.

After a couple of false starts, where Gordon stood and paced, then sat again, he spilled the beans at last.

"Something I've never explained to you before. Vampires are not immortal. We may live for hundreds of years..."

I got that little tingle of anticipation again – would I finally find out just how old Gordon is?

"But we don't last forever. I know you've been curious, so I'll tell you now. In life I was part of Oliver Cromwell's New Model Army."

I let my breath out as a gasp.

"The point is, that there comes a time when our powers and abilities fade. The other night was the first sign this is happening to me. Without our *skills* vampires are impotent. My days, or should I say nights, are numbered, though hopefully it'll be a few years yet."

My nerves shattered. I'd had no idea. I studied Gordon's face, but there was no lie there. This was real. "I...I don't know what to say."

His tone sharpened. "You say nothing. I've told you now, and don't want to discuss it further. You must not breathe a word of this to anyone else either. This remains between us. Understood?"

"Um, er, yes, of course. Is that why you killed him, in case he told someone? You're glamouring is compromised too?

"Probably. And that's my last word on the matter.

CHAPTER 14 – DEATH OF A VAMPIRE

At the turn of the millennium, the world was fired up for some kind of miracle, but in the end, it was a bit of an anti-climax. Well, why wouldn't it be? The 1st of January 2000 was just another day. But for me, everything really did change.

Gordon tended to get bored easily. More so in recent years I'd noticed, as he sought to compensate for his dwindling vampire skills. It was why we travelled so much, but we saw in the new year in our home city. He'd been taking more risks. Staying out longer, mixing with humans more, and being just that little bit less careful when he fed. I tried to talk to him, but he'd either laugh it off, or snap at me, depending on his mood. It was like he had a death wish since the incident with the blond man from the nightclub a few years back.

When the clock struck midnight, and all the people cheered and sang 'Auld Lang Syne', he was right there in the middle of it. Nobody batted an eyelid at his strange appearance, after all, many were in fancy dress, so he didn't stand out. I tried to encourage him to come home, but he wouldn't listen.

"If you want to go home, then go. Don't let me stop you." Gordon said.

I'd had enough of the evening – I was never really much of a party-goer. Gordon was drunk. It was a strange thing for a vampire. We couldn't get drunk by actually drinking, but we could be affected if we fed on someone with alcohol in their blood, or drugs for that matter. I guess that could have been it, because I'd never seem him so wasted. Nothing I could do would convince him to come with me back home, to the point where he took a swing at me. He missed, his arm flailing wildly in his inebriated state. It made me so cross, I stomped off, and headed back to the flat.

I never saw Gordon again.

There was a newspaper report of a man miraculously bursting into flames. Many humans claimed to have witnessed this, but it was put down to the drink and drugs, as there were no remains to verify their claims. I knew why that was, as did the rest of the vampire community. He would have turned to ash and been blown away in the wind.

I stayed in the flat, drinking more than I should, not that it mattered, it had very little effect, and nipping out to feed when the need arose, and generally moping around. I was lucky I suppose. I had a roof over my head, Gordon's assets were available to me, so I had money – more than expected actually – but oh, how much I missed the cantankerous old git.

I went to see Anna several more times during the last few years. I watched her grow older, and her kids grow up, until finally I saw no point in going any more just to peer sadly at a grey-haired woman. She wasn't quite seventy the last time I saw her, but the years didn't sit well with her, and she looked much older than that. I always remained hidden, after all, how could I let her see me, when I still appeared to be in my thirties?

In Spring 2023, when the days began to lengthen, I travelled alone to the Andes once more – the first time for twenty-five years. It just wasn't the same, so I tried finding different places to visit in South America. It didn't help, so the following November I headed back to the Jones's place. I always enjoyed my time there, and we'd been many times since that first visit, but I hadn't continued to go after Gordon's ending – as vampires called it – until now.

CHAPTER 15 – HOW I CAME TO BE HERE

November 2024 - Jedd and Helen's second eldest son, Kobbi, had become a particular friend of mine, especially after my previous year's visit. He was now as old as Jedd was when I first met the family, though he'd never found himself a nice sasquatch wife. His older brother and his sisters were all married with their own families, just young Jimbo was not yet married, but courting apparently. But that was not for Kobbi. He was a wild one, even in his human form, preferring to be out and about in the forest, swimming in the lake, fishing, climbing the hills, and so on. He taught me many things about the countryside – in fact he taught me to swim, something I'd never done before in my life, or my unlife. As a newbie vampire, the cold had been invigorating, but since my human physiology had become completely non-existent, something that had taken a surprising number of years, I no longer felt the cold at all, so swimming in those northern lakes in the middle of winter was one of the simple pleasures I could enjoy, with no downside, just like when Gordon and I used to bathe in the small pools in the Andes – when they weren't frozen over of course, and the chill would eventually get through to me then, despite my being largely a 'cold one'. Now I felt nothing, but enjoyed swimming nonetheless.

Kobbi had a desire to travel – unusual for his kind. Though they spent much of their lives in their human forms, they suffered greatly if they didn't 'embrace the beast and answer the call of the wilding' as they put it, on a regular basis, once a day, and for a couple of hours at least was the norm. This made any thoughts of travel nigh impossible. Kobbi and I spent many hours working out how he could fulfil this particular wish. In the end we had a plan and we booked our flights to England.

I'll leave it to him to tell you what happened after that, but suffice to say, once I got the call from a witch friend of mine asking to meet up, it seemed the ideal opportunity for Kobbi to fulfil another of his desires – to meet a *bona fide* witch, and see how 'the other half lives'.

*****

"Well, that's my story. I'll get another round in, and then it's over to you my friend," I said, gazing at Kobbi, who was bobbing his vast hairy head to the dulcet tones of someone called Miley Cyrus.

THE END... at least from me.

KOBBI THE SASQUATCH:

It was interesting to hear Bob's story at last. I'd asked him a few times to tell me about how he became a vampire, and he'd always fobbed me off with 'another time maybe'. Well that time had been tonight, and I felt closer to my friend because of it.

It was my turn now. The witch gazed at me with her beautiful, penetrating eyes – well, actually it was a little disturbing I have to say.

I was umming and arring about whether to shift to human form to tell my story. Speech isn't so easy in sasquatch form, though I'd mastered it better than most over the last two or three years, having spent more of my life in this form than is usual for my kind. The rest of the family went squatch for an hour or two a day, and headed for the forest and mountain slopes. I spent a lot of time in the wild too, but was also quite happy remaining in this form at home. It made light work of some of the chores I had to do. Anyway, in the end I decided to remain as I was, they'll just have to listen carefully – besides, I had my big coat on, but other than that hadn't brought my clothes in from the car, and couldn't be bothered to fetch them. So here goes nothing...

SASQUATCH ON HOLIDAY

What happens when one minute you're a happy-go-lucky kid, the next you're sprouting fur?

A Bit of a Preamble:
In the chill wilds of Canada and North America, amidst the vast forests of conifer, cedar, maple, hemlock, other trees and scrub, exists a living legend, or at least it is so according the local folklore. Bigfoot, AKA Sasquatch, roams quietly through the woodlands and the misty slopes of the mountain foothills.

Come on, you can picture it can't you? Imagine a film reel. Great hairy beasts, walking upright like human beings, yet despite their size, camouflaged among the trees, and able to vanish from sight in an instant when spotted. There's haunting music on our imaginary film that builds to a crescendo, as finally that elusive creature is sighted in the distance, and the music fades as the vision dissipates. Okay, so I'm getting a bit carried away here. Mum always says I do, but then lets face it, Mum was the one who got captured on a photograph back in the 60's, so who's she to criticise? My people do our best to remain hidden. Generally it's not that hard, yet folk travel from all over the world to try to get that next, more convincing, picture or video. A whole arm of the tourist industry has built up near our home, based around catching just a glimpse of us. Ludicrous really, we're just people in our own way.

But remaining discrete has a major downside. We can't go anywhere outside our territory – or at least that's what my people believe. I've decided to prove them wrong. My name's Kobbi, I am sasquatch, and this is my story.

CHAPTER 1 – FIRST CHANGE

I'm a Big Hairy Lummox – What the Hell!

So you're a small boy, interested in small boy things – you know, digging up and eating worms, riding on the back of wolves, climbing trees just to hear how your howl echoes down the valley – I'm sure all little kids do this, don't they? Then one day your body betrays you to the *wilding*.

I was five years old. My brother Denny and I happily played a game of hide-and-seek in the woods near our house. Mum always warned us not to go anywhere near the caves in the foothills, but hey, where better to hide than a cave? I saw the narrow entrance, and the darkness beyond. Denny was a scaredy-cat, he would never think to go near the place, let alone go inside.

I listened carefully. No sound emerged – it must be empty. My heart rate increased, and a little shiver of trepidation ran down my spine as I stepped into the blackness. A musty, if not unpleasant, aroma wafted up my nostrils. I couldn't identify the smell, but guessed it must be bear – long departed from its den, surely. In late spring and summer they're out and about hunting aren't they?

My eyes adjusted to the faint light emanating from outside and I scanned the inside of the cave. There wasn't much to see. Runnels of water dripped down the walls interrupted by patches of moss, liverworts and the odd toadstool – yes I know, five-year-olds wouldn't normally know about, or pay much attention to such things, but then other five-year-olds didn't have parents like mine. Not that I knew then just how different our family was to other folk. I simply assumed every forest-dwelling family *changed* to go hunting.

It was a deep cave, sloping downward slightly, and reaching back a fair distance into the mountainside. Hide-and-seek, and indeed Denny, forgotten, the curiosity of the young took over. Slowly I edged down the slope, using my hand on the wall as a guide in the increasing darkness. My nose twitched as the smell became stronger, and more acrid. Though I was shaking now, I was committed to my mission, and I pressed on. I guess it wasn't really that far in, but my steps were short and slow, so it seemed longer than it probably was. Not being able to see the back of the cave didn't help, yet suddenly it loomed before me.

As the weight of the mountain seemed to press down on me, the bear-scent became overpowering, and small sounds, that I'd hardly even registered before, became almost intrusive, rattling around in my head as I tried to identify the noise. Then it came to me – cubs.

Well, I can tell you now, it didn't take long to put the pieces together. Where there were cubs, the big mama bear won't be far away. I slipped a couple of times on the muddy cave floor as I abandoned my cautious movements in favour of fleeing. At one point I completely missed seeing a bend in the route out, and slammed into a rocky corner. This jerked me sideways and down to the ground, at which point I tumbled several feet back down the slope, bleeding from my shoulder. If the racket I made didn't bring the mama bear running, then the smell of my blood certainly would. I scrambled back to my feet and ran as fast as my little legs would carry me back to the cave entrance.

There she was – one hell of a big angry bear. I tried edging along the outer wall of the cave in the hope she'd be more concerned with checking on her cubs, but that was a forlorn wish. Her body swung back and forth where she stood, her nose up in the air catching all the scents in the immediate area, then her eyes found mine.

As my underpants flooded with warm fluid – *come on now, I was only five* – she rose up onto her hind legs. It was the most terrifying thing I'd ever seen. Not that I'd seen many terrifying things in my short life, you understand. She was close, I knew this even though I'd shut my eyes tight in anticipation of an attack, but I could feel her warm breath – which happened to be somewhat pungent I have to say.

Suddenly I was racked with pain. I didn't think she'd come at me just yet, and it wasn't like the pain of being bitten, or so I assumed, having never actually been bitten by a bear – it was more like my whole body convulsed. Shaking in terror I forced one eye open to find the bear watching me, but not yet approaching.

There was a ripping sound as my shirt tore at the back. My soggy pants became tighter and tighter until they too ripped. *Mum's going to go mad.*

The next thing I knew, the bear turned tail and ran back to the tree line. There she stood watching both me, and the entrance to the cave. I finally turned my attention away from her to my body. I almost jumped out of my skin when saw how far down the ground was, the fur on my arms was the next thing that caught my eye – well eyes, they were both open now. I scratched my hairy face and knew immediately what had happened – at last.

Five is actually quite late for a sasquatch to turn for the first time. The *wilding*, Dad called it. I'd seen my parents and Denny change many times, and I'd imagined this would happen the first time for me in the comfort of our home, with everyone around supporting me, and cheering me along. But no, here I was in the middle of nowhere – and where the hell was Denny anyway?

As it transpired, when Denny hadn't been able to find me, he'd gone home. Now the whole family had come searching – even Mum, with Cally, my baby sister, strapped to her back. Mum had been reluctant to be outside when she changed ever since she'd been caught on camera when she was young. Her photograph had been splashed all over the newspapers, and it had brought countless tourists to our area coming in search for the elusive 'bigfoot' as our kind were sometimes called. They were dangerous times, so I'm told. Sasquatches need to change regularly. If we don't do it at a time of our choosing, it can happen spontaneously, and almost certainly at the most inconvenient time possible. Imagine if it happened at the store, or the gas station or something! Anyway, Mum left the hunting to Dad, and rarely headed into the forest.

Mum hugged me first, before tearing me off a strip for going into the bear cave. "What the hell were you thinking? How many times do I have to tell you to stay away from bears?"

"We were just playing hide-and seek," I pleaded, though it seemed lame even to me.

CHAPTER 2 – DIFFERENT

"Do I have to?" I whined.

"Everybody has to go to school," Mum stood with her arms crossed and her head tipped to one side.

"But you keep telling us other folk ain't like us."

"Don't say 'ain't'."

"Why not?"

"Because I said so, that's why not."

I sighed as I pulled my satchel over my head.

"And remember, if you feel the 'wilding' calling..."

"Go to the bathroom. I get it."

"And don't *tut* at me," Mum said.

I just managed to dodge the slap that came my way. Denny and I ran the half mile or so to the road just in time to flag the school bus down. There was no official stop there, but that wasn't unusual in these parts.

My first day at school didn't go well. As it transpired, even when in human form, our family were regarded as 'different', and different doesn't seem to go down well with most folk. I didn't understand it at the time, but our people have an aroma that turns other folk off, plus our mannerisms and general demeanour apparently set us apart.

So there was I, sat at my desk in class, minding my own business, when a small projectile hit me on the cheek. It didn't hurt or anything, but I looked across to see where it came from, to find a couple of boys grinning maliciously at me. One had a small catapult that he didn't have the sense to hide. This was a new experience for me. No one had ever been nasty to me before, though Denny had warned me on the bus that not everyone is 'nice'. I decided to ignore the affront, and turned back to see what the teacher, Miss Bennett was up to. Not a lot – she was still droning on about something that hadn't registered at all with me. Trouble was, I should have been listening as the next thing that happened threw me right out of kilter.

"Kobbi Jones. What do you think?" asked Miss Bennett.

As I didn't have a clue what she was asking about, I utilised one of Dad's strategies when dealing with similar questions from Mum. "I don't know Miss, What do *you* think?"

The class erupted. For some reason they found my polite enquiry hilarious.

"Have you heard anything I've said this morning?"

"Of course Miss," I lied.

"Good. And do you have anything you'd like to add?"

I shook my head.

Another titter came from a few of the other kids.

The bell sounded and everyone scrambled.

"Kobbi – a word," said Miss Bennett.

I went up to the front of the classroom. "What word is that Miss?" It seemed a reasonable enquiry to me.

"Are you trying to be funny?"

I frowned, giving her question serious thought. "Well, actually no, but everyone seemed to find me funny, not sure why though."

Miss Bennett's eyes narrowed.

Clearly I'd said something wrong, but what?

"I'll be watching you young man."

"Okay. Can I go now?"

She gestured towards the door with a sharp head movement.

Well, she seems nice – looking out for me and all, I thought.

CHAPTER 3 – THAT WAS CLOSE

On the way home I told Denny about my day. He simply told me to try to listen to the teachers, and to keep a low profile. Our family weren't popular, I'd probably not make any friends, and I should do nothing to draw attention to myself – *hadn't he already said that with the whole 'low profile' thing?*

"How was school?" asked Mum.

"Okay." Well, what else could I say?

I couldn't believe I had to keep going off to school so often. It seemed a complete waste of time to me. I lived for the weekends when I learned to chop wood, tend stock, forage in the woodland, make stuff for the house like shelves and whatnot. I also got to run through the forest, go swimming and climbing and so on. Everything I needed to know, I could get from Mum, Dad and Denny, and as my little sisters grew up, she'd learn from them, and me too. What else was there?

It was month's later I nearly slipped up at school.

The two boys with the catapult, from that first day, had continued to try and pick on me – and I continued to ignore them. I could have floored them in moment, but 'low profile' was ingrained into my mind. Unfortunately they decided to up their game. They waited for me outside the cloakroom one afternoon. Denny was a senior at the time and his last class of the day finished half an hour after mine. The boys must have worked this out over time, even though I always waited for my brother up a tree where I couldn't be seen.

They followed me to the edge of the woods. I hadn't realised they were behind me until I heard footfall crunching on dead leaves. As I swung round at the sound, a baseball bat walloped me on the head. It stung a bit, but sasquatches aren't built the same way as humans. I'm sure the blow would have floored anyone else. I have to say, the expressions of disbelief on those two boys' faces was priceless. They stood and stared at me, glanced at each other frowning, then back at me.

The attack, however, triggered my instinctual defences, and the familiar discomfort that preceded the change rippled through my body. It wasn't as bad as it used to be, it got easier over time as my body got used to the metamorphosis, but it was still painful.

One of the boys laughed nervously. "Like pulling on a dinosaur's tail," he said.

The other boy turned back to him. "What the hell are you talking about?"

"Delayed reaction. Pull on a dinosaurs tail, and it takes a couple of minutes for the sensation to reach its tiny brain. Looks like Kobbi's a dinosaur."

How would he know about dinosaur reactions?

He was laughing now. He thought my pain was from the bat.

I struggled really hard to stop the change in its tracks, but it was no good. I could feel my limbs extending and my hair sprouting. My eyes were shut – for some reason I always closed them when I shifted. I was sure by now they must be watching the spectacle, though I couldn't hear them, wrapped up as I was in the change. But once I'd turned full-on squatch, and opened my eyes, the only person staring at me was Denny.

I scanned around, barely stifling a roar, and realised I was deeper into the woods than I had been when the shift began. I wanted to run, to expend some of the energy coursing through my body, but the sight of Denny, and his calming words, brought about a reversal. I changed back to human form, changed into my spares clothes – we always carried spare just in case – and picked up my torn shirt and pants, – *Mum's going to kill me!* And we headed for the bus.

"What happened? Where did they go?"

"I came up on them from behind so they didn't see me," said Denny, "then I just banged their heads together. They went down like a dream," he laughed, "then I propped them up against a tree. They'll wonder what happened, of course, but they saw nothing apart from you acting a bit weird – or at least that's how they'll see it – and they'll wake up with headaches, and serve then right."

I glanced round again.

He understood my unsaid question. "I took your hand and led you here while you were shifting. You're still a bit out-of-it when you change. You need more practice little brother. Come on, or we'll miss the bus."

That was the last time I got any bother from those two.

CHAPTER 4 – CALLY

I was much more careful after that close call, especially after Denny had gone up to 'big school' a few years later.

When I was nine years old, Cally too started school, and now it was up to me to look after her and make sure she didn't get into any bother. Cally was quite the wild one – I was so proud of her – but this did have the potential to cause difficulties in public. She too was unable to make friends with the other kids, but unlike with Denny and Me, this really upset her. Wild she may have been, but she was also caring and sensitive. It was heart-breaking to see just how hurt she was at being excluded. I'd never had feelings of any kind about humans before, but watching dear little Cally being ignored, or even picked on, in the playground at lunchtime was enough to instigate a nugget of dislike, that would later become an intense distrust in the human race.

Even the parents that came to pick up their kids after school would glare at us, and shuffle the kids away, like we were infected or something.

I can remember standing in the bathroom staring at my reflection, trying to figure out what was so different about us – when we were in human form of course. Nope, couldn't figure it out. I asked Mum, she said it was our homespun clothes and our musky scent. Personally, I thought it was a nice smell, but Mum told me humans wash their bodies every day – yes that's right – EVERY DAY, just to make sure they had no animal smell. How weird is that? The fact is, it didn't work. Our heightened senses meant we could whiff them a mile off, even when their natural aroma was masked by all the soaps and deodorants they used.

When Cally came out of the bathroom one morning before school stinking of some cosmetic stuff she'd cleaned herself with, I'd had enough, and I talked to Mum and Dad about it.

"Honey, you are what you are, and you are beautiful. You shouldn't be trying to be something different just to please a bunch of bigoted humans," Dad told her.

"But everyone hates me."

"They don't understand you, that's all. You have to remember we are sasquatches, and we have to keep that hidden. They'll never get it."

"But why do we have to hide what we are?"

Mum piped up then. "Because they'll never leave us be. I was photographed once when out in the forest, and years later, people still come to hunt us."

I squeezed Mum's arm, I knew she was still traumatised by that event. I then glanced Cally's way and found her eyes wide and brimming with potential tears.

"Hunting? Do they want to eat us?" Cally shook in fear.

"No honey. Humans are a cruel species that don't just hunt for food, but for some kind of perverse pleasure. They call it sport," said Dad.

As Mum and Dad slowly calmed my little sister down, and convinced her of the logic of remaining secret, my thoughts went elsewhere. That little nugget of dislike was growing.

CHAPTER 5 – TOURISTS

Coming of Age: Sasquatches typically follow a very specific path – keeping ourselves to ourselves within our family groups. But we mature earlier than humans, and at fourteen I came of age and could make my own decisions. It was then I realised my life would follow a different path…

At fourteen, and now at big school, I headed for the bus one day when something caught my eye. There was a sign in the hardware store advertising for part-time help at weekends. I'd never really considered that I might need money for anything. For us, the forest, the river and lakes, and the land around our house where we grew crops, provided everything we needed. But I'd overheard some of the other kids talking about all the things they could buy when they went to work and earned a living. The sasquatch in me didn't understand when the land provided all, but there was another side of me that was curious. I concluded that the best thing for me to do was to earn some money. If I found I didn't need it, I'd just put it away in my drawer – nothing ventured, nothing gained, as they say.

I went into the store and asked about the job. It transpired I was perfect for it. They wanted someone to show tourists around the forest trails, show them the wildlife and talk about Bigfoot.

For me this was the ideal situation, with multiple benefits. I knew the forest well, could teach them stealth so they could photograph wild animals, talk about the bigfoot 'legend' whilst playing it down as nothing but stories, and steer them clear of our territory – all the while collecting dollars that I may or may not find some use for.

Mum was horrified at first, but I managed to convince her of the wisdom of taking the job – especially the bit about keeping them away from our home and surrounding land – apparently land that we 'owned'. Whatever that meant. It defied all sense to me that people thought they could 'own' land that had been there since – well, forever – and will still be there when they'd long turned to dust – but such was the absurdity of human beings I suppose.

Anyway, I convinced the storeowner, Jack, that the trail leading by our house was impassable because of a rock fall. It wasn't true – oh there'd been a rock fall alright, but anyone could get around it. Jack would never deign to set foot anywhere there was no pavement, so there wasn't any chance he'd find out otherwise.

My first day on the job went pretty well, though I hadn't realised just how frail humans were until that day, and just how many of them had no idea what to wear, especially on their feet. Less than ten miles of walking had them wiped out. This made my job all the easier. Oh yeah, and Dad told me not to take them swimming, as humans don't strip off in front of each other, so they'd get their clothes wet, and the water was too cold for them anyway. I could hardly stop laughing.

Being given money every week just to lead half a dozen folk along a pre-prepared trail, stopping at various points to point out the odd squirrel, deer or even occasional bear, while they snapped away with their cameras, was a doddle. Fending questions about Bigfoot was a little more tricky.

"Have you ever seen one?" asked one guy.

I hated lying, but secrecy was so important to us. "No sir," I said. "Sasquatch is just a legend."

"But what about that famous photo? Wasn't that taken somewhere near here?"

Mum's picture again! Well, I guess I'll have to get used to

playing that one down. “I’m certain it was a fake, just someone trying to get their name in the papers. To the best of my knowledge, such beings don’t exist.” I hoped I wasn’t turning pink in the cheeks from the lie, it wasn’t something I was used to doing.

“But we came all the way here to find one.”

I hesitated for a while as I gauged a suitable response. “Sir, take a look around you. The forest is beautiful, the trees majestic, the birdlife abundant,
you’ve got some lovely pictures, and even caught a glimpse of a black bear. Is this trip not worth the effort?”

The man twitched his nose trying to find fault in what I was saying. “The bear was a long way off,” he said.

I sighed. “You can be grateful for that. They can be dangerous creatures.”

Finally satisfied, I led the party back to the store, where they gave me good reviews, and I got paid ten dollars and a couple more as something called ‘tips’.

On another trek, we’d only gone a couple of miles into the trail when we came by a family of beavers. There was a hide set up already just to watch them, and the whole group went no further than that. I still got my ten dollars.

Most tourists were happy watching moose, wood bison, beaver, and the occasional lynx or bear. All asked if they would get to see Bigfoot. All got the same answer – such creatures are the stuff of legend and don’t exist. Until one day, one man in the group I was leading spotted a footprint that didn’t match any of the iconic species I did my best to find for them.

“That’s it!” the man pronounced. “Come and look at this everyone. It rained only last night, so this print is fresh. There’s a sasquatch near here. It must be from some time this morning.”

The group were all so excited, they spread out, straying form the trail path in search of their quarry. Trust me to get a self-proclaimed expert in animal spoor in my group.

“Please, everyone, keep to the path. I need to keep you all in sight. Please sir, don’t go that way, you’ll get lost. Ma’am there are dangerous animals in the woods."

I was frantic as I tried to pull the group back together. They weren't listening to me at all – determined as they were to be the first to photograph a sasquatch since that unfortunate incident with my Mum in the sixties. I took a quick glance at the print – yes adult squatch. Probably Dad or Denny, damn them, they knew this was a tourist trail, what were they thinking?

My voice, like all sasquatches, would carry, so, trying to keep the natural roar at bay, I projected a demand that they came back to me, now. The call of a sasquatch cannot be ignored, and seven semi-frenzied tourists gathered once more in front of me. But there should have been eight. There was a fallen log next to the trail. I directed them to it and selected one of the women who looked more or less sane.

"Please ma'am, keep everyone here together. Don't let anyone leave this log. I need to find..." I couldn't remember the man's name.

"Jim," someone said. "Jim's missing."

They began to get agitated again.

I appealed with a look, to the woman I'd chosen as their guardian.

"Don't worry Kobbi," she said, "I'll keep everyone in check. You go get Jim."

With my heightened sense of smell, I caught human scent on the wind and headed east in pursuit. After about fifteen minutes I heard Jim's heavy breath, and diverted slightly to the southeast, following the sound and the strong aroma of human sweat.

The sight that greeted me as I passed around the rock almost brought on a shift. *Where the hell had Jim got hold of a gun? Everyone's bags were checked before the trek started. He must have kept it hidden.* The stupid human leant with his back to a rock, sweat dripping down his face despite the cold air. Denny in full sasquatch form stared, paralysed down the barrel of Jim's gun.

Denny spotted me approaching from the side. His eyes were wild, even more so than normal. I raised my hands to him, trying to affect a calming gesture, whilst at the same time fighting to supress my own change.

Jim was babbling incoherently whilst holding the gun in one hand, and trying to operate his camera with the other. I didn't know if he managed to snap any pictures, so I had two things to do now.

Having got myself under control, I crept slowly towards Jim.

"Sir, please put the gun down."

"It's…it's…" he waved his arm at Denny.

I was only a few feet away from him now. "Sir, I want you to drop the gun now."

Jim's breath was coming even faster as his panic rose. Denny was in real danger of being shot. I knew what I had to do. I leapt in one swift movement, landing on the ground with Jim beneath me, but a loud shot went off, the sound reverberating in my head. Jim lay on the ground staring wildly at me, the gun no longer in his hand, but on the grass just beside him. I grabbed hold of it and flung it away so that it was out of his reach. The other thing I needed to do was prevent his photographs from finding their way into the public domain. Jim watched, stunned, as I opened up the back of his camera, extracted the film and exposed the frames.

"What are you doing? You idiot," said Jim. "I had proof, and now…"

His face held amazement, shock and finally anger.

I heard a groan behind me and turned to Denny. He leaned naked in his human form against a tree – bleeding from his side.

Jim forgotten, I leapt up and ran to him as a wave of panic convulsed my body. "Denny!"

He breathed his next words. "I'm fine. It was a glancing shot. I can make it home.

I gently touched the wounded area.

Denny cried out.

"It looks serious to me."

I took hold of his chin and studied his eyes. They weren't

glazed – they were clear and focused.

"You need to find a way to sort this mess out for me little brother."

I tore my gaze away from him and looked back across to Jim. How the hell was I going to explain this away?

I turned back to Denny.

"Really, I'm okay. Just get that one…" he indicated my charge, "…back to the store with the others. You're just going to have to try and discredit what he saw somehow."

"What were you doing out here anyway?"

"I was following a young moose and got carried away with the hunt."

I was cross now. "What's the point in me telling you all where I'm going if you're just going to ignore it?"

With that, Denny shrugged and loped off.

A few moments and a number of deep breaths while I gathered my thoughts, then I went over and helped Jim to his feet.

Once standing he snatched his arm away from me. "Why? Why did you protect that wild beast, and why did you destroy the pictures. This is what we're all here to find. You just wait 'til we get back," he said marching off – in the wrong direction.

"Er Sir, it's this way."

He stopped, turned, and stalked away in the direction I pointed out.

We finally made it back to the others waiting obediently on the trail.

Jim ran the last few feet. "I found it. I found Bigfoot, but this idiot exposed my film. I had good pictures, I'm certain of it.

He couldn't see me behind him, so I took the opportunity to begin my deception. The other tourists in the party all stared at me, so I shrugged, turned my finger in a round and round movement next to my ear, trying to indicate Jim was a little bonkers. I hadn't heard much of Jim's ranting, but he finally drew to a close with his passing shot:

"So, what do you have to say for yourself young man?"

Feeling a little guilty I turned the tables on him. "Sir, there was no sasquatch. You probably saw a bear or something."

"Huh! And what about my camera? You deliberately destroyed the images."

He thought he had me there. "Sir, I'm sorry, but your camera hit the ground hard, the back flew open and the film spilled out."

"You're lying. You know what happened. Bigfoot was there. I had him in my sights. I know you saw him too. In fact you seemed to be talking to him. I shot him and you took my gun and camera away."

"Everyone was checked for weapons before we left. There was no gun, and your camera got dropped when you fell," I said, as convincingly as possible.

"No, you leapt on me. This is all your fault."

He was so agitated. I needed to get the others in the group on side. "Did anyone else see the animal this gentleman thinks he saw?"

They all passed looks between them, then the woman I left in charge answered by first glancing apologetically at Jim, then she turned to me. "We didn't see anything," then almost as an afterthought she said, "but we did think we might have heard a shot."

"There, see," said Jim.

I had to think quickly. "Well, there was a distant tree-fall. Sometimes that sounds a bit like a shot," I lied, hoping beyond hope nobody here had ever heard a tree-fall in a forest as the sound was quite different.

"Tree-fall? Nonsense," said Jim, "You're trying to cover this up."

I decided to revert back to the standard mantra. "I'm sorry everyone, I know how much you want the sighting of Bigfoot to be true, but the simple fact is, this is a creature of legend only and it does not exist in reality. Now, we need to be heading back."

Jim grumped away for the whole return walk back to the store. He went on about his sighting so much, that by the time we got back, no one believed him, even the bit about having a gun – much to my relief.

Jack, the storeowner eyed me suspiciously, but supported my stance from the tourists' accounts. Once they left he questioned me about the event. "So, what actually happened out there?"

I needed to tread carefully, and perhaps give a little bit of truth – not too much of course – on my version of the story. "I'm sure he must have caught a glimpse of a bear, and convinced himself it was Bigfoot. The bit about the gun was true though. He got a shot off, I knocked him just intending to dislodge the weapon from his hand, and he lost his footing and fell. I threw the gun into the bushes – I can go and find it if you like."

Jack rubbed his chin. "I'm not sure if I should sack you for assaulting one of my clients, or promote you for diffusing a difficult situation."

I sat heavily on a stool behind the store's counter waiting for the outcome of my day's work.

Scratching his head, Jack finally concluded I'd done the best thing under the circumstances, but also decided to refund Jim's fee for the tour, which would come out of my wages. All in all, I thought that went better than expected, and I sighed in relief.

CHAPTER 6 – A SEED IS SEWN

I continued working for Jack, and even set out some new trails, always ensuring they went nowhere near our house. I stashed the money I earned in a box under my bed. I had no use for it that I could figure out. Jack provided me with a tee-shirt sporting something called a 'logo' on the front. The rest of the time, I preferred to stick with my comfortable homespun clothes. It was an easy lifestyle for me, especially as the family continued to grow, so the workload at home was spread between us. I'd had additional tasks while Denny recovered from his injury, but that was only for a few weeks. Sasquatches heal easily.

That whole trouble with Jim the tourist made me somewhat ambivalent about humans. On the one hand, I decided they weren't to be trusted, and certainly my experiences at school supported that. On the other hand, I met literally hundreds of them working as a guide. Most I found to be predictable, not very interesting and typically unfit, but there were also some that piqued my interest.

Oh, and by the way, before you go thinking that big words like 'ambivalent' seem unlikely for country folk like us, well you can keep your snobbery to yourself, because our parents made sure we were educated in ways that even school didn't teach us. They said it was important that we were never seen as dumb animals – not that I've ever considered animals to be dumb. You want dumb, just look at ninety-five per cent of the tourists I met.

Anyway, like I said, some of the humans got me thinking about things that maybe sasquatches shouldn't think about.

One cold but sunny day, we'd been quietly observing a flock of waxwings feeding on the berries of the cotoneaster bushes. I decided as we were all settled in a comfortable spot where soft mosses grew, we might as well have an early lunch break. As we all broke out our flasks and packed sandwiches, one of the tourists came over and sat with me.

At first I wasn't easy with that, I tended to prefer my own company when on a break, just so long as I kept the group in sight. She said nothing at first as she unwrapped her food. Part of me wanted to get up and move to another patch of mossy grass, but that would have been rude, so I sat and waited for the usual questions about Bigfoot. But that was not what she talked about.

"So, young Kobbi. Where is life going to take you?"

I was completely taken aback. I had no idea how to answer such a question. I gauped at her, dumfounded. She looked like so many other tourists I'd guided around the trails. Middle-aged, brown hair going grey at the temples, slightly overweight. She'd been puffing up the steeper slopes along with everyone else. But she had deep, kindly eyes. The upward crows-feet indicating she smiled a lot.

"Ma'am, I'm not sure what you mean."

She patted my knee. Under normal circumstances, that would have annoyed me a bit, but I found myself drawn to this woman – not in some weird 'young lad attracted to older woman' sort of way, just in a 'two folk getting along' kind of way.

"You strike me as a bright young man. You know so much about these forests and mountains, and all that lives here. You have an instinctual affinity for this place. I wonder, have you considered broadening your horizons?"

I still wasn't quite sure what she was getting at, so I simply said, "This is my home."

"Indeed it is. There's probably very little you don't understand about it. But you are young, and there's a big wide world out there. Do you not want to see what other forests look like – the trees and the wildlife are very different in, say, the tropics, or the deciduous forests of, for example, Europe. And you said earlier how you enjoy swimming in the cold lakes," she shuddered a bit at the thought, which made me smile. "Would you not like to swim in warm seas where bright colourful fish and corals live?"

I frowned, giving her words some genuine thought. "Well Mrs…"

"Call me Ann."

"Well, Ann, it sounds fantastic, but you see, folk like us don't travel to such places. We are kind of…rooted to our home land."

"I see. Well, at least promise me you'll think about it. I've travelled a lot, and I can tell you there are many wonderful places to explore. Beautiful as it is here, it's not…all there is."

"Sure, I'll think about it Ma'am."

"Ann," she reminded me.

"Ann," I repeated back.

At the time I had no intention of giving travel a moments thought. I'm a sasquatch after all. I have to shift to the call of the wilding at least once a day. If one of our kind tries to hold that off for too long, the change comes upon us unbidden, and we can't allow that. We have to keep control of our shifts so that we can choose the when and where of it.

Yet Ann's words kept resounding in my head – 'there's a big, wide world out there'. We'd learned about such places in school, and the library had many books we could study.

Slowly but surely the seed Ann had sown in my psyche, germinated and grew.

CHAPTER 7 – STRANGE VISITORS

At the age of seventeen, and having left school behind some while back, I did a lot more tours around the trails. Jack was pleased with my work, I got good reviews, he upped my wages and I got bigger and bigger tips. I had to make a bigger box for all my dollars, though I still had no idea what to do with them.

Our family had grown a lot. There were now nine of us kids. Well, when I say kids, I guess you couldn't really describe Denny, me or Cally that way, we were grown up badass sasquatches now. But I suppose 'badass' wasn't a good description for Cally. She was just as gentle and sensitive as ever. Even in squatch-form, she was so different from my other five sisters, or even little Jimbo. She hated hunting, but just loved to run, climb and swim. No one minded that she didn't do her share of bringing home the meat. It was always plentiful.

I got home one day to find two visitors in our house. This was a first. In all my life, no one ever came to visit. We did a bit of bartering with a couple of the local homesteaders from a few miles away, but they never set foot inside the house. All business was conducted in the barn. And if anyone came knocking, usually tourists sans guide, they were repelled at the front door.

Anyway, surreptitiously sniffing, I couldn't sense these two men were other sasquatches, though many others lived in Canada and the northern reaches of North America. But they didn't smell like humans either. In fact, they had no scent at all – most peculiar. I eyed them sidelong waiting to discover what they were doing here.

It was an odd conversation they were having with Mum and Dad. One of them, the older man, talked about my grandparents and great-grandparents, and even further back, almost as if he'd known them, but that was impossible of course. This man couldn't have been more than Dad's age, maybe even a little younger. The other man stayed silent, appearing as confused as I felt.

The conversation moved on and now this guy, Gordon, he was called, told a tale of his companion making an ass of himself with some woman. He was so eloquent in his description that we all fell about laughing – all except the subject of his story, Bob. He looked pig-sick.

Little did I know at the time that Bob would become my best friend.

Anyway, back to the strangeness of the day. Not only had these two men been invited into our home, but Dad, quite out of the blue, stood up and shifted – right there in front of them! I could hardly believe it. He then gave Denny and me a signal to do the same. Well, I can tell you, I had my doubts about the wisdom of this. We'd always hidden what we are from everyone except our own kind. The importance of secrecy had been pressed on us all our lives – now here we were giving a demonstration. We did it, of course, because Dad wanted it.

As it turned out these two guys weren't human – well, I'd already suspected that much – they were actually vampires. Can you believe that? I never knew such beings existed. But then I guess it was equally important for them to keep their identities secret as it was for us. And the older guy, Gordon, well he actually did know several generations of our ancestors. He'd been kicking around for centuries.

Our visitors made a few more trips to see us over the next few years, and we struck up good friendships with them, and looked forward to their winter stays. Then quite suddenly they stopped coming. It was a long time before we found out why.

CHAPTER 8 – BIG, WIDE WORLD

I never saw the tourist, Ann, again, but she'd influenced my life in a big way. My people don't normally mix with humans, and I was already living contrary to all the sasquatches, over generations, that came before me by getting a job leading tourists on forest and mountain trails, and even earning money. But now I took it a step further. Ann's words resounded in my mind all the time – *"there's a big, wide world out there."* I could almost hear her gentle voice.

I began to take more interest in the people I was taking out. Where they came from, what their home states or even countries were like, what kind of wildlife and plants lived there. The idea of the sea fascinated me. Water, undrinkable as it was infused with salt, and yet many species had adapted to live in that environment. I had never seen the sea, but I was determined to swim in the ocean one day. I had no idea how I would pull that off.

We rarely saw wolverines, largely because they hunt at night. But on one trip, early in the day, we found a large male feeding on a deer it had taken down. We stayed quietly hidden to observe the spectacle, but when the wind direction changed he caught our scent on the breeze and ran off leaving his prize behind.

The tension in the group, as we'd observed this ferocious beast, eased visibly. Shoulders relaxed, held breaths exhaled, and quiet conversation resumed. I began my talk – when it came to wolverines, this was not a speech I got to give too often.

"The wolverine is the largest of the weasel family. It has powerful jaws and a vicious reputation, and you can see why when it's capable of taking down prey much larger than itself. But like almost all wild animals, it would always choose to avoid confrontation with people. As soon as this guy caught our scent, it skedaddled..."

"Huh, you mean your scent," said one rather pompous man with a broad Texan accent.

"James, don't be so rude," his wife responded.

He ignored her. "Don't you wash boy?"

"James!"

I'd come across this issue before, though folk were normally a little more subtle about it. It was another thing I had a standard response to.

"Sir, I apologise if my natural musk offends you. I am *OF* this land. My people were here long before the white man arrived. We are not at odds with nature, and the wildlife here *knows* us."

"So what are you saying boy? That we all have to stink to fit in with the countryside?"

"James!" His wife was beside herself now.

I calmly replied. "No sir, I'm saying that human scent from other environments are unfamiliar to the animals here. The unknown is a potential danger to them, so they steer clear. That's all." I understood the animals completely. I wanted to get away from this annoying man myself, but we all continued along the track, where I dearly hoped we'd find something of interest to distract everyone away from this uncomfortable conversation.

I'd felt the first signs of my own predatory tingle running down my spine, but had learned to easily supress this now.

This was otherwise a good trip, with a sighting of a huge skein of migratory geese, then in the afternoon, we were able to observe a lynx, though at a distance. This particular trail was circular, and when we had about an hour left before getting back to the store, James' wife trotted forward and joined me.

"I'm so sorry for what my husband said to you."

She was genuine in her apology, there was no doubt about that, though I smiled to see her nose twitching a little. My musk smell would be heightened after a long day on the trail.

"It's really okay Ma'am." I didn't want this conversation, so I steered her away from it. "So what's it like where you live?"

"Well, Texas is a big state, but we live on the edge of the desert. We've got foxes, jaguars, prairie dogs, oh and pronghorns – the fastest land animal in the States, only the cheetah in Africa is faster. The desert can be a harsh environment, though when the rains come in the spring, the flowers are a tapestry of colour."

I was impressed. I'd asked this question of many people over the years I'd been guiding, and this was one of the most expansive answers I'd had. It was almost poetic. This woman loved her home, that much was certain. By the time we got back, I had a powerful image of the Chihuahuan Desert that expanded into the western part of Texas from Mexico. Now, not only did I want to swim in the ocean, but I wanted to see the desert in bloom too.

As I guided more and more tourist groups I learned about other places in the world that I wanted to see for myself.

CHAPTER 9 – COVER BLOWN?

Later in the season, as my group of tourists sat by the river watching a herd of moose drink, a young man nervously approached. I wasn't sure why he was nervous, I did my level best to ensure my groups were comfortable around me – musky aroma notwithstanding!

"You have a question sir?" I asked.

"Please, call me Trevor."

"Trevor it is then," I said gazing at him curiously.

"It's just, well the scent..."

Oh here we go! I was about to launch into my usual blurb about that when he stumped me completely.

"You're not human are you?"

My heart skipped a beat as I stared at him. "Sir?"

"I can tell, you know."

Shit, was my cover blown? I had to get this particular conversation under control. I glanced around at the rest of the group. No one could hear us from where they were standing or sitting.

"Sir, what is it you think you know?"

He bit his bottom lip as he braced himself to... to what? Accuse me of something? I wasn't sure. That he wanted me to call him by his first name was likely a good sign. At least I hoped so.

"I'm an anthropologist with a notable reputation for my studies in cryptozoology. I study humans and their behaviour and compare them with some of the more unusual zoological findings. You…you are different… to all of them."

There was that tingle again. I shoved it down before Trevor found out just how different I was. I stayed silent waiting for him to continue.

"Your…musk is animal, not human."

"Humans are animals."

"Well, yes of course, but humans have evolved away from their natural animal instincts. We have separated ourselves from the rest of the Animal Kingdom. But not you."

Okay, so back to the standard blurb after all. "I apologise if my natural musk offends you. I am *OF* this land. My people were here long before the white man arrived. We are not at odds with nature, and the wildlife here *knows* us."

"Oh, believe me, I'm not offended, far from it. But maybe you are human, just of an ancient type, now largely extinct."

"Phew, at least he doesn't know what I am."

But then the next blow.

"Tell me about sasquatches. Do you think they're human's underneath?"

Again, I recalled my usual mantra. "Sir, Trevor, Bigfoot is a legend, nothing more. Sure, the legend brings the tourists here, but they rarely go home disappointed once they see all the *real* animals they can encounter."

Trevor nodded sagely. "We'll talk later," he said.

Not if I could help it. He'd put me on a back foot. That didn't happen much these days, as I'd become quite adept at dealing with humans and their questions over the years.

We got on with the trek in the usual manner, but my mind kept wandering back to the conversation with Trevor, and I ensured I was never with him, out of earshot of the group for the rest of the day.

That evening, as I was leaving the store to head home, Trevor accosted me.

"Kobbi, please could we talk some more?"

"I'm sorry Sir, I'm finished for the day, and I'm heading

home now."

He looked so disappointed I almost relented.

"Then could I come back tomorrow before the tour starts for a chat?"

"I'm not working tomorrow. I'm not working again until Saturday, and I'm sure you'll be heading back home before then," I hoped.

"Oh no, I've got another week. Saturday it is then."

Trevor skipped off before I had a chance to protest further. I needed to get home and talk to Mum, Dad and the others. See what their take on all this was.

It made Mum nervous. "I knew it was a bad thing, you taking this job. I just don't understand why you do it."

"Oh, come on Mum. I've been doing it for years now. This is the first time anything like this has happened."

"It only takes one breach to expose us, then our lives will change forever. We'll never be left alone."

Dad chimed in. "Let's keep this simple shall we. You get to work late on Saturday, just ten minutes or so before you head off with your group of tourists. You explain to this guy that you are of an ancient tribe of the First Nations, and that our people happen to exude a little musk. It's actually not that uncommon in humans, you know that, some have a more distinct aroma than others. Also, I suggest you get up early, shift, and go for a run before heading to work – just in case you get a little irate with the man. It'll ensure you don't have any spontaneous changes in front of him."

I did it all just as Dad said. Trevor seemed to accept what I told him, and I thought that would be an end to it.

Saturday's trek came and went without incident, and I felt confident the whole thing had blown over. Feeling happy and energised, I decided to shift and run home rather than get the bus. I headed back into the forest, well away from the road and the store. Stripped and stashed my clothes in a bag under a rock, to retrieve them the next day as I worked Sunday's too, so would be back in the morning, then I answered the call of the wilding, making the change with my usual ease.

Little did I know at the time I'd been followed.

I caught Trevor's scent almost immediately. He'd clearly seen me shift as he was scrambling and stumbling his way fearfully in the opposite direction with no thought to where he was going, or to navigating the forest safely.

No time to retrieve my clothes, I had to stop him. I quickly shifted back to human form – all the better to try to convince him he hadn't seen what he indeed did see, and I ran after him. If anyone had seen us, it would have made a comical sight. One panicked man being chased through the woods by another man – stark naked. Perhaps I should have gone back for my clothes. I could run a lot faster than Trevor, but I too was in a bit of a panic as Mum's words came back to me.

'It only takes one breach to expose us, then our lives will change forever. We'll never be left alone.'

I had to catch Trevor. But what would I do then? How would I explain? How would I stop the world from crashing in on our lives?

Then tragedy struck. Never would I have wished such a thing to happen. As I neared Trevor, I could see the whites of his eyes as he glanced sideways and saw me gaining on him flanking his position. I could smell his fear, even in my human form. He redoubled his efforts.

"Trevor stop, please. Let me explain," I called.

He made a sound – not words, more of a strangled jibber, then he fell. Rolling down a steep slope, he tumbled awkwardly. I followed. In my haste I hadn't kept track of where we were headed, and as I scooted down the bank to where Trevor had fallen, I realised too late he'd found the road.

The loud noise of a horn, and the screech of brakes, the vague impression of a large vehicle, then all went black.

CHAPTER 10 – HOSPITAL

Strange bleeps, the smell of disinfectant and call for a Dr. Martinez over a PA system brought me swiftly back to consciousness.

I kept my eyes closed. I didn't want anyone to know I was awake until I'd assessed what condition my body was in. Slowly I lifted my arm to my face. Well, that was something at least – I was in human form. Tentatively I opened my eyes as I couldn't hear anyone nearby.

I'd never been inside a hospital before, but I read a lot, novels as well as non-fiction, so I had some idea of what they looked like and what they did. Turning my head, I could see I was hooked up to some kind of monitoring machine. I went to get up, but the agony all down my right side was so great, it caused me to flop back down.

I lay on the bed pondering my situation. Mum's going to freak, Dad'll be really pissed with me, and what would Trevor do?

Suddenly the thought of Trevor sent me into such a panic, I could feel the call of the wilding pressing in on me. Shifting would heal my wounds all that much quicker, but I could hardly do that here. I did need to find out what happened to Trevor though, so I strained to push down the change, having already got almost past the point of no return. My limbs had started to lengthen, and hair sprouted on my body. If I didn't calm myself down, I wouldn't be able to turn it around. Closing my eyes,

I thought about swimming in the mountain lake, and running through the forest, Slowly but surely, my hair retracted, and my limbs shrank back to human size, just in time before the door unlocked – *unlocked?* – and opened.

I peered through the door. There was a man in uniform just at the edge of the doorframe. A doctor came in with another uniformed man by her side.

"Hello, my name's Dr Hamblin. How are you feeling?" she asked.

"My side hurts. What happened? Is Trevor okay?"

She gazed curiously at me. "Can you tell me your name?"

"Kobbi Jones. Please tell me if Trevor is alright."

"I'm sorry. Mr Campbell died from his injuries last night. He never regained consciousness. Was he a friend of yours?"

I flashed a quick glance at the policeman. *What do they think happened?* "Well, no, not really. I work as a trail guide. He was one of the clients." I had to think quickly. "He went off track, so I had to find him."

The policeman was the next to speak. "Do you normally work in the nude Mr Jones?"

Shit! "I'd finished work for the day. I like to run – free – in the woods. When I saw Trevor, I thought he'd get lost if I didn't catch up with him and put him back on the trail."

"So you chased him, naked, into the road, where you both got hit by a truck."

Shit, shit! Trevor was dead, and it's my fault. Part of me – a small part, was relieved that the only person, the only human person that is, to ever witness one of our folk making the change, would never be able to tell his story, but that thought did little to assuage the guilt I was feeling at that moment.

"Sir, the forest can be a dangerous place. I panicked when I saw him roaming about so far off the trail. I would never harm him, or anyone for that matter."

"I see. And yet you can go off the trail, in this *dangerous* forest, and run naked."

"Yes sir. I know these forests," back into work blurb – it

always served me well, "I am *OF* this land. My people were here long before the white man arrived. We are not at odds with nature, and the wildlife here *knows* us."

The policeman scribbled something is a little book. I wanted to see what he wrote, and craned my neck, but couldn't catch a glimpse from my bed.

The doctor spoke again. "Who can we call?"

"Oh, that's okay. I'll just go home now." The urge to shift was almost overwhelming, *why?* "How long have I been here?"

"You were brought in about seven thirty last night. It's now five o'clock."

I glanced at the clock above the door, hardly able to believe her without checking. "I've been here a whole day?" No wonder I was struggling. The call of the wilding was knocking at my door. I had to get the hell out of here before I lost control. "I really need to leave now. My folks will be worried, and I've missed my shift at the store. I should have taken a group of tourists out today."

The policeman took all the details down – my address, who my family were, and where I worked. This wasn't good, but he wouldn't let me leave until I told him. He said he'd be round to see me at home the next day. I had to warn everyone. Humans never came into our house – the occasional tourist knocked on our door, usually hunters looking for Bigfoot, but we had answers for them, to fob them off.

Dad was brilliant. He did a lot of fast-talking, and finally the policeman was convinced I was just eccentric in my behaviour, and not in anyway responsible for Trevor's demise.

It wasn't true, it was all my fault. I would have to learn to live with that.

Mum got her way. I gave up my job. I'd worked there for eight years by this time, and I would miss it. Especially all the stories I heard from the tourists about the wonderful places I would never be able to see for myself.

CHAPTER 11 – TAKEN BY THE WILDING

What happens when a member of a closed tribe wants – something more?

Following the incident with Trevor, I was consumed with guilt. What if I'd got the bus home that day as normal? What if I'd checked more carefully before shifting? What if I'd stopped to get dressed before tracking Trevor down? Would things have turned out differently? But then what if he'd survived? The implications to my kind had he exposed us would have been devastating, not just for my family, but for all sasquatches. Then again, would anyone have believed him? After all, the fact that we're shapeshifters didn't feature at all in the commonly held legends, so we could easily enough hide our identities. I just couldn't stop beating myself up over the whole situation.

The only relief I had, was when I shifted to sasquatch form. The beast in me took over when I answered the call of the wilding, and the beast ran more on instinct, with less of the moral dilemmas than human-kind wrangled with.

The more time I spent as sasquatch, the less I felt the pain of guilt, so I remained in that form more and more.

Mum and Dad, and in fact, all the family, were becoming concerned.

Cally was the first to air her worries. She caught up with me on the edge of the trees by the lake as I finished a light marmot snack. "Kobbi, are you alright?"

Speaking wasn't as easy in this form, so I just nodded and

grunted.

Cally shifted back to human form, her naked body covered in goosebumps against the winter cold.

I shifted back too so we could talk. For some reason I found it harder than normal to shift. I guess I was just reluctant.

"Please, you need to spend more time at home."

"Why?" it seemed a genuine question to me, but she bit her lip as the frown, which didn't suit my gentle sister, creased her forehead.

"We...I'm worried about you. You're away so much. Please come home with me."

I didn't want to upset her, so we both shifted back and ran home.

"Son," said Mum, "I want you to stay in human form for at least the rest of the day."

This made no sense to me.

Dad explained. "Your mother is right. The more you stay as sasquatch, the harder you'll find it to shift back."

I had to admit, that hadn't occurred to me, though it would explain why I found it harder than normal earlier.

I stayed home that night, sleeping in my own bed. Only then did I realise it was the first time I done this in over a week.

The urge to shift again came upon me in the early hours of the next morning. I sneaked out of the house, shifted straight away and headed for the mountains. There was a particular tree, beside a cave – one without a bear in residence – where I liked to hang out. It was well away from the trails followed by the tourists, and was far enough away that even the hunters didn't usually make it up there, and definitely not in winter. It was difficult ground at any time of year for humans, but now, there would certainly be no one about, not even the more intrepid. This suited me just fine.

I fell into a routine of hunting, fishing, foraging, swimming and climbing. I was completely taken by the wilding, and I loved every minute of it. Slowly but surely I forgot my other life. I was a beast, a contented beast. What was the point of anything else? My mind relaxed, maybe it even became supressed, and my instincts took over in all aspects of my daily life.

*****

Spring came, then Summer, and before I knew it, the year had slipped by, then another and another. How many, I wasn't even sure.

Until one day, I saw humans again for the first time in so long, I'd lost track. A group of hunters beat their way through the undergrowth in the foothills of my mountain. Three had rifles, and two others had cameras slung round their necks. They had no chance of seeing me as I'd caught their scent on the wind long before they neared my position. I knew all the best hiding places, though part of me balked at the idea of hiding. This was my home, my mountain. Why should I hide from these intruders? But the sight of those rifles stirred a memory I couldn't quite grasp hold of. I simply knew there was a danger, so I remained stealthy.

Watching these men from my tree, I noticed one kept crouching, and touching the ground. I'd never really thought to hide my tracks, having arrogantly supposed no human would make it all the way up here.

"Hey Jack, take a look at this," said one of the men.

"Yeah, that's Bigfoot alright. Just look at the size of it!" said another.

They all crowded round my footprint. One I could have easily scrubbed out. I'd have to be more careful in the future.

I spent the next few days following the group from a distance, keeping out of sight, and checking they came nowhere near my cave. They camped at night and searched by day.

At night I crept a little closer and listened to their conversation. Much of their talk was about the hunt, their weapons and the tastelessness of their trail rations. But they also talked about where they came from. As I listened, I discovered that the three hunters were all Canadian, from somewhere nearby, and they were escorting the two Americans with cameras, who, it transpired, were from the same university where Trevor had worked. He must have told them why he'd decided to visit our area.

Trevor's name jolted me into remembering at least parts of my other life, thoughts that came in brief, but poignant flashes. The remorse I'd supressed for so long hadn't gone. It was still there, just masked by the beast in me.

By the time these men had given up and headed back down to the town, more memories had surfaced. I thought about my family, and the grief of not seeing them for so long induced a roar so loud it echoed through the valleys.

CHAPTER 12 – RETURN TO CIVILISATION

My stricken roar was heard. Not by the humans, but by the sensitive ears of the sasquatches.

Despondent, I sat on a rock just outside my cave as I fought to regain yet more memories of the past. How long it had been since I'd taken human form, I had no idea. Could I even shift back? I had no notion of that either so I tried.

Nothing happened. Perhaps I was too weak. I hadn't hunted for days, intent as I was watching the human party that invaded my territory. So I went off to seek prey. I'd become very adept, but winter could be tricky for hunting. Other animals were more cautious, many hibernated, or at least remained in their lairs unless hunting or foraging. Also, I could be more clearly seen, with my brown fur, against the white of the snow. Yet I got lucky that day. Mountain goats were skittish and easily spooked, but there were lots of them. I wasn't keen on goat, it's pungent flesh left an unpleasant aftertaste, but I was hungry, they were easy to track with their powerful aroma, so that would have to do.

I took the goat carcass back to the cave after I'd had my fill. It would do for the next meal too, but I had to keep it away from scavengers. As I piled heather on top of it to try to mask at least some of the smell, I caught wind of another scent. And light footsteps – lots of them.

Scrambling up into my favourite tree, I watched the approach of many sasquatches. They came to a stop outside my cave. Two went inside. I snorted in disgust at the invasion, and the head of one individual snapped my way – a large male.

With a shimmer, he shifted, shrinking to human form, naked and shivering in the freezing snow-covered mountain.

"Kobbi? Can you hear me? Can you understand me?"

I shook my head a little, as if trying to free up a memory. Feelings of kindness, and familial connection dripped into my consciousness. I knew him.

"It's me, Denny."

The two that had gone inside came back out, and now they were all looking in my direction.

Denny. It sounded familiar. Two more shimmered into the shift, another big male and a female. I watched, studying them carefully.

"Kobbi, please come down from there," said the female. She was older, and the sound of her voice felt safe and soothing as it pricked at my memory.

Yes, Kobbi, that's me. I eased my way down from the tree and stood before my mother.

The older man reached up and put a hand on my shoulder. "Son, it's time for you to come home."

At the time, I struggled to account for the joy I felt at that moment, but I knew I would go with them.

My parents and Denny changed back, and we all loped down the mountainside, through the forest, and to the place I knew to be home.

CHAPTER 13 – HOME

The house looked different. Bigger. And there were two other houses nearby that hadn't been there before. *How long have I been away?*

Everyone but me had resumed human form. I couldn't do it. As I gazed around the people in the front room, there were both familiar faces, but older, and there were unfamiliar faces.

I tried to speak. It was always difficult in squatch mode, but I hadn't uttered a word in – how long? And now I couldn't bring forth language. Try as I might, all I achieved were grunts, the odd squeak, and the occasional roar that vibrated the crockery on the sideboard into motion.

I sat on the two-seater sofa, taking up all the space, as my family looked on with worry creasing their brows.

The back legs of the sofa gave way under my elevated weight, and I rolled backwards off it, landing in an undignified heap. A young boy I didn't know couldn't supress his mirth, snorting as he tried to hold back laughter, but in the end it burst forth. At first I felt my anger rise, but as others joined in, I too saw the funny side, I huffed my own amusement at the ridiculous scene I'd created, and the tension in the room dissipated.

Dad righted the broken sofa, indicating with his finger for Denny and another man I didn't recognise to carry it out to the barn. He then sat on the floor beside me as the laughter slowly faded away, and most of the people resumed whatever business would be their normal daily tasks.

"You've been away a long time," said Dad. "I guess you stayed squatch all the while, which is why you're struggling to shift now, but you have to keep trying." He waved his arm about the room, at those who remained. "Being surrounded by your family, doing normal things about the homestead – all will help bring you back to us. It'll take time. And son, it's good to have you home."

I wondered what 'a long time' actually meant, but couldn't form the question, so pointed towards an unfamiliar woman standing nearby. Dad caught my drift.

"Denny's wife Marianne." He nodded towards the boy who'd started the laughter earlier. "And that little monster-from-hell is their son Brodie. He's the middle son of three. Cally's also married, well and all the others too, except Jimbo who's just started courting. You'll soon get to know who everyone is."

If my human visage had been visible, he'd have seen the blood drain from my face. *Just how long have I been away?* Jimbo was just a whipper-snapper when I last saw him and now he's going out with girls? Huh!

Dad continued. "First things first though. We need to get you shifting forms again. It used to come so easily to you. Remember how that felt and work on it."

I grunted and headed outside to look around the homestead. The new buildings were now home to my brothers and sisters and their families. I wondered how they'd met their partners, other sasquatch families lived many miles away, and tribes rarely mixed, but now that I thought about it, mixing had to occur sometimes or none of us would be here.

Watching Denny replacing the back legs of the sofa was such a normal scene, I stood and drank it in. He grinned up at me.

"Hey brother. Good to have you back, but if you don't shift soon, we'll have no furniture left, oh, and none of the beds are long enough for you."

I huffed again – my version of a laugh at that time.

He hesitated a moment, chewing on his bottom lip before speaking again.

"Um… you could do with a bath. Quite honestly Kobbi,

you stink."

It hadn't occurred to me. We were quite aromatic, even when we had a daily shift to squatch form, and I'd been like it for goodness knows how long. I huffed again, headed out of the barn and ran to the nearest lake. Behind me I heard Mum call my name, her voice agonised. I was about to turn back, when I heard Denny tell her I was just going for a bath in the lake. Poor Mum, she thought I was leaving again.

CHAPTER 14 – WORST SHIFT EVER!

I'd been back over two weeks, and still remained sasquatch. I'd tried over and over to shift, but with no success. I had to sleep in the barn, hunt for fresh meat as my sasquatch stomach couldn't take cooked meat or any other human food. Other members of the family came with me on hunts. I suspected, correctly as it turned out, that Mum had instructed everyone to keep an eye on me. Clearly she was still terrified I'd run off and never be seen again. Dad told me they'd been searching for me, but only half-heartedly, as he'd decreed that I would return when I was ready. The truth, however, was that I'd all but forgotten everyone as the wilding took me. Maybe I'd have returned sooner otherwise. When my agonised roar had echoed down from the mountains, he decided it was time, and the whole family followed the call.

I could feel everyone's concern like a hum in the back of my mind. Would I ever be able to change? I could only keep trying. In the end, it was the most unlikely thing that made the difference – blueberry muffins.

I'd been carrying tree trunks down from the forest all morning so Dad and Denny could mill them into planks for the next house to be built – this time for my sister Katia. She was pregnant with her first child so needed her own home with her husband Bill. We were all taking a break from the work, stretching out to take in the rays of the early spring sunshine.

Katia and Mum were in the kitchen baking blueberry muffins. The aroma was divine. They say smell is the most poignant of the senses when it comes to evoking memories, and I'm happy to declare that to be true.

As sasquatch, I couldn't eat muffins, I could only consume the diet of an obligate carnivore, oh, but that smell!

It had been many years since I'd felt that familiar tingling sensation that initiated the shift, but I knew immediately what was happening. My bones, my organs and my skin had been fixed in a single form for so long, they did not give up their structure easily.

I screamed – well, it was still more of a roar in fact. It shook the very ground, and everyone came running. The agony was almost unbearable, and as I caught a glimpse of the horrified faces of my family, I tried to put a stop to it, but it was too late.

Dad, ever empathic, understood. "Go back to what you were doing," he commanded, "Denny and I will look after Kobbi."

They all hesitated, both concerned and fascinated – after all, none of my in-laws or my nieces and nephews even knew what I looked like in human form.

Dad's growl came, almost as if he was in beast mode. "NOW!"

They scattered like swatted flies.

"Try to relax son," said Dad.

He had to be kidding!

Pain ripped through my body as everything within my frame shifted and shrunk. My fur receded and disappeared leaving my skin red-raw. The change took only minutes – it felt like hours, but finally I felt the chill of the air on my naked body. A sensation I hadn't experienced for longer than I could remember.

For some inexplicable reason, it was the pain in my face that hurt the most, and I raised my hands to cup my cheeks, and to manually direct my head to the kitchen door, where Mum stood watching, her face a mix of worry and relief.

And the first word I uttered after years with no speech? "Muffin."

Mum ran out carrying a blanket, and she and Dad led me,

stumbling in pain, into the house. I sat on a stool in the kitchen, now certain it wouldn't give way under me, and devoured four muffins one after another.

"Careful," said Mum, "your body isn't used to such food."

I grinned at her, already sensing a bit of a stomach ache, but I didn't care. I was back, and I could shift. It was the worst shift ever, and I wasn't sure how long I would go before I'd pluck up the courage to do it again, but finally I was certain that my life would get back on its normal track. And now I could get to know our extended family properly.

CHAPTER 15 – SANCTUARY

Though my kind normally shifts at least once a day, it was four days before I changed again. Normally that would be impossible. If we didn't shift voluntarily on a regular basis, the change came unbidden. This could cause problems, as you can imagine, if it happens when we're anywhere that humans are to be found. But it was as if I was so overloaded with squatchiness, that I was able to go so long before my next change.

When I did finally shift, it was like putting on an old coat. Dad reckoned our folk spent around ten per cent of our lives as sasquatches. For me this was very different, and as such, it was the form I felt most comfortable with. Apparently I'm not the first to lose myself to the wilding, but he thought I might be the first to successfully return. Either way, it was a joy to be able to run and hunt again.

The cave in the mountains and my tree next to it had been my home for many years. I decided to head up there for one last time – or so I thought. Brodie came with me. He was eleven years old, and very competent at hunting, so we decided to have camp-out there. We saw no one, the sun shone, we had good hunts, climbs and swims, didn't speak at all and headed back content after three days.

Brodie was a curious boy. "Do you mind that I came with you to your sanctuary?" he asked.

This stopped me short. Sanctuary. I hadn't thought about it that way before, but he was right. That's what it was, and from now, what it would remain.

"Not at all," I said. "I was alone there since well before you were born. It was nice to have company."

Brodie's insightful comment filled a hole I hadn't realised was there. As the years passed, I went to the cave on a regular basis. Sometimes alone, and sometimes Brodie or one or two of the others in the ever-extending family came with me. It truly became a sanctuary. Though I was always happy to have a bit of company, the wilding had taken me in a way that would never be completely lost to me. I did my chores at home, I helped build houses for what was now becoming a real family community as more and more squatchlets were born, I taught the youngsters skills they needed, and when everything became a bit too much for me, I headed for the cave – my sanctuary.

CHAPTER 16 – BOB

November 2023: We hadn't seen Gordon and Bob – our vampire friends in many years. We often wondered why they stopped visiting, we'd always made them welcome in our home, then one evening, there was a knock at the door.

"Bob!" said Dad, delighted. "Come on in." He looked over Bob's shoulder. "What, no Gordon?

"I'm sorry to have to break this news to you, but he met his ending over twenty years ago."

Mum came into the room. "I'm so sorry to hear that Bob. How did it happen? I thought your people were immortal."

"Almost," said Bob, looking a little cagey. "We went out to celebrate the new millennium, and he wouldn't come home with me. He stayed out until dawn – I think it was deliberate. I'm sorry, I should have written, but I was so lost. It's funny, I hated him at first, but I came to care deeply for him."

"Well, we're glad you're here now. I'm afraid we haven't got any blood packs for you, but we can arrange for that tomorrow. Meanwhile we have goats out on the paddock."

Bob creased his nose. I remembered he wasn't fond of goat blood.

"We can hunt if you like," I said, "find something more palatable?"

"Thanks Kobbi, I have to say, a bit of deer blood might go down well."

"Consider it done."

We headed out straight away, despite Mum's protests. All the better to make the most of the night hours. I shifted and ran for the trees. It always amazed me just how swift vampires are,

Bob easily kept pace with me.

In the event, we brought down a deer within the first hour, and I watched in fasciation as Bob bled it dry whilst I tucked into a hind leg.

Now we had the rest of the night, so I thought it might be nice to go for a swim.

"I've never actually learned to swim. Gordon and I often bathed in mountain pools, but they were small. Not suitable for swimming. In fact I don't know if Gordon could swim either," said Bob.

"It's as good a time as any to learn."

*****

Over that winter and the early part of the next spring, Bob and I struck up a profound friendship. I taught him to swim, better stalking methods, climbing, and something of the plants and wildlife, though I wasn't certain if these last things were of any real interest to him, but he heeded my words nonetheless. In return, Bob told me about the world. All the places he'd been, the things he'd done, and the people, human and otherwise he'd met. Two things really piqued my interest – well, everything he talked about did that, but these two things really had me going. Firstly, he told me about his home town. He spoke with such passion and longing that I knew I had to go there with him, some day, some how. The other thing – there were witches in the world – *can you believe that?*

"Witches? Seriously?"

Bob went cross-eyed. He did that sometimes when he thought I was being silly.

"There are vampires and sasquatches – so why not witches?"

"Tall, pointy hat, broomsticks and all that?"

He chuckled. "No. They look just like humans. Well, actually, I think they *are* humans, just with…you know… a bit extra. Some are a bit weird and creepy, though I wonder if they're just putting it on. Mostly, you wouldn't tell them apart from anyone else unless you've got the ability to see auras. Do you have that talent?"

I cocked my head as I gave that serious thought. "I really don't know. I've never actually seen an aura, but then maybe there are no witches hereabouts." Now, not only did I want to find a way to visit Bob's home town, I wanted to meet some witches too.

Spring had arrived, the days were getting longer, and Bob had to leave, promising to return the following Autumn.

CHAPTER 17 – HATCHING A PLAN

November 2024: I'd spent the last year pondering how someone like me, who had to shift to sasquatch form at least once a day, could possibly visit all the exciting places I'd heard about. My people had always restricted themselves to the forests and mountains of Canada and North America. It was the only way we could remain hidden and safe.

I thought back to the time when I'd returned to my family after years away – taken by the wilding. When I'd finally managed to change back to human form, I remained that way for four whole days. The trouble was, I didn't want to repeat that. It would mean a lengthy period away from my family again, and maybe I wouldn't have anything that would trigger my return to civilisation next time as it did before. Also I couldn't guarantee succeeding when it came to changing back, and I'd be stuck in that one state of being. Or, even if I did, would it again be four whole days before I needed to change? It couldn't be guaranteed. No, that was not the answer.

So when Bob returned as promised, I grilled him on how he managed to travel when he couldn't even go outside in daylight – and how he fed when travelling.

"I had concerns, I can tell you, when Gordon first told me we were going on a trip, but actually it's not too hard to make sure I stay in the dark. As for feeding, I carry a few blood packs if I can, and I can feed on humans, then glamour them into forgetting. It's quite entertaining actually. They know something strange happened to them, but they wander about aimlessly, unable to put their finger on it."

"Fascinating," I said. "And they don't become vampires too?"

"No, I stop short of killing them."

All the years I'd known Bob, it had never occurred to me to ask him about such things. "You know, I'd love to hear your story – you know, how you came to meet Gordon and become a vampire."

"Humph! Another time maybe. Right now I feel the urge to run. Coming?"

"You bet!"

Later in the winter, I took Bob to see my cave. We had to spend the day there, as we wouldn't make it there and back in the dark.

I gathered firewood so that I could shift to human form, making it easier for me to talk. Sasquatches could talk, but it wasn't easy, and in human form, I would freeze up there without a fire.

"Do you know I've never seen this cave through my human eyes," I said.

Bob was wistful. "You must have felt so free all those years up here."

"Free, yes, but deep down, not... complete." I hesitated a moment, then, "Bob, there's something I want your help with."

"Name it."

"I want to travel. I want to travel a lot, but first I want to visit your home town and meet witches."

He stared at me then burst out laughing. After a while, He gazed into my eyes and realised I wasn't joking. "How, when you can't go more than a day in this form?" he said, waving his hand to indicate my human body.

"Well that's just it. I'm not sure. You travel by ship sometimes, couldn't I do that?"

"Sure, and when your hunting instincts kick in, they'll be

a few tasty sailors to munch on."

"I'd never hunt humans."

"Kobbi, my friend, what else do you expect to find on a ship for days or even weeks. No, that wouldn't work."

He scratched his head, and chewed his bottom lip. "It could only be by plane," he finally said.

"Hmm. I've thought of that, but it's at least two hours to the nearest international airport, then three hours at the terminal, the flight time, then getting through customs at the other end. One small delay, and I wouldn't make it. Can you picture the scene at Heathrow? There'll be me, standing at passport control as they compare my face to the photograph, when suddenly I have a major growth spurt, and sprout fur."

We both fell about laughing, and making up silly scenarios involving screaming kids, fainting old women, panicked flight attendants, and confused cops trying to figure out what law I'd actually broken.

"Oh, and that's another thing. I would need to sort out a passport."

"That's the easy bit. We'll get a photo done, and I'll get that sorted for you. The main thing is working out how to shorten the time needed at each stage of the journey. Firstly, we can find somewhere for you shift much nearer the airport, that'll cut out most of those couple of hours. Second, don't worry about the three-hour thing. If you get there an hour or so before the flight, you'll still get on okay. There's nothing we can do about delays. Hopefully that won't happen, if it does, and it's a long period before the flight takes off, we'll just have to go for walk. Of course, I'll be with you, so we have to time it all so that we are only outside at night."

For the first time I really felt this could actually happen.

We headed back home the next night where we had the even more difficult task of telling Mum and Dad what I planned to do.

"Absolutely not," said Dad.

"Son, you can't possibly go. It's never been done – and for

good reason," said Mum.

"It's alright, we've got it all worked out."

An argument ensued, that included all of the family by the time we were done, but nothing was going to dissuade me. And in the end, I simply announced, "I'm doing this, and that's that!"

CHAPTER 18 – ENGLAND HERE WE COME

The day had arrived, and I can tell you, I was nervous as hell. Mum was a complete mess, still trying to convince me not to go. Bob's status as family friend was strained, though Mum beseeched him over and over to look after me and ensure I wasn't discovered.

We drove to a large wood only a half hour or so from the airport where, after checking all around in this unfamiliar territory, I shifted. There wasn't much to hunt in this woodland, and I had to manage on a few squirrel snacks. As I chomped my way through my third, there was a scream.

Jumping up, I clambered up the nearest tree to get a better look. A woman in hiking gear ran away from my position – I'd been seen. A moment of panic shivered down my spine, yet just as I pondered what I should do, Bob snagged her by the collar of her coat as she ran. I watched, fascinated as his eyes turned a deep red and he stared deep into the woman's face. Finally, she wandered off in a mild stupor.

I leapt to the ground and caught up with him. "Was that a glamouring?"

"It was. I can't imagine what she was doing wandering around in the dark. Anyway, she spotted you feeding. Poor woman was terrified – probably thought she'd be next on the menu."

"I don't hunt humans."

"I know that, but she doesn't."

Potential disaster averted, I changed back, got dressed, and we headed to the airport. So far so good.

My stomach churned as the plane took off, such that I started to regret that third squirrel, especially as I'd shifted back to human form so soon after eating it – it wasn't fully digested. I coughed up a fur-ball, which I quickly hid in my pocket. But soon we were above the clouds, and the night sky was full of stars. The flight attendants brought round drinks and little salty snacks in packets, instructing us to pull the blinds down. I didn't want to. It was good to see the sky so clearly, but I complied, not wanting to draw attention to myself.

I pulled on my headphones and watched an in-flight movie – something called 'Deadpool and Wolverine'. Whoever made this film had clearly never seen a wolverine! But it was an entertaining way to wile away the hours.

We landed at Heathrow almost two hours before sunrise. Apart from the incident in the woods, all was going to plan. We just had to get through passport control, baggage and customs, pick up Bob's car then head for one of his safe houses nearby to see out the daylight hours. Simple.

Or was it?

"First time in the UK Mr Jones?" asked the woman on the desk at passport control.

I wasn't sure if this was some kind of trick question. I gave her a sidelong look. "Yeeesss."

"Business or pleasure?"

"Excuse me?"

"Are you here for business or pleasure?"

"Oh, er, pleasure. Visiting friends."

She gazed at me a little suspiciously. "Where will you be staying during your visit?"

I hadn't thought to ask. "Er, I don't know. My friend invited me to his place, I'm not sure where that is." I scanned around to find Bob at one of the other desks, three up from me, as a British citizen he didn't have to jump through the same number of hoops, or go through the international arrivals desk. I called to him, but it was so noisy, he didn't hear me. Only one thing for it. I roared – yes, even in human form we could do that, but to a lesser extent.

The woman almost fell off her chair, and all the people nearby backed away.

Oops! So much for keeping a low profile.

Bob got his passport stamped, and rushed over – though he was on the other side of the barrier now.

I gazed at the woman, who seemed to be recovering quite well, though she still eyed me suspiciously, just like everyone in the queue.

"Sorry. I just wanted to call my friend so he could help with your questions. I'm staying with him."

She swung round and gazed at Bob. Despite his overall human demeanour, and some flesh-tone stage make-up, he always looked a little vampish. But he had this covered.

"Madam, please let Mr Jones through. He's a bit of a roughneck from the wilds of Canada and doesn't comprehend the niceties of decent behaviour."

Well, I was a little offended by that, I can tell you. But I had to trust he knew what he was doing. He gave his address, and after a longer time than we'd hoped, we were finally free to leave.

After collecting our bags, we got the bendy-bus to the car park where we picked up Bob's Mercedes.

He glanced at his watch. "No time now to get to the safe house. We'll have to book into one of the local hotels."

I too peered at my watch. "By the time the sun sets…"

"I know," he interrupted. "As soon as we can leave, we'll need to find the nearest stretch of woodland we can find so you can shift."

"It doesn't have to be woodland. It just needs to be somewhere I can't be seen," I pointed out.

"Kobbi, this isn't the wilds of Canada. I don't think you realise just what a busy country this is."

For the first time I started to question the wisdom of this trip.

The hotel receptionist passed us a knowing look as we booked a room for the day. It made Bob a little bad-tempered. "Sir, we've had a long and tiring journey, and I just want to get some rest to ensure I'm safe driving my car."

"Of course sir," the man said.

I was at a loss to understand what the man was implying, but again, I just had to trust in my friend's knowledge and experience in such matters.

Honestly, I'd never seen so many people, the hotel was abuzz with humanity, but I was curious, so while Bob slept, if that's what you called it – looked more like just being dead to me – anyway, while he was out for the count, I was impatient to explore this strange place.

CHAPTER 19 – FIRST TASTE OF A FOREIGN LAND

I had my money that I'd earned all those years as a guide, and I'd brought the box I'd stuffed it all in with me. I was thirsty, for more than just the bottled water provided in the room, or the tea in a little bag. I fancied a beer, so I headed for a bar.

"Beer please."

"Anything in particular?"

Hadn't I made myself clear? "Beer please," I said a little louder.

The barman raised one eyebrow, then poured my beer from a tap. "£3.35 please sir."

I opened my box of dollars.

The barman's shoulders slumped. "Sir we don't take Canadian dollars. You need to get that changed."

"To what?"

"To British pounds sir." He sighed. There's a foreign exchange booth at the airport. Didn't you think to do that there?"

"My friend's been taking care of everything. I guess he didn't know I had my own money."

"Well, we take cards."

"What kind of cards?"

"You know, debit cards, credit cards. American Express will do nicely Sir." He tittered as if he'd said something funny.

Not wanting to seem too ignorant, I laughed along with him.

"Are you staying in the hotel?"

"Yes."

"We can charge it to your room if you like."

I didn't know what that entailed, but if that meant I could drink my beer, I'd go along with it. "Yes, please do that."

"Your room number?"

"428."

Six beers later, that for some reason I hadn't had to pay for, I was feeling quite mellow, and a little wobbly on my feet, so I thought perhaps I should get something to eat to soak it all up. After all, aside from some scrambled eggs on the plane, hours ago, I'd had nothing substantial to eat since my last squirrel. I went to the hotel restaurant. I knew of such places, but had never been to one before. The bar in my home village did pies, biscuits and gravy and sandwiches, so I guessed it would be a bit like that.

A waitress showed me to a table and handed me a menu. I read through all the unfamiliar options, and finally, thank goodness, came to steak and mushroom pie. I pointed to it when she came to take my order.

"Anything to drink?"

I ordered more beer. Had a second helping of pie, followed by something soft, squidgy and fruity, called trifle. It was delicious. Then I had more beer.

Once I was done, I stood up, and then fell down. Hell, I was drunk, and here I was drawing attention to myself again as everyone in the restaurant stared. The waitress helped me to my feet just as I lost control, and a wodge of my fur sprouted on both my wrists. She jumped back in surprise, but then seemed to reacquire her composure.

"I think you should go to you room and get some rest sir – sleep it off."

I grinned, and just managed to turn away before throwing up on the floor.

The manager came and told me to leave.

When Bob woke up, he saw me dozing in the chair by the window. "Have you had a good rest after the long flight?" He asked.

I woke with a start at his question. "Huh, what? Oh, well not exactly."

We were in the car heading north on the A1 before Bob finally deigned to speak to me.

"What were you thinking? Which bit of 'don't draw attention' don't you get?"

"I just fancied a beer or two and some food, that's all."

"Fifteen beers, two dinners and a charge for cleaning up."

"No, it can't have been that many."

"Look at the bill yourself." He thrust the invoice at me.

"Oh, well, you could have told me I needed to change my dollars to British money."

"Firstly, I didn't know you even had any money, but we can get that done later, and secondly, it's not about the money. I hear you lost it a bit and sprouted. There was…talk when I went down past the restaurant. Though I have to say, the waitress was pretty cool about it. "Goodness knows what she thought was happening. Good job this is England. Anywhere else in the world and everyone would have been running for the hills."

"What do you mean? Why is England different?"

"Anything weird happens here, British folk would not admit to 'never having seen it all before'. It's one of the things that makes it easier for people that are… different to live here unnoticed."

"Humph. I've not met many Brits. Very few came out on my guided walks. It was mostly Canadians, Americans, some Australians, and a few Europeans. Had a lovely group of Germans once."

"Stop changing the subject. The fact is, you were almost compromised on your first day here. You have to be more careful."

"Well, if the Brits are so cool about things, maybe I don't have to be so secretive."

Bob just sighed and left it at that.

CHAPTER 20 – TRAFFIC JAM

There were roadworks on the A1. Bob said that's normal, there were always roadworks on the A1, but that at least we didn't have to go on the M6, which was even worse. I had no idea what he meant by that, but decided just to nod sagely.

I had more important things to worry about. The familiar tingling was running down my spine.

"I'm not going to be able to hold off the shift much longer," I said.

"Shit, I was worried about that. There's nowhere to pull off, and even if there were, there's nowhere we can go around these parts where you won't be seen."

The cars were at a standstill. I scanned around, only a thin row of small, bare trees lined the road, and there were a few fields and houses the other side of them. Nowhere that I could shift, or hunt, even under the cover of darkness, because, truth to tell, with all the streetlights, and lights in the houses, it really wasn't all that dark. Hopefully the food I'd eaten in the hotel would stave off the hunger, such that the hunting bit wasn't going to be a problem, but trying to hold off the change was causing significant pain.

Another hour later, and I don't think we'd moved more than a mile or so, my fur sprung from my arms, chest and head. "I'm sorry, but I'm not going to be able to hold back any longer." I pulled off my shirt, and tried to wriggle out of my trousers and underwear.

"Oh, bloody hell," said Bob. "Okay, down beside you is

a lever on the side of the seat. It'll tip the seat into a near horizontal position and you can slide back a bit too. You'll just have to change where you are."

I'd never shifted in an enclosed space before, but I had no choice. I managed to get out of my clothes as my body elongated to my eight-foot sasquatch stature, and fur sprouted all over my body. The car rocked insanely, causing some other car drivers to beep their horns. Finally the shift was complete and I tried to sit up, but could only raise the seat so far as the inside of the car wouldn't accommodate my full height.

I sat there, in full-on squatch mode, as the cars in the other lane next to us began to move. Despite the dark, my profile must have been visible, and it elicited stares and more beeps from everyone going by.

"Okay," said Bob. "Just stay calm, no one will catch more than the a cursory glance at you. How long before you can change back."

I grunted my answer. "Minimum one hour, more is preferable."

"Make it the hour, and we'll find somewhere else for you later."

I could hardly believe we got away with it. Yes I got stared at, but no one could really get a proper look at me, and people's natural defence mechanisms would hopefully cause them to find logical explanations for what they thought they saw. *'It was a big teddy bear' 'It was someone dressed up as an ape, or even a sasquatch.' It was just a shadow, a trick of the light.'* Either way, no one would ever think they saw a genuine, *bona fide* sasquatch sitting in a car on the A1 in England.

We finally arrived at Bob's place in the early hours, and long before dawn.

CHAPTER 21 – THE PUB

After my questionable incident in the hotel at Heathrow, Bob gave me the run down on acceptable behaviour, he got my dollars changed to pounds, and finally he was satisfied I could go out on my own during the day when he was resting.

I enjoyed the experience of life in a small English town. This included gaining lbs of weight as I enjoyed the delights of the local tearooms – to include sampling cream teas, carrot cake, chocolate cake – okay, I'd had chocolate cake before – and a personal favourite, sticky toffee pudding – they served this literally everywhere.

I only went out at night to shift, with Bob there to keep an eye on my privacy, and all worked out well.

Spring was knocking on the door by the time Bob announced that he'd been in contact with some witches he knew, and that we would meet one in a pub later that week.

I was so excited. The thought of meeting a real witch was the stuff of dreams to me.

"We'll go to the forest first, so you can change, then head out to the pub. It's in the country, and is frequented by quite a lot of witches, and a few other so-called supernaturals. I've been there a number of times and my appearance doesn't faze anyone."

I was surprised though. Bob normally wore very standard, mundane clothing, with a bit of stage make-up so he didn't look quite so pallid. But this night, he had his black and reds on and his silk-lined cape, and hadn't applied the make-up. He looked every bit the vampire.

I'd eaten quite a hearty dinner so that I had no need to hunt when I changed that night. It was a bit of an issue in these British woods anyway – not much wild game, just the odd rabbit or hare, and occasionally I was lucky enough to find a deer, but Bob discouraged that as I couldn't consume it all in a single night, and a half-eaten deer was yet another thing that would draw attention as it seemed very little of the British woodlands remained free of humans for any length of time.

We got back to the car park on the edge of the forest, and found two other cars parked up.

"Dog walkers probably. They may not be long as it's dark, you can't spend time changing here in case they return mid-shift."

"Why not take a risk?" I said.

"What do you mean?"

"If this place, as you say, attracts folk that are different to most humans, why don't I go in like this?"

Bob gazed at me. "I know your speech is a little awkward when you are sasquatch, but it almost sounded like you're suggesting you go in the pub like that!"

"I did."

We argued for a bit, but I'm a stubborn sod when it came down to it, and finally Bob relented.

"Well, if you're going to do this, at least wear your big coat so that if you shift back to human form, you're not stark naked."

"It doesn't work like that. I can't resist shifting to sasquatch after a certain amount of time, but it's not the same the other way around."

"Humour me."

I agreed, donned my big coat, though it wouldn't reach right across my massive chest, and we headed into the pub to meet up with a witch called Kitha.

THE END – so far...

KITHA THE WITCH:

I was intrigued when my adoptive sister, Venus, told me Bob the vampire wanted to meet up, and he was bringing a 'friend' with him. For years I hadn't known vampires were real, but Venus knew a number of them, and told me Bob was actually quite an affable chap – as vampires go, so curiosity got the better of me, and I wanted to take a look at this mysterious creature for myself. Little did I know the friend he was bringing along was possibly even more enthralling. Venus would curse herself when she found out she'd missed out, having opted to stay at home that evening.

I got to the pub early. It was still light, so I knew they wouldn't be along just yet, but I just felt like sitting quietly by myself for a while. I was half way through my second spritzer, when the atmosphere in the main bar shifted to one of amazement. In came Bob with a huge hairy creature beside him. I couldn't help but stare at it – him – whatever, even as Bob got in a round of drinks.

I'd met many different supernatural beings before, but had never suspected sasquatches were real.

Anyway, after we agreed to tell each other our respective stories, Bob went first, and then Kobbi took his turn.

I listened to both their stories with keen interest. Although Kobbi's speech was a little off, it wasn't too difficult to follow. Each laid out a whole other world I'd been completely unaware of. I hoped they would find my story just as interesting as my tale wasn't just about me. In fact it spanned centuries. So here goes...

GREY WITCH

What happens when everything and everyone you know is so different to what you thought...?

A Bit of Preamble:
History and legends abound with tales of witches. Always they are white witches – those benevolent by nature, out to bestow good things on all people. Or they are creatures of the dark that follow the black arts and are bent on seeking power. Either way the stories tell of their persecution throughout time. Indeed almost all the women hanged, burnt at the stake or subjected to the ducking stool for witchcraft had no such power at all. They were simply wise women with knowledge of herb lore, or with an understanding of the natural world. Yet the truth is, such power does exist. Its practitioners typically had the sense to keep their abilities hidden. In reality, witches are neither wholly light nor wholly dark. Like almost every other person, they possess traits of both, and could therefore be described as grey. My name is Kitha, and I am one such grey witch. This is my story.

CHAPTER 1 – MANIFESTATION

I'm a Witch – What the Hell!

I was a quiet child, solitary by nature. This never seemed a problem to me, I was happy that way, but the teachers at school worried over my lack of inclusivity. Why didn't I want to play with the other kids? Why did I not contribute when forced to do group work? Why did I sit alone in the playground during breaks? In truth, school seemed no more than a necessary evil to me. The tasks we were assigned ranged from pointless to downright stupid, and as for the other kids – well, their company offered me nothing of interest, and many demonstrated a cruel streak when confronted with anyone with a bit of imagination.

There was one exception. Matthew. Matthew was a kind boy, with a talent for drawing intricate and fascinating patterns, mostly in ink, on white paper. But we were never partnered for joint work – the teachers liked to spread us oddballs around rather than 'encourage' us by putting us together.

Matthew, however, had a 'disability'. A spurious term I think, as he was notably more 'able' than most, it was just that his legs didn't work properly. He compensated with sticks – it worked for him though it made him the butt of lame jokes from our classmates. Sorry, no pun intended. On the day a gang of said class 'mates' went too far, my own nature erupted unexpectedly and disastrously.

I came out of the toilet block just in time to see Josh, Ben, Terri and Tania kicking Matthew's sticks away, and laughing as he toppled to the ground. But they weren't satisfied, with that. They all got their phones out to film him trying to get up. When I saw him attempt to cover his face with his arm, making him slump back to the ground, an uncontrolled hatred built inside me, roiling around in the pit of my stomach. It was more than just anger at the injustice. It was a sheer loathing for these kids and their mindless, abysmal behaviour. A burning sensation grew from a mere spark deep within, as a wellspring of previously untapped power arose from inside my body. It was a kind of shockwave. It swept from my chest and abdomen, flattened the nearby bushes and floored Matthew's assailants.

Unfortunately the headmaster witnessed my first manifestation of witchcraft. And all five kids stared at me from their prone positions. Yes five, even Matthew gazed at me wide-eyed and terrified. It's true what they say, 'no good deed goes unpunished', and that was certainly the case on that day.

CHAPTER 2 - RESCUE

After the incident at school, I spent the next year or more in some kind of institute being prodded, poked, analysed, tested and questioned. I had no answers. I didn't know I was a witch. No one had ever told me, and my parents were notable by their absence.

My sister Penny was my first and only visitor. It had taken her that whole year to be allowed in to see me, and by the time she did, my anger at the injustice had me coiled like a tight spring. I snapped at her delay in coming, even though I knew it wasn't her fault.

"I'm so sorry Kitha. We should have taken you under our wing long ago. I just hadn't realised you were one of us."

"What? What do you mean?"

Penny pursed her lips and her forehead crinkled as she closely analysed the whole room top to bottom, under the bed, behind the only picture in the room – that of a tropical beach – and under the lampshade.

As I watched her, I could feel my own frown deepening. "What are you looking for?"

She put a finger to her lips and continued her search.

I sat on the bed and waited, watching as she lifted the rug and then checked out the en suite. Beckoning me through, she shut the bathroom door.

"This room's clean."

"Of course it is."

Penny sighed and tipped her head as if I were being dense. "They're listening in."

"What!"

"For goodness sake Kitha, they've been studying you all this time, do you really think that stops when you come to your room?"

A little prickle worried at me between my shoulder blades and I too glanced about the room. But this was the first time anyone else had been there. "Why would they bother? I've had no one come to visit and I'm not in the habit of talking out loud to myself."

"You're a witch Sis. I can guarantee if you'd started chanting, they'd be in here like a shot."

"A witch? What are you babbling about?"

"Why do you think you're here? Do you think just anyone can do what you did?"

I wanted to argue, but she shushed me again with a wave of her arm.

"Never mind all that now. We have to get out of here quick before they wonder what we're up to."

"How? I've tried to leave before, they won't let me out."

Penny opened the window. It was small, barred, and oh yes, my room was on the second floor. "Through there," she said.

I just laughed and went to go back into my bedroom. She grabbed my arm, muttered something incoherent, and before I knew it we were sitting on the branch of a tree in the garden. Shock coursed through my body as my feet dangled in empty space twenty-five feet off the ground. I stared at the beads of sweat on Penny's forehead. Whatever she did, she was paying for it.

"One more and we're home free."

My knees gave out as, in a flash, we landed on the grass in the park across the road and I fell to the ground. I glanced up at Penny. She looked awful. Her red face was framed by sweat-soaked bangs of wispy hair, and she leaned over putting her hands on her thighs.

"Are you alright?"

She didn't answer the question, but took hold of my arm again. "We need to get away from here – fast. My car's in the next street. I thought I could do a third jump, but I'm afraid my energy's sapped.

I could see Penny didn't have any 'fast' in her. I stood and lifted her arm across my shoulder. "Which way?"

She waved her hand in the general direction to the left, and I helped her first into the treeline so we couldn't be seen from the building we'd just exited, and then across to the road. She still had her yellow VW Beetle. There it was, parked behind a big white van.

"Keys?"

She rummaged in her pocket and pulled out a key. I couldn't drive, and I was pretty sure Penny wouldn't let me if I could. She adored her little Beetle. I unlocked the driver's door with the key – no push button gizmo with a car this old – and somehow managed to manoeuvre her into the seat. I handed her the key and rushed round to the passenger side while she got the old jalopy fired up.

Now I wanted answers. "Okay, so now are you going to explain how the hell you did that? And what was with the whole bathroom window business?"

Penny was breathing hard. I felt a bit guilty questioning her, but I was bursting with curiosity, and my righteous anger hadn't yet dissipated despite the rescue.

"Line of sight. I could see the big beech tree through the window, it was the focus for the jump."

"Jump," I said flatly, trying out such a normal word in a thoroughly different light.

"Jump. Transport. Whatever you want to call it." Her breathing slowed and her colour returned to normal as she put the car in first gear and pulled away. "We're going to a friend's house. I need to recover my strength. Later I'll explain everything.

CHAPTER 3 – OUT OF THE FRYING PAN AND INTO THE FIRE

Darbie and Kat lived together in a substantial cottage on the outskirts of the town. Huh! Darbie and Kat – it sounded like a bad comic duo! I studied them surreptitiously while Penny went upstairs for a sleep. Darbie was tall for a woman. Her near black skin was perfect as it stretched over her high cheekbones. Strangely her eyes were a startling green, an unusual and beautiful contrast. She could only be described as elegant in her plain, dark brown trousers and simple peach-coloured top. Kat was completely the opposite. A kind of 'earth-mother' type. Average height, slightly overweight – in a comfortable sort of way – unruly brown hair with red highlights, and a face that shone with joy. You simply couldn't look at her and not smile back. She was dressed in a long purple skirt, flowery yellow blouse and blue, crocheted jacket. Nothing matched, and yet somehow it was a good look for her.

Kat patted a stool. "Sit yerself down lass, I'll make a cuppa."

Darbie glided over and sat next to me. She ran the back of her hand down my cheek. It was a surprisingly sensuous gesture that made me shiver with pleasure. Concern creased her forehead as she gazed straight down into my inner being. "We will take your suffering from you Kitha."

I stared into Darbie's penetrating eyes, and was shocked

to feel a tear welling. I couldn't hold her gaze for long, so I concentrated on the mug of herbal tea Kat had given me as I wrapped my fingers around it's comforting warmth. I started to wonder just how long Penny would sleep, and hoped, selfishly, it wouldn't be too long before she joined us.

After that slightly awkward moment, the conversation turned to the mundane, so by the time Penny entered the kitchen a couple of hours later, she found us chatting about cake recipes. Not that I knew much about those, I only knew my mum's carrot cake was the best – ever.

Penny smiled at the, now easy-going, interaction. "Shall we go and sit in the front room? We need to fill my sister in before the others get here."

Others?

Darbie floated – not literally – through the door as Kat gathered up one of the three tabbies from its slumber on top of the washing machine, and gestured with her head for me to precede her.

My emotions were a complex mix of happy to be out at last and anger that it took so long. So first I demanded to know why, if Penny could do this 'jumping' thing, she didn't come for me before. She explained 'line of sight' to me again like she was talking to a five-year old. The three women starting talking all at once as I swallowed this explanation. I didn't know where to look as they kept finishing each other's sentences, verbally tripping over each other in their attempts to get me to understand.

Mental numbness crushed me into silence as Penny, Darbie and Kat brought me up to speed.

So here are the highlights. My mum's a witch, but my dad forbade her from using her talents. Yes that's right, I said 'forbade'. What the hell! I was never close to either of my parents, and clearly missed all the signs that their relationship wasn't all it should be. Penny held Mum in contempt for allowing herself to be suppressed in that way. Personally I thought back to my

Dad's quick temper and found myself sympathetic towards her. Not that I could do anything about it – it was her bed, and she'd have to lie on it. Whatever!

Penny, it seemed, had her talents discovered at an early age when Kat 'felt' the protective shield she put around me in my crib as a baby. Apparently she had no idea what she was doing, it was just instinctive, but the thought tapped a well of tenderness in me towards my sister. Kat had introduced Penny to their coven, and she spent her early evenings learning to understand and control her talents before heading home. Mum and Dad never knew, they probably assumed she was doing after-school activities, and clearly weren't interested enough to find out one way or the other.

The coven was made up of fourteen witches – fifteen now with me, they say – which I have to admit fills me with both excitement and trepidation. There are a number of different types of witch, but they all try to master at least some skills outside of their own speciality. We needed to discover what areas I have the most talent in, but I will take on other teachings too – so they said anyway. Penny told me that up until a year ago, I'd demonstrated no signs at all of being a witch. After I was taken away to the Institute, it was months before Penny even found out where I was. She'd tried to visit me many times, but had been turned away. Only after she threatened to seek a court order now that she was officially an adult, they relented, and finally she was allowed in, and was able to extract me. However, as a minor, the coven would have to keep me hidden until I got to eighteen. None of these people, not even Penny, were my official guardian after all. I guess my parents would be fine with me being hauled back to the Institute. But still, I wasn't happy about having to remain in hiding.

My anger and frustration started to rise again. "Wait. You can't keep me cooped up in here for over a year. I'll go nuts. That'll be like swapping one prison for another."

Darbie's amazing eyes found mine again. "Never a prisoner Kitha. We just need to keep you safe so they don't take you back to that place. We'll change your appearance. Restyle and colour your hair, put on makeup before you go out anywhere to make you look a little older, and, if you can bear it, to always have one of us with you."

Kat chipped in. "Don't go to any place on a regular basis, don't stay anywhere for too long, and don't go to places where you might be seen by people who know you. Just be like everyone else, but don't draw attention to yourself."

Penny's turn. "It'll all be much easier as we train you. You'll come to sense any potential danger, and quietly move away from it. But one of the key things, especially in these first few months while you learn to control your magic, is to avoid getting upset or running to anyone's rescue." The reference to Matthew wasn't lost on me. It's what got me into this mess in the first place. "Now, I want you to get some rest before the rest of the coven arrive. They're all anxious to meet you, and I have a feeling it'll be a long night.

My new bedroom was rather stark. After all, I owned nothing but the clothes I stood up in. There was an old wardrobe made of dark wood, full of woodworm holes – empty but for an old-fashioned nightdress and a knitted cream cardigan. Other than that, there was a single bed with flowery bed linen, a tatty green armchair, a bedside table with a lamp and a colourful woven rug. I sensed Kat's influence in this room. Penny said she'd take me clothes shopping the next day after Darbie had 'sorted my hair out', and that as time went on, I'd fill my 'space' with nik-naks and the tools of my witchcraft.

I lay down, only now realising just how tired I was, and before I knew it, there was a banging on the door.

"Up you get sleepy-head," called Penny. She didn't wait for me to respond. The door swung open and she came in still towel-drying her long red-blonde tresses. Fully revived now, Penny sat on the end of the bed. "Get yourself showered. You can borrow some of my undies for now, then come on down and meet the others. There's food in the kitchen – what am I saying? There's always food in the kitchen." She rolled her eyes, but with a joyful smile.

"Kat?"

"You guessed it." She'd dropped the wet towel on the floor and finger combed her hair.

The bulky silver ring Penny wore snared my attention.

She saw me looking and held out her hand so I could get a better look. The figure of an owl was half the length of her middle finger. "My spirit guide."

It was like something out of a fantasy novel, or something. "Spirit guide? Seriously?"

Penny grinned. "Don't worry. You'll understand soon enough." With that she grabbed the towel from the floor and left, but just as I was about to undress for my shower, she rushed back in with a bra that was a little too small for me and matching knickers.

I bit my lip a bit too hard, *ouch*, as I went downstairs and headed for the kitchen after my shower. What would these people be like? Lively chatter emanated from the living room, getting louder as I got closer. There was no one in the kitchen, but though my stomach rumbled insistently, the salads, quiches and bowls of nibbles on the table lost their appeal as nausea took over. Even a room full of aloof whitecoats with probing instruments hadn't made me feel this intimidated. I grabbed a glass and went to the sink for water. As I swallowed a full half pint, the back door suddenly looked quite appealing. I put the glass down and went to make good my escape, but as I grabbed the handle and pulled at the door, it only opened a short way, then it resisted. Yes, that's what I said. It resisted! I tried with both hands, but it was like it was being sucked back to the frame. *Trapped.* My vision blurred as unexpected tears flowed. I lost any purchase I had on the door as it finally slammed shut and I fell back against the kitchen table. I hadn't realised there was anyone else in the room.

"Come on. Everyone's dying to meet you," said Kat.

Queasiness drew me back to the kitchen sink. I thought

to fill another glass of water, but I'd had enough, and besides, my hands were shaking. I glanced under my arm at Kat as I leaned over the edge of the sink. Her eyes shone like diamonds. Kat who'd seemed so homely and comfortable to be around. My instincts had been to trust her, but now they riled against her. There was a powerful witch behind this apparently cheery house-frau. Talk about 'out of the frying pan and into the fire'. What had Penny got me into?

Kat's voice took on a kind of weird, deep echo. "I see fear in your eyes child. You do well not to take any of us for granted, but I assure you, we mean you no harm. You'll see." Her voice returned to normal. "Come now."

After another quick glance at the back door, I saw little option but to comply, so I followed Kat into the living room. Everyone fell silent and turned towards me as I walked in. My gaze wandered across the eclectic mix of women in the room. No. Not just women. Two were men. For some reason I couldn't fathom, I found that comforting.

Kat piped up. "Everyone. This is Kitha – Penny's little sister. Now, for goodness sake, stop gawping at her, she's spooked enough as it is."

Slowly the chatter started again, and a few members of the coven passed a word of greeting or a nod to me before re-engaging in their previous conversations.

Penny came over. "You look like a rabbit in the headlights. Come and sit down."

I followed Penny to one of the three sofas. It was a big room that comfortably accommodated all fifteen of us. I found my gaze drawn to a girl who looked about my age, maybe a little younger. She sat alone on a stool by the sideboard, with a glass of juice in her hand. We smiled shyly at each other.

Darbie glided onto the sofa next to me. "That's Venus, Shirley's granddaughter." She pointed a long, manicured finger at a woman standing near the window talking to one of the men. Darbie then changed tack. "Don't worry about Kat. She's good people, just takes some getting used to. It won't be long before you know everyone here really well. Tonight is just a friendly gathering…" *friendly?* "… to show you off. It's been a while since the coven had a new member. On Saturday we'll meet again for your initiation."

My stomach reeled as I wondered just what was involved in an 'initiation'. Nobody had asked me if I even wanted to be part of this coven, and I wasn't sure I did. I needed time to think. I glanced around the room again. As my eyes fell on each person, they all in turn looked back at me and responded with a smile or a nod, or, in a couple of cases, a stare. It was as if they'd felt my eyes on them and, one after the other, reacted accordingly. Spooky.

I searched out Penny. Where was she? Just as panic started to rise again, she came into the room. I hadn't realised she'd gone out. She was chatting to tall woman in her late forties or early fifties with spiky silver hair and too much mascara. Then Kat clapped her hands and everyone fell silent. All eyes turned to me at once – again with the mixed expressions. I wasn't too sure this welcoming committee was unanimous in its benevolence.

"Everyone, you've now had a chance to see our latest member. In time you'll all get the chance to chat with her, but for now, let's sing her into the coven."

You've got to be kidding me!

From somewhere, Kat produced a weird drum thing, made of wood with carvings around the rim, and started tapping out a beat. Everyone began to sing. I couldn't make out the words, but the harmonies were complex and, I have to admit, quite beautiful, such that it sent shivers through my whole body. By the time the song ended, tears streamed down my face yet again. Penny came over and hugged me.

"I have to get out of here Sis." I whispered, "I need time to think."

Penny bit her lip as her forehead creased a little. "People will be looking for you. The Institute probably called the police. You need to stay here, just for the time being. We'll get you ready for a trip out tomorrow, I promise."

I pursed my lips and nodded my compliance.

*****

I awoke wondering why I hadn't heard the loud buzzer that always sounded at 6.30 at the Institute. Then the memory of the previous day came crashing through my thoughts and I sat up with a start. I scanned my new bedroom once again. Yes, it was rather empty, but at least it wasn't white and sterile, and Penny had promised to take me shopping. I glanced at my watch. It was almost 9 o'clock. I hadn't lain in so late since I lived back home. I dressed quickly and went downstairs. Kat was in the kitchen causing me to pause briefly at the door.

"Good morning Kitha. What would you like for breakfast?"

"Oh. Er..."

"I'll bet you like pancakes."

My mouth watered at the thought despite my trepidation. "Well, yes actually."

"Excellent. I'll get right on it. There's tea in the pot, help yourself."

She seemed so normal and homely again, yet I'll never forget the way her eyes sparkled brightly as she ripped the backdoor from my hand with just a thought, or a spell, or something – and as for that weird voice, ugh! I poured a cup of tea, and then remembered my manners. "Can I pour one for you too?"

"Oh. How kind. Two sugars, but no milk."

I passed Kat's tea over to her and perched on a stool watching her busily beating the eggs in a bowl, and dumping in the flour, some of which puffed into the air and then clung to her cheek and apron. It made me smile, and I tried to remember the last time I'd done that.

Kat couldn't have seen me, as she was facing the cooker, yet she knew somehow. "It's good to see you more relaxed. Your pretty face lights up when you smile. Did you know that?" It was rhetorical. "I realise last night was a little overwhelming, but you'll get to know us all, and we'll all be friends – more than friends."

After breakfast, Darbie took me to the bathroom where she was ready with a stool, comb, scissors and a packet of hair dye. She got to work with hardly a word, then took me into her bedroom where a dressing table was strewn with a hair drier, styling rod and more make-up than one person was likely to use in a lifetime – odd, because her own pure skin looked untouched by such products.

By the time Darbie was done, a dark-brown bob replaced my long red-tinged blonde ponytail, and my face looked years older. I liked the new colour, though wasn't sure I was too keen on the hairstyle, but the makeup was cool. One thing was for certain, no one would recognise me.

"Wow!" said Penny from the door.

Darbie acknowledged the approval of her work with a tiny smile and a sideways nod.

"Okay Sis, lets get you some new threads."

CHAPTER 4 - SISTERS

Well, I thoroughly enjoyed our day in town, and Penny was clearly in her element too. We went from one shop to another, trying on clothes and shoes, and laughing as we put on elaborate hats we had no intention of buying, whilst pulling silly faces and poses in the mirror. It was the sort of thing sisters do – but we'd never done. We had lunch in a lovely little bistro overlooking the river. At the time, I didn't wonder for a moment where the money for all this came from, but she must have spent more than a grand that day.

My one moment of distress came when I peered through the window of a jewellery shop. There was a bangle on display designed with etched daisies. It reminded me of the one Gran had given me on my twelfth birthday, just before she died. I missed Gran, and wondered, not for the first time, why Mum wasn't more like her. Penny said she'd go home and get it for me. The thought warmed me. At least it would be something that was really just mine from the only one bit of the past I could never let go.

Anyway, by the time we got back to Darbie and Kat's place, we were loaded up with goodies. But when we were packing away all my new stuff into the wardrobe and drawers, reality came crashing back down on me.

"Don't forget to hang this up too." Kat was standing at the door brandishing a hooded black cloak.

I stopped in my tracks. Saturday's 'initiation' had temporarily slipped my mind. Now my fun day was ruined.

Penny's smile dropped too as she saw the distress on my face. I couldn't hear what she whispered to Kat as she took the robe from her and shut the door. "Let's not worry about this for the time being," she said as she hung it at one end of the wardrobe – largely out of sight behind my other new clothes.

"No one's asked me if I even want to be in this coven of yours. I feel like I'm being railroaded into something without the slightest idea of what I'm letting myself in for."

Penny sat on the bed and patted the space next to her.

I hesitated a moment before I joined her.

"Actually you're lucky. This is the best coven in the area."

There are others?

"We all look after each other. It's nothing to worry about." She chewed her top lip for a moment and then continued. "Witches without membership of a coven are considered rogues. Rogue witches are shunned at best. Driven out of town...or worse. Kitha, you have a strong magical power. It's a form of talent, if you like, but it's undisciplined, wild. We keep what we do secret. Out in the world, without the protection of the coven, not only would you be rogue, but without training, your talents will manifest randomly. Look what happened before. One flash of magic and you were hauled off to that awful place. If you draw attention to yourself using your talents in public, with no control, you'll be banged up again in no time. Or worse, if any witches from other covens get hold of you, they will do whatever they think is necessary to stop you. We have to remain secret, you understand that right?"

My mind reeled as I conjured up a whole list of images of what could happen to me – none of them good. I was trapped by my own nature. But was I? "Is there anyway to put a stop to it? Take away the magic?"

Penny stared at me. The shock, plain on her face, almost made me laugh for some reason. Gathering her wits, she took a few deep breaths and put her arm across my shoulders. "Never, ever, say that again. Firstly no. Magic is in the genes. It can't be removed. Secondly, as witches we consider ourselves to be more than human – better. You can't change what you are, and honestly why would you want to? What you have is a gift. Once you're trained in how to use and control it, it will enhance your life beyond anything you can imagine."

I wasn't convinced, but I was clearly getting nowhere talking to Penny about this. She was brainwashed, that had to be it. Until I knew more, I'd have to play along. I changed tack. "So what does this ceremony involve?"

Penny's shoulders eased, and the worry line on her forehead smoothed back out. "The ceremony's a simple matter. Each member of the coven will surround themselves with their particular aura of magic, call in their spirit guide, then give you a blessing to formally welcome you into the group. Once done, you'll have to swear allegiance to the coven. It's just a short promise..." *sounded like the Brownies.* "...I'll teach it to you on Saturday before we get started. After that, well, we just party."

"Well that doesn't sound too bad." Secretly I was wondering where I could go. Somewhere they couldn't find me. And I'd have to get past Kat.

Penny smiled happily, clearly back in her comfort zone now that she thought she'd won me over.

CHAPTER 5 - ESCAPE

Saturday morning – it had arrived. *Well, of course it has. Not even a witch of my considerable talents, ha ha, could have stopped that.* I dressed, donned the bracelet Penny had retrieved for me as promised, and went downstairs. Everything looked normal. Kat's apron was splattered with oil as she happily fried a load of eggs. Darbie sat on her usual stool with her hands wrapped round her coffee mug, and Penny poured tea for the rest of us – actually, I'd have rather had coffee. Why had no one asked me what I prefer to drink when I get up?

"Good morning Kitha. It's a beautiful day. Pop some toast in. I'll do you some eggs."

I'd come silently into the kitchen, and Kat hadn't looked my way. How did she know I was there? How did she always know? I put two slices into the toaster in the middle of the table.

"Are you ready for your big day? It's so exciting, isn't it?"

You'd think Kat was talking about a trip to the zoo or something. The homely, cheerful act was really starting to get on my nerves as, yet again, she seemed to see right through me.

"Now now. No need to fret. We'll all be there supporting you. Oh, and I invited Venus over to have a chat with you. She was the last initiate, though she was only eight at the time, and the ceremony's a little different for children."

Eight? "You forced an eight year old to join the coven?" Shock at such a terrible thought had brought on the outburst. Dammit, I was trying to play it cool while I planned my escape.

They all stopped dead in their tracks and stared at me.

Penny was the first to speak. "I thought you were cool with this – you know, after our little chat."

How was I going to smooth this one over? *They'll watch me more closely now. Shit!* "Well. Yes. Of course I am. It's just, well, I'm not eight years old. I'm old enough to decide for myself, after all."

Darbie's penetrating eyes found mine. Well, honestly, I'm not gay or anything – at least I don't think so, but I still get that little tingle of excitement when she turns her attention on me. I don't know, but perhaps it was the way I was drawn to her or something, but she seemed immediately satisfied I was good with all this. She turned to Kat. "It's fine," was all she said.

Kat nodded, and resumed her mumsy stance, dishing up the eggs onto my plate.

Phew, got away with that then. I'd just cleared away the dishes when Venus arrived.

*****

"Naked? What do you mean naked? They've given me a robe to wear." I was struggling to breathe as Venus gave me her run down on the initiation ceremony. Then I remembered Venus was initiated when she was only eight, and rage took over. The sideboard started to shake and a vase fell off, smashing noisily on the floor. "They made you strip off?"

Venus gave the broken vase a quick, startled glance before turning back to me, wide-eyed. "Oh! Er, no. Because I was just a child I got to wear a petticoat type thing. They called it a shift. Mind you, it stuck to me when it got wet, and it was a bit see-through, so it didn't make much difference."

"Wet? Why would it have got wet?"

The sideboard had stopped rattling, and Venus took another glance at it just to make sure. "Oh, it's nothing really. As each of the coven members gives you their blessing, they douse you with a cup of equally blessed water. There's a lot of 'blessing' that goes on in the coven. They see it as important." She shrugged.

"So what kind of witch are you? – If I'm allowed to ask."

"Honestly, I don't know. My Gran's convinced I'm a witch. She says she's 'felt' it, but that I haven't 'manifested' yet. Whatever that means. I think it's just wishful thinking."

"You don't think you're a witch at all?"

"Who knows? My Mum died and my Dad cleared off. Gran's all I've got, and I guess I'm all she's got too, so she's determined to witchify me somehow!"

I looked at Venus with new eyes. She'd had to put up with this crap for years. I changed tack. "So how do you get on with the other members of the coven?"

Venus shrugged again. "Oh, okay. Mostly they ignore me as I haven't got anything to offer. They just see me as some kinda hanger-on. They're not wrong. The two fire witches don't seem to like me. But they're pledged to protect me like everyone else is, so that's okay I 'spose."

"Fire-witches?"

She tittered nervously, and her voice dropped to a whisper. "They're really weird. You must have spotted them the other night. Spiky red dyed hair, too much eye-liner, black lipstick and faces that look like they've just been slapped."

I couldn't help but laugh. Her description of the two women who'd stared at me without a smile was so accurate, and beautifully cynical. "Yeah, I saw them. They looked at me like I'd just farted in a lift with them."

Venus laughed too, and before long we were both in tears pulling fire-witch faces and making up stories about fire-witch mannerisms and behaviour.

The door swung open. Kat bumbled in. "I'm so happy to see you girls getting on so well..." she beamed. Then her expression changed, just a little. Oh the smile was still there, but her eyes were stony, "...but don't ever let me hear you disrespecting Alina and Julia again."

"Sorry Kat, "said Venus.

I wasn't apologising. All this coven business did nothing for me. I felt no allegiance to these people, and quite frankly I couldn't muster up any respect for those two fire-witch weirdoes. As far as I was concerned, they took themselves way too seriously.

Kat frowned as she stared at me, chewing the inside of her cheek. "Mmm," was all she uttered as she shuffled back to the kitchen.

Venus grabbed my arm. "Come out to the garden with me."

I followed her outside.

"Listen Kitha, you need to play the game. They may all look stupid and puffed up about themselves, but they're real witches. They've got a lot of power. All of them – except me of course. You don't want to go pissing them off."

"Is that what you do? Play the game?"

"Sure. But unlike you, I've seen some really weird stuff. You have to be more careful around them."

"Your frightened of them?" I accused.

"Damn right. And so should you be."

Once again I shifted the conversation. "So what do they use their magic for anyway?"

"Oh all sorts. Mostly they're like a secret club. They 'help' each other get stuff. You know, power, success. They've all become pretty rich. None of them work, but they've all got money somehow. They go where they want, do what they want, buy what they want. I don't really understand it all, but I think they've got business investments that they conjure into big successes."

"Bloody hell, they sound like crypto-freemasons!"

"What?"

"Never mind."

"Kitha, if you're planning on making a run for it, don't. Or if you do, go a long long way from here, and go now."

I was startled at how sharp this girl was. She'd gone right to the heart of what I was thinking when I didn't think anyone else had. Also, I thought back to all the things Penny bought for me when we went shopping. She was just like the others, even though she seemed normal – the sister I remembered – but she wasn't of course.

Venus followed my thought processes without a word, then made up her mind to help. “I can cover for you for a couple of hours. I’ll tell them you’ve gone for a lie down so that you’re well rested for tonight. Have you got anywhere to go?”

“I’ve got an aunt…”

She held up her hands. “Don’t tell me. They’ll get it out of me. Better I don’t know.” Venus delved into her pocket and pulled out a wodge of notes, stuffing them unceremoniously into my own jacket pocket. She was prepared for this. “Go.”

I gave my new best friend a quick hug, then I just walked out the back gate and headed for the station, hoping Venus wouldn’t get into too much trouble.

CHAPTER 6 – SANCTUARY GONE BUST

Towns, villages and countryside passed by the window. From my seat on the train I gazed out, barely registering any of it. My mind was abuzz with everything that had happened in the last few days. Sure, I'd hated being at the Institute, and no way was I going back there, but I suppose the routine had at least become familiar. Nothing they did really harmed me, and I never showed any further signs of, what I now knew, was witchcraft. Perhaps what happened at school that day was a one-off. Perhaps I wasn't a witch after all, although there was the rattling sideboard earlier that day. Hmmm! If I'd stayed at Kat & Darbie's place, I'd be like Venus. Forced to hang out with a bunch of creepy, hippy wanabes, splashing water and 'blessing' all over the place. I chuckled at the thought, incurring a frowned stare from the man on the seat opposite. But it wasn't funny. What was I going to do now?

I didn't know my Aunt Ellie all that well, though she seemed alright when we had those rare family gatherings. Would she be okay with me turning up on her doorstep? I didn't know. So it was with some trepidation that I tapped on her door. There was no answer. Stupid of me, why would I assume she'd be at home in the middle of the day? *She's probably at work.* Well, it was just gone three o'clock. I'll go and get a coffee in the village, then come back later.

As if I hadn't done enough pondering about my situation, I sat over my latte thinking. There was Penny. My sister had rescued me from the Institute, and then thrown me to the wolves. Well, I guess she didn't see it that way. She was totally into all that coven stuff. Once I'd got myself sorted, perhaps it'll be me rescuing her. Talking of which, what about Venus? She was about my age, maybe a year or so younger, and clearly not sold on what was going on there, but making the best of a bad situation. Then there was Kat. All mumsy one minute, with her baking and her herbs and stuff, and so scary the next. Apparently she's a hedge-witch, whatever that means. She seemed like she was the coven leader or something, if they even have a leader, I don't know. And Darbie. Wow – Darbie. I didn't know at the time what it was about that woman. She was just so sensual to be around. It felt good just to be near her. Years later, once I had a better understanding of the different types of witches, I realised just how dangerous people like Darbie actually were. She was some kind of mind-bender who messed with your emotions, and could get you to do pretty much anything for them. I was deep in thought when a familiar voice filtered through the haze.

"Kitha?"

"Aunt Ellie!"

Ellie sat down opposite me. "I had a call from your mum, She's worried sick about you. Said you'd run away from the hospital."

"It's not a hospital. It's a prison where they do experiments on the inmates."

"Oh, come now. Surely..."

"Aunt Ellie, listen to me. Penny broke me out of there, and took me..." Well, I won't repeat what I've already said, but I sat there and poured everything out to Ellie from the moment I flattened the kids and the bushes to the ground at school over a year ago, to my escape from the coven with Venus' help. She listened intently and without interrupting. It felt so good to be able to offload all this shit.

Ellie paid for the coffees and took me to her home. We sat in the conservatory. It was pleasantly warm under the glass.

"I need to let your mum know you're safe."

"Why? I've not seen or heard from her in a year. She couldn't care less about me."

"That's not true Kitha. It's not her, it's that... it's your father. He stopped her from seeing you."

"No. I'm sorry, but she could have come when he was at work, or at least written a letter."

"She wrote letters. It was only recently she found out you weren't getting them. Once Penny knew where you were, she practically tore the door down trying to find out what had been going on. Your mum was devastated that you'd been so alone all that time. The staff at the Institute told her that isolation was part of your treatment."

"And yet even then she made no effort to see me, and as for Penny, she took me to Kat and Darbie's house. One prison to another."

Ellie's forehead crinkled as she chewed her top lip. Finally she answered. "You were not a prisoner of the coven. They were trying to protect you. In order for you to get the full protection of the coven, you had to be initiated, then no one in their right mind would do anything to harm you."

My world just spun out to space as the implications of what my aunt was saying hit home. She was in on it. She knew everything already, and was all for me being swallowed up by these crazy people. I found myself staring at her with new eyes. I'd gone there thinking it would be a sanctuary, and after this revelation, I had to get away – again. But where?

"You knew I was coming here," I accused.

"Penny called me. She'll be here soon and we'll talk this all out."

"No!"

I got up and made for a quick exit, but then Ellie pulled a 'Kat' on me and somehow prevented me from opening the door. No amount of pulling at the handle would budge it. I scanned around me quickly. There was a potted plant on a little table nearby. I grabbed it and threw it at one of the windows. It was toughened glass, so the window didn't break, but it was enough to distract Ellie for a few seconds. I was through the door, down the hall, and out the front door before she could regain control.

I ran until I could run no more, then I scooted into a shop.

"Can I help you?"

The shopkeeper's question made me jump. Suddenly aware of how I must look to the old man – out of breath, dripping sweat and clearly not perusing the hardware he had to offer, I just stared at him. He had a kindly face, but curiosity was a normal human trait, right? I had to say something.

"I...I thought I was being followed. It's probably nothing." Damn he probably thought I was a high-strung paranoid idiot. "If there's a back way out, I won't trouble you any more."

The man gazed at me for a moment or two. "Come through the back and sit down. I'll make some sweet tea and you can tell me all about it."

"Oh. No. Really, I'll just catch my breath a minute then I'll be out of your hair." I took a sharp intake of breath. *Shit, he's hardly got any hair, perhaps that was a bit tactless.*

But the man just ran his hand over his head, wiggled his eyebrows and chuckled merrily. It made me laugh too, easing my tension a little.

Well, I couldn't exactly tell him my story, so I made up a yarn about visiting a relative, but they'd moved, and the householder was angry at being disturbed, so he chased me down his drive, and I was so scared I ran here.

"I see," he said flatly.

Hmph! That meant he didn't believe me, didn't it? Well there was nothing I could do about that.

"How old are you lass?"

"Eighteen," I lied. One raised eyebrow indicated he didn't believe that either. *Shit, now he thinks he's got a juvenile delinquent on his hands. I need to get out of here.*

I glanced up and could just about see the street through

the open door of his storeroom in the back, and through the shop floor. Aunt Ellie was peering in through the window. Then there was another face. Penny was with her. *Damn, she'd arrived quickly.* The little bell on the shop door tinkled as they came in. *How did they know where I am?* I turned and studied the shopkeeper's face suspiciously, but there was no sign he was aware the two women in the shop were anything but customers. They must be able to sense me somehow. Penny did say they had such abilities, didn't she? I understand it all now, but at the time it just felt like a trap closing in on me.

"It looks like you have some customers," I said to the shopkeeper, "so I'll go now. Thank you for the tea." I didn't wait for a response. I left through the back door and out into an ally. Which way? Well, *just pick one Kitha*, I told myself. I turned left as this seemed like the best route back to the station. I didn't know where to go, but anywhere away from here would have to do.

*****

By the way... *I may have forgotten to mention that all this was twenty odd years ago, when I was just a kid. Right now, I'm in my house, looking out the window at the turbulent winter sea on the south coast. My dad's probably in the nick again, but he'd disowned me anyway, which was fine by me, and Mum and Venus are living with me and Bandit. Bandit is my collie-cross, named for the black hair around his eyes in his otherwise white coat.*

CHAPTER 7 – EVER NORTHWARD TO JOY

Anyway, after escaping Aunt Ellie and Penny, I decided if I put a couple of hundred miles between them and me, it would surely be far enough away, so I bought a train ticket and a sandwich and I was off again.

It was freezing that first night on a bench in the park. I hardly slept a wink, though somehow I got through the night. What the hell was I to do? I still had a bit of the money Venus had given me, but it would only buy one night in a B&B, then it would be gone. I bought myself a coffee and a bacon buttie in a café nearby. It was lovely and warm in there, so I sat pondering my precarious position as I thawed out.

"Mind if I join you?"

Startled out of my reverie by the woman's voice, I just nodded slightly as she sidled into the chair opposite.

"Bitterly cold night last night."

"Yes." I studied the woman. She was middle-aged, average height, average... well, average in every way really. Her hair was kinda nice though. Near black and shot through with silver strands. The crows-feet at her eyes indicated she smiled a lot.

"I saw you this morning in the park. Alone, running away and nowhere to go?"

Well, maybe she wasn't so average after all. She'd gone right to the heart of my problems.

"How old are you?"

"Eighteen," I lied about my age again. Last thing I needed

was some do-gooder turning me over to the authorities.

"Huh! You lie like a hairy egg. I'll bet you're barely sixteen. Am I right?"

Hairy egg? Weird expression! I bit my lip and slid my legs sideways in my chair ready to bolt if needed. "What do you want from me?"

The woman's face softened. "Don't worry. I won't be calling the police or anything. I want to help."

"Why?"

"I sensed your warming blanket when you were on your park bench. It was weak, but just about enough to keep you from getting hypothermia."

"What? What do you mean?"

The woman gazed at me for a while. I could almost hear her thoughts churning through her mind. She looked up briefly as her tea and toast was brought over, acknowledging the server with a nod and a smile.

She turned back to me. "Did you not know you have magic?"

I stiffened. *Have I got a sign on my back or something?*

She raised a hand. "Calm down, it's alright."

It wasn't alright. It wasn't alright at all. And who doesn't hate it when someone says 'calm down'?

"I can see from your face that you are aware you have… something, but you're not sure what that something is. So let me see. You're running, that much is clear. You're a long way from home with nowhere to go, and no money. You don't trust whoever you're running from."

I just sat and stared at the woman. How could she know all this? And what was all that business about a blanket?

"My name's Joy. I realise you have no reason to trust me, so how about this." She took a card from her purse and handed it to me. "This is my address and number. I live not far from here. I won't put any pressure on you, but I can help you. You are free to choose if you want my help or not. But I will say this. You have fledgling magic. You are lucky it was me that sensed it first as there are some very unpleasant covens out there seeking to increase their ranks and exploit the abilities of naïve witches. If you come to me, I will show you the way of the wyrd, and you will be free to leave any time you wish. Would you do me the honour of telling me your name?"

Wyrd? Honour, What? "Oh, er, my name's Kitha."

"Kitha," she repeated back. "Well, Kitha, I've said all I'm going to say now. Choose to come to me and you'll be safe."

With that Joy left. I stared after her for a moment then left too.

*****

I wandered around the town for most of the day wondering what to do next. I must have been getting paranoid or something as I was sure people were staring at me. You know, like those psychological thriller movies where people turn to stare with fish-eye-lens faces. The Christmas lights were coming on all over town as the winter sunset came before the shops were even shut. There was a street seller vending hot soup in polystyrene beakers. I bought tomato and basil soup with a granary roll and sat on a bench with it.

Two women came and sat, one either side of me.

"Hello little witchling," said one.

Joy's words came back to me '*...unpleasant covens seeking to increase their ranks...*' and boy did these two fill me with dread. I looked first at one then the other. They were both smiling, but their smiles didn't reach their eyes. Fear rippled down my spine. I jumped up and bolted. I had no idea at first if they pursued me. I just kept running. At the far end of the High Street I stopped to catch my breath leaning against a lamppost. Scanning round, there were quite a few end of day shoppers about. Everything looked normal. Then I heard them – laughing.

"Well, little witchling, where will you run to now?"

I could hardly breathe. Not from the running, I'd recovered from that, but from panic. "What do you want from me?" I yelled.

A few heads turned my way, but nobody stopped. No one wanted to get involved in someone else's problems. People just kept walking on by as the two women ambled slowly and confidently towards me.

I grabbed my phone and quickly dialled Joy's number. "Joy, it's Kitha. Help me please. I'm at the top of town, there are two weird women..." I didn't hear if she answered.

One of the women knocked the phone from my hand, and the two of them took one of my arms each. I struggled frantically, but I couldn't free myself from them. I called for help, but no one wanted to know. In a moment of clarity I wondered if I could use my magic somehow. I thought back to how I felt when I saw Matthew back on that day at school being picked on. I took a deep breath and pushed. Pushed what? I didn't know – yet it was just enough. The two women let go their grip. One fell backwards, the other just staggered. But I wasn't out of trouble yet. The one on the ground got back to her feet, her face like thunder. The other still wore a fixed grin.

"Oooh! The puppy bites. What fun!"

Heart thumping in my chest, I ran again, knowing they were right behind me. Just then a little red hatchback pulled up just ahead, and the passenger door flew open.

"Get in," shouted Joy.

I didn't hesitate. I ran for the car, jumped in and we were away before I could even pull the door shut.

CHAPTER 8 – DIFFICULT STUDENT

I was hesitant at first. I'd already poured out my troubles to Aunt Ellie, and look what happened there! But Joy wasn't pushy. She patiently took care of me, and asked for nothing.

She told me about the women from the town. They were in a very dodgy coven that targeted young witches. I was lucky, she told me, to have escaped them. Well, it wasn't luck was it? She'd rescued me. I'd have been in serious trouble otherwise. Yes, she was a witch too, but didn't seem to be part of a coven.

No one came to the house during those first three weeks. It was a peaceful place. We had a Christmas dinner, but even that was a no-fuss affair.

I wondered that there appeared to be no one in her life, so in the end I just had to ask.

"I have a son, Tom, in New Zealand. He's married to Gianna and has two daughters, Millie and little Flo and a son, Shaun. I've been planning a visit in the new year," she told me.

Disappointment wriggled its way into my thoughts. I knew it was selfish, but I realised this meant I had to move on. I tried to hide my feelings. "That's wonderful. You must be so looking forward to seeing them."

"I am." She gazed sideways at me. There was a notable twinkle in her eye. "However, I haven't booked anything up yet, or fixed a date with them. I think I might wait for a while. I don't want to be there in the height of their summer season anyway, and I think I might have a bit of a project here at the moment."

"Oh. Please don't change your plans for me."

"It's fine. I do what's needed. And right now, what's needed is...right here."

*****

Bottom line – Joy, not only saved me from a coven of dodgy witches, but she was happy to sacrifice her trip to see her family, just for me – a girl she hardly knew. It was one of those pivotal moments in life – you know, when everything that had gone before has led you to where you are now, and things would change from that point onward.

Joy was a lone witch – not a rogue, as Penny had told me unaffiliated witches were, not someone out for their own gain, just someone who was willing to take a lost soul like me under her wing.

*****

My training began. I wasn't an easy student – in fact I don't know why Joy ever put up with me. When I wanted to learn the big stuff – spells, scrying, potions – that sort of thing, she was teaching me to meditate, do the gardening and do chores around the place. My impatience got the best of me many times. I stomped around in a huff, locked myself in my room and even smashed crockery on occasion. Then after about four months, I totally blew my top.

"That's it. I'm done. I'm leaving."

When I think back on it now, I could laugh at my stupidity – except hurting dear Joy wasn't funny at all.

Joy listened calmly as I spat my teenage tantrum into her face. When I'd finally and cruelly vented all my frustrations, and had, at last, gone quiet and headed for the door, Joy spoke.

"Now that you've finally got that off your chest, perhaps we can continue?"

"Continue? Don't you get it? I'm off."

"Oh! Okay. Well, I'll be here when you get back then."

Her nonchalant attitude and placid manner simply served to make me all the madder.

Who was I to talk about attitude?

I slammed the door on my way out and headed towards town and the station intending to, once more, go somewhere, anywhere on the train. But where to this time?

You can imagine my shock when, coming towards me, was one of the two nasty witches from a year ago, accompanied by my sister Penny. Gliding along beside them, the sight of Darbie still sent little tingles through my body. What were they doing with the bitch witch?

"Kitha!" called Penny, "Oh thank goodness. Jo here told me you'd taken up with a rogue witch. I was terribly worried. We all were. I'm so happy we've found you."

I stared first at Penny, then at this horrid Jo woman for a few moments before I spoke. "She's no rogue. She's a wonderful woman who saved me from her..." I spat that last word, "...and her nasty friend. She's done nothing but help me. She took me in and has been teaching me. I won't have a word said against her." As I finished my speech, it was only then I realised just how much Joy meant to me, and how selfish and petulant I'd been.

Darbie spoke. "I'm sure she seems that way to you, but you have to understand how irrational and unpredictable rogue...lone witches are. In a coven we all look after one another and make sure no one steps out of line and abuses their power."

I could feel myself drawn to Darbie. I wanted to touch her. Not in a creepy way, you understand, I just wanted a connection. And her words made so much sense to me at that moment. As she held out her hand, I automatically stepped forward and almost took it, until Joy's words came back to me.

'Each coven has at least one psyche witch. Those with the power of the siren. They are almost impossible to resist.'

I stared at Darbie. That was it! This was her power, her

magic. She'd sucked me in before, such that I was nearly ready to give myself up to their rotten coven, and now I almost lost it in her presence again. It then dawned on me that all those innocuous, ordinary chats with Joy in the evenings, once the chores were done, were actually part of my training. How could I have been so dense? She'd been slowly drip-feeding me the information I needed. It had sunk in, and I hadn't even noticed.

Snatching my hand away, moments before it connected with hers, I just yelled, "No".

It was the first time I'd seen anything other than quiet confidence on Darbie's face. The shocked expression disappeared almost immediately, and I heard Penny gasp.

"What has that woman done to you Sis? We need to get you home as soon as possible. Kat will know what to do."

"I'm not going anywhere near her. I don't trust her."

Jo piped up, her smirk plain on her face. "Seems the little witchling has a mind of her own."

Penny scowled.

"What are you doing with that bitch anyway?" I refused to look Jo's way.

"There's a code amongst covens. She let us know where you were."

"Huh! I've been here a year almost. She wasn't in any hurry then."

"Yes. I had noticed that," said Penny with a brief glare at Jo.

Jo just laughed. "I've done my bit. There's nothing in the Book that says I had to snap to and do it straight away."

"Enough of this. We need to get her back to Kat." Darbie's demeanour had changed so completely since I'd resisted her wiles, I hardly recognised her. Yes, she was still elegant and attractive, but now she seemed just, well, ordinary. I grinned, feeling pretty smug. I'd broken the siren's spell. She had no hold over me now.

Jo and Darbie grabbed one of my arms each.

"Don't hurt her," cried Penny.

"Oh, for goodness sake." That was the last thing I heard from Jo as her fist connected with my chin.

CHAPTER 9 – ENEMY CAMP

I couldn't make out the words, but the muffled chatter of a collection of voices brought me back to the world. I groaned before I was sensible enough to supress reacting to the pain.

"Kitha. Are you okay?" asked Penny.

I peeled one eye open, and stared back. Her face was right in front of mine. "Where am I?" My hand went to my sore chin as I wrenched the other eyelid open and took in the unfamiliar surroundings.

"We're at the house of the coven leader, Amber." *Huh! In the enemy camp then.* "I'm so sorry Jo hit you. Amber's tearing her off a strip even as we speak. She should never have done that. I'm so sorry," Penny repeated.

I swung my legs round and sat up on the sofa. I could hear angry words emanating from another room, and Jo's whiny complaints. I got a tiny bit of satisfaction out of that.

"I'll get some more ice," said Darbie, leaving Penny and me alone. The strange look she gave me as she headed out the door sent a shiver down my spine.

It took me a while to gather my thoughts, meanwhile Penny was babbling on. She was giving me a headache.

"It's all my fault. I should have explained everything to you better. I should have given you more time to get to know everyone, it was just that we wanted you initiated so that the coven would fully commit to watching your back. I was so frightened I'd lose you again, that I hadn't realised I'd already lost you. I can see why you were scared, but honestly, there was never anything to be concerned about. Darbie and I will take you home, then we'll give you what time you need."

Penny's concern for me was genuine, I had no doubt about that, but still, I couldn't see her as anything other than one of the enemies at the moment. I needed to contrive a way to get out of here without being caught again. Later I'd have to find a way to get Penny out too – if I could convince her she was playing for the wrong side.

"I need the loo," I said. *A place to think.*

"Of course, come with me."

Penny led me upstairs to the bathroom. "I'll be right outside."

Of course you will.

I sat on the toilet seat chewing my thumbnail and biting my bottom lip. First I thought I should call Joy, but that wouldn't do at all. What would all these crazy witches do to her if they thought her rogue? Besides, I didn't actually know where I was. I could try to bolt for the door, but no, they'd be right behind me, and I wasn't sure I'd even escape the house. What then? I just didn't know what to do. My witchcraft wasn't up to anything I could use against a whole coven, plus Penny and Darbie.

"Are you okay in there?" called Penny. True to her word she was right outside the door.

"Fine." I stood, flushed the loo and turned on the tap. The mirror above the sink gave me a fine view of the swelling on my chin. I rinsed my face in cold water. It gave a momentary relief from the pain. "I was just checking out my bruise."

"Kat will make a herbal poultice for that. It'll clear up in no time."

"Poultice? – what is it, the middle ages or something?"

"She has an extensive knowledge of herblore."

"Right. Hedge-witch."

I patted my face dry on a towel, and gazed again at my reflection. I still didn't know what kind of witch I was, so had no idea if I could use craft to affect an escape. By the time I'd opened the door, I'd made up my mind to go along with them and hope an opportunity presented itself.

Jo was coming out of the front room as I went down the stairs. She glanced at me and muttered, "I'm sorry I hit you."

The utter lack of sincerity was plain. "No you're not. You've been told to say that, so your apology means nothing."

Penny rounded on me. "Kitha!"

And there it was again. For the second time in my life, I felt that intense wellspring of rage building. But it was more this time. I tried to contain it as my breath came in great gasps.

Penny's face went from anger to fear. "Kitha, No."

Too late. It was like a giant ball of energy that needed somewhere to go. It burst out of me from my chest, abdomen and lower body. Jo went flying back into the front room, Penny hit the wall so hard it knocked her out, and the front door blasted outwards. Cracking wood, smashing glass and a kind of hurricane wind surrounded me. People were shouting, both inside the house and outside, where a car skidded and crashed into a lamppost.

Maybe I should have checked on Penny, but all I could think of was running. I ran into town and stopped to get my bearings. Now I knew exactly where I was, so I headed back home to Joy's house.

CHAPTER 10 – UNEXPECTED VISITORS

"Pop the kettle on. We'll have a cuppa and you can tell me all about it," said Joy.

I'd never been the demonstrative sort, what with having such cold parents, but the simple acceptance and support afforded by Joy was more than I could resist. I flung myself into her arms. Her eyes widened in surprise, but she returned the affection wholeheartedly. We sat with proper tea, not herbal, and a packet of chocolate biscuits and I told her what happened.

"You broke a siren's spell, impressive! Some of what I've told you must have sunk in then."

"I'm so sorry for earlier. I understand now."

Well, I mentioned pivotal moments earlier, perhaps this moment was actually the one that mattered more. Joy had no agenda except to help me. Oh how I miss her!

My training took on a different turn from that day. I still didn't know what type of witch I was, but Joy described the various types. From this I could at least work out what I *wasn't*. No way was I a hedge, hearth, kitchen or green witch. I could never picture myself gardening month in month out for spell ingredients, or being all homey, like the dreaded Kat. Joy wasn't worried, she said I'd find my calling when it was time. Still, she thought it wouldn't hurt for me to learn a bit about herbs and stuff, and I didn't mind pottering a wee bit. And anyway, it seems that even if they're not my 'thing', they can always help enhance my magic.

A lot of what came next, and for the following six months, was more about control and focusing my thoughts. Joy never criticised the coven Penny was in, and indeed told me many of the same things, such as keeping my talent secret, and learning to 'act not react'. I found meditation difficult at first, and a little of the teenage angst came to the fore, as it had when I first moved in. Getting control of my automatic frustration when things didn't go my way was one of the biggest lessons to learn. That was another thing about the herb stuff, some of the tisanes were quite calming, while others helped by focusing the mind.

Tisane, by the way, is apparently the proper name for herbal tea. Who knew?

So I found myself steeping rosemary in vodka, drying feverfew, fine-chopping sage and so on and so on. Humming happily as I was absorbed in my work, I was suddenly snatched away from my reverie by the sound of the doorbell. It occurred to me that in all the time I'd been at Joy's, I'd never heard the doorbell chime – not once. Joy was out, so I went to answer the door.

All the peace and contentment instilled in me over the last year and a half or so came crashing down in an instant.

"Mum? What are you doing here? And with her!"

Aunt Ellie stood at my mum's side.

"Well, actually, I was going to ask you the same question. May we come in?"

"No. What do you want?"

Mum bit her lip, and worry pulled her forehead into a wrinkled frown. I, meanwhile, had butterflies in my stomach, and was trying desperately to avoid throwing up. I hadn't seen my mum in well over two years, not since I was sent to the Institute. She looked older than I remembered, much older. I swung my gaze to Aunt Ellie, and felt my eyes narrowing at the sight of her. She betrayed me, and now she stood there as bold as brass.

"And you," I said to Aunt Ellie, "why are you here?"

"If you'll let us in we can talk. We'll explain everything."

Huh! Where have I heard that before?

"No way. I have nothing to say to either of you."

"Then don't talk, just listen," said Mum.

I folded my arms across my chest. "I think you should leave now."

Joy was coming up the path. My relief at the sight of her was short-lived.

"You must be Kitha's mother and aunt. Won't you come in?"

I was incensed. "What? No."

Joy smiled at me in her usual patient way. "Kitha, your family are part of your life. Of course you are cross with them – I'm rather annoyed with them myself," she said turning from Mum to Aunt Ellie then back to me, her expression stern, "but you need to deal with this once and for all, and for better or worse."

Mum stared at Joy. She was shaking – well, she always was a bit of a nervous wreck.

Aunt Ellie wasn't about to miss out on the invite. She stepped up, and I reluctantly moved aside to let her in – hoping Joy knew what she was doing.

Mum and Joy followed her in and we all went to the living room.

"Kitha, why don't you go and pop the kettle on?" said Joy.

I glared at her for a moment, but I'd got kind of used to doing as she said without question. By the time I came back in with the tray of tea and biscuits, the tension in the room could've been cut with a knife. Mum studied me like I was a stranger – and in many ways I was.

"She's still a minor," said Aunt Ellie.

It was true. I wouldn't be eighteen for another four and a half months. I'd hoped not to see any of my family before my birthday, as this was the obvious point they would make.

I was about to defend my position when Joy stood up from her chair – all the better to physically, as well as morally, take the high ground.

Joy pointed first to Mum. "You allowed you daughter to be taken to an institute where she was treated as a lab rat for more than a year. "She turned then to Aunt Ellie. "And as for you, Kitha came to you, poured out her heart, told you of all the terrible things that had happened to her, and instead of taking care of her, you turned her over to that Witch-Prime."

Aunt Ellie started to speak. "Now wait jus...."

"You think I don't know what you're up to?"

My mind was reeling now, *Witch-Prime?*

Joy continued. "You all know how powerful Kitha is, how much potential she has, and you just want a piece of the action."

Sweat erupted from my brow as my breathing went haywire. *What's she talking about?*

Aunt Ellie almost snarled. "Oh, and you aren't after the same thing."

"Kitha is at liberty to leave when ever she wants. I ask nothing of her in return for the training and nurturing I have afforded her. I've never held her captive, sneaked behind her back," she looked back to Mum, "or abandoned her to strangers."

My heart was beating fast in my chest as I finally found my tongue. "Joy, what's going on?"

Joy's face softened as she turned her gaze back to me. "I had no idea at first, then I suspected, but wasn't sure, but it would seem you may be a Witch-Prime."

"A what?"

"About one in a thousand or so witches have exceptional power. We call them Witch-Primes, and I think you may be one, though I'm still not certain." Again turning to the two women opposite her, her eyes narrowed once more. – the expression didn't suit her at all. "It may account for why everyone is so keen to get their hands on you."

Finally Mum spoke. "Kitha, dear," that made me balk,

"Ellie explained what happened at Kat's place. I had no idea Penny was caught up with that lot – you have to believe me – and Ellie genuinely thought Penny had your best interests at heart. In fact she probably does. She believes in the coven."

I felt my dander rise, as anger replaced the hurt and confusion. "I wasn't even quite fifteen when I went into that bloody place. You never came, and I've been out of there for ages as well. Where have you been all this time?" My emotions flipped again, as tears streamed down my face.

Mum came over and knelt on the floor in from of me. She gripped my knees and stared up into my face. "Your father wouldn't let me. You have to understand, love, he controlled me, and I had no will-power to overcome him."

I was confused again. "But he's just a man, how could he have such power over you, and, for that matter, if that's the case, how have you broken it now?"

Mum broke down. She buried her face on my lap and sobbed, unable to speak.

I could feel the heat rise in my face from this awkward situation. I was so shocked at this turn of events, I had no idea what to say or do. I found Joy's face, and appealed to her with my eyes.

"It seems your father is a warlock," she said.

Almost too dumbfounded to speak, I squeaked at first before I found my voice. The old film 'Warlock', or at least part of it, replayed in my head. "You've got to be kidding me. Next you'll be telling me there are vampires and fairies."

"Don't be silly, Kitha, of course there are no such things as vampires," said Aunt Ellie.

Joy cringed at that, pursing her lips, "Um, well..."

I stared at Joy. She clearly wasn't expanding on whatever she was thinking on the vampire front right now – *what did she know that eluded Aunt Ellie? – probably quite a lot knowing her.*

That aside, that Aunt Ellie hadn't denied the existence of fairies was a conversation for later, though a thrill tingled its way down my spine. Meanwhile, Mum had pulled herself together a bit, and went back to sit on the sofa. But my question still stood.

"Okay, so 'warlock' then. How have you managed to get away from him now when you couldn't before?"

Mum glanced at Aunt Ellie before turning back to me. "Your father's in prison."

"Whoa, Dad? Why? What did he do?"

"He was furious the Institute lost you," she drifted into thought for a few moments, "Hmm, I wonder if he knew what you are." She shook her head and came back to the present. "Anyway, he stormed down there, demanded to know how you got away, and, well, he kind of blew the place up in his rage."

"He did what? How?"

"The police and fire service are still trying to figure that out. I can only assume he used magical power to do it. Obviously he won't tell them that, but he's looking at attempted murder charges."

"'Attempted', well, at least then, I assume, no one was actually killed?"

"No. But two of the scientists have second-degree burns, and the Institute is damaged beyond any likelihood of rebuilding. The police are also looking into what they were up to in there."

"So, you're free of him then."

She bit her lip again. "I hope so." The worried frown from earlier returned.

Aunt Ellie piped up. "Kitha, your mum wants to take you home. It'll be safe for you there, and she can train you in the art."

Something close to panic drove me to a standing position next to Joy. She and I both said a resounding 'No' at the same time.

"You're only seventeen, we could force the issue," said Ellie.

I dug my heels in. "Joy's been looking after me and training me for more than a year and a half. I'm staying here. If you want to do something useful, I suggest you find a way to get

Penny away from Kat."

Joy studied Mum's desperate face and sighed. "You may come and stay whenever you wish, but I assure you, this is the best place for Kitha right now. Taking her away at this time will just disrupt the good work she's doing here. I'm sorry, I didn't catch your name."

Mum took a while to respond, then answered as though distracted. "Oh, yes, of course, I'm Jacqueline, but everyone calls me Jacqui."

"Well, Jacqui, what do you say?"

"I agree. If you're okay with it, I'll come every other weekend."

"Agreed."

I couldn't have felt any less in control. "Don't I get a say in this?"

"You have a problem with this arrangement?" asked Joy.

Try as I might, I couldn't identify a flaw in the plan. "No, I suppose that'll be alright." I couldn't help but notice the invitation didn't extend to Aunt Ellie, Good!

CHAPTER 11 – SEA WITCH

Never Underestimate Mum

At this point in my life, something I never would have predicted happened. Mum and I became family. She'd never been much of a parent to me or to Penny, and I'd had nothing but contempt for her. She'd always seemed weak, and totally under my dad's thumb – yet now we began a new relationship – one of mutual respect. Who'd have thought..?

At first I wasn't comfortable on the weekends Mum was there. I'd never really felt close to her, but over time I found myself looking forward to her visits. Her magical knowledge came from a whole different place than Joy's. It seemed she was a sea witch – probably why Dad had bought a house about as far away from the coast as possible. I asked her if that made me a sea witch, that seemed pretty cool to me, but she said that if I was a Witch-Prime, I wouldn't have a designated field, I'd have skills across the board. She did, however, suggest a trip to the coast, and it dawned on me then that I'd never actually seen the sea, except on the telly. How crazy is that? Nowhere in the UK is that far from the sea, yet I'd never been. I guess Dad wanted to keep Mum away from her power-base or something.

It was the end of October, though warm-ish for the time of year, and the three of us set off in Joy's little red car, loaded up with a picnic basket and towels, for a jolly to the Northumbrian coast.

My heart soared at the sight – a vast sandy beach, a huge castle on a hill at the southern end, and the waves – the sound, the smell, the taste of salt on my tongue. It was heaven on earth to me.

"Are you sure I'm not a sea witch Mum? I feel like I've come home."

Mum and Joy glanced at each other.

"It's possible of course, we still don't know if you're a Witch-Prime, you may not be, and though your training is going well, to be honest, you haven't manifested all that much power except in your emotional outbursts, at least not yet, though initial assessments did deem you quite powerful. But you're still young, we will see what happens," said Joy.

I went for a swim. It was cold, yet exhilarating, and the seawater made me quite buoyant, so I could float without my legs sinking. You can keep those chlorine boxes full of splashing, noisy kids – well I guess that was me once too - I never wanted to get out of the sea – except I was shivering now. While Joy set out the picnic, Mum joined me. I'd never seen her so relaxed. Arms at her side, she rapidly dolphin-kicked over to me. It looked pretty impressive I have to say.

"Concentrate on spreading warmth through your body."

"What?"

"Even if you're not a sea witch, you're my daughter, so you must have some talent in this realm."

Realm?

For this short while and in this element, Mum became my primary teacher. Who'd have thought? I remembered the night in December, when I'd first come to the north, and slept on a park bench. Joy had told me then that I'd wrapped a magical blanket around me. I hadn't even realised I'd done it at the time, but now I drew the energy of the waves to me and made it my own. Warmth crept across my prickling skin, and my muscles relaxed.

Mum smiled in satisfaction.

We swam, and bodysurfed, and dived, and found

beautiful shells on the seabed. Fish came by to see what we were up to. I was happy beyond belief. This had to be my element. One day I would live by the sea, I decided.

Yet another of those pivotal moments I talked about before.

When we finally got out, I watched as Mum shook a little. All the water left her, and by the time she got back to where Joy was sitting on the beach, she was completely dry – skin, hair, swimsuit, the lot. Okay, I can do this too. I mimicked her movement, but remained dripping. I tried again – nothing.

"How did you do that?" I said as she handed me a towel.

"Practice."

"Huh!"

CHAPTER 12 – OWN TWO FEET

It was late in the year, and Christmas was looming once more. A few weeks after that, I'd be eighteen and officially an adult. Joy announced that she would be heading to New Zealand to visit her son and his family shortly after my birthday. Something close to panic came crashing down on me. I tried to hide it, after all, she'd delayed her trip just for me, but she saw straight through me, as she always did.

"You don't have to leave," she said. "This is your home now. Take heed of what I've taught you. You can do almost anything. You just have to concentrate on control – remember 'act don't react'. Look after the place for me, and start thinking about making a living for yourself."

I stared at Joy as I realised things would never be the same. "I don't have any skills. What will I do? I'm unemployable." My breath came in gasps as I stared into, what seemed, a dark abyss.

"Nonsense. Review all the things you know now, that you didn't know when you first came to me. You'll figure it out."

I'd relied on Joy so much. She guided me in all things, but now she was leaving. But I owed it to her to stand on my own two feet – and I owed to myself too.

Joy pursed her lips. "Make a list."

I did. Gardening, cooking, herbal remedies, tisanes and toiletries, money management, computer skills – well, spreadsheets anyway – flower arrangements and various haberdashery crafts.

Joy perused the list. "Excellent. There's a little shop unit in the high street. I covered the first six months to get you started."

A shiver ran down my spine. Whatever did I do to deserve being in Joy's life? Trying and failing to hold back tears, I threw myself into her arms.

"By the time I come back, I expect to see a thriving business. Your mum will help you get started, then I suggest you employ some local help."

Joy, Mum and I had dinner in a local pub for my eighteenth birthday – another first for me. It's amazing the kind of things that other people take for granted that are nothing less than adventures for me. A few days later, a taxi arrived to take Joy to the airport, leaving me with her car – that I had yet to learn to drive. My sense of loss was so profound, it took me almost a week before I could bring myself to get dressed, go out of the house and pick up the keys to my new shop.

Mum came over that weekend, and we shopped for materials to make up the stock I would need to open up. We set up three small tables for tea-tasting, decorated the shop in bright boho colours, inside and out, and furnished an office in a small back room. In three weeks we were ready to open.

On that first day I had visitors.

A shiver flew down my spine when I spotted Penny in the doorway. I was kind of pleased to see her until Kat swept in around her.

Penny smiled.

Kat said nothing at first – just wandered about the shop picking things up, turning them over a few times and carefully placing them back. I watched her, waiting for whatever it was she had to say to me. By the time she'd studied pretty much all of my stock, I was ready to scream.

"Lovely to see you Kitha. Has it really been more than a year?"

Kat's tone was so matter-of-fact I could have laughed at the absurdity of it – had I not been in a state of near panic.

"Why are you here?"

Penny came over. "Come on Sis, don't look so worried. We wanted to celebrate your new venture, that's all."

"How did you know?"

"Mum's been keeping me up to date. Where is she by the way?"

I felt a little betrayed, though I guess it was me that convinced Mum to reconnect with Penny. I tried, and probably failed, to keep my tone casual.

"She's just popped out. She'll be back shortly."

Kat came over to the counter. "So, now that you've grown up a bit, and started your training, are you ready to rejoin the coven?"

I was staggered. What was it with this woman?

"Why on earth would I want to do that? Everything's worked out just fine without you and your band of weirdos. Besides, I live up here now. I'm not moving back south."

She raised one eyebrow at the insult, but otherwise didn't change tack.

"Is that what you think? Hmmm!" She pulled on her glasses, leaned forward a little and took her time studying the packs of herbs on the shelf behind me. I had her sussed now. These pregnant pauses were designed to unhinge me. Now I'd figured that out, I was having none of it. I folded my arms and waited.

Finally she delivered her blow. "I understand you've had a couple of encounters with one of the local covens. There are three in this town by the way. Had you not wondered why they've never troubled you again?"

Actually, I had to admit, I hadn't given it a moment's thought.

Kat, at last, made eye contact. Her steel-grey peepers made me shudder. "Even though you refused to go through the initiation, we'd already sung you into our coven. Our protection was yours, whether you thought you needed it or not."

Penny, ever reconciliatory, piped up. "Kat's not actually a hedge witch, she's a Witch-Prime. Amber and the other coven leaders were instructed to leave you be." She swept her arm around the room. "Do you think any of this would have happened otherwise? I know how much you think of Joy, but to the covens, she a rogue. She's powerful, of course, that's why she never got driven out, but, for the most part, witches don't do well outside the coven system."

Apparently I was supposed to be impressed. How could I believe anything Penny told me? I loved my sister, but as far as I was concerned, she was brainwashed.

Mum bumbled in through the door right at that moment, loaded up with shopping. We'd decided on elderflower champagne and cupcakes for the opening day. Exhausted, she dumped the bags on one of the tables, and flopped into a chair – all before spotting my 'guests'.

Penny rushed over, knelt on one knee and gave her a hug.

"You made it then. I'm so pleased." But then she spotted Kat. "You!"

Penny stood. "Now Mum, don't get worked up. Kat only wants to help."

"Help! I've had her brand of 'help' before."

Whatever does she mean?

Mum glanced at me and nodded, clearly satisfied in that one moment, we were on the same page. Then she rushed over and drew up to Kat. "We don't want you here. Leave my daughter alone. Get out."

Kat didn't look at all perturbed, but, much to my surprise, she about-turned and headed out the door. "Good to see you again Jacqui," she said on her way out.

Penny was wringing her hands, her eyes wide with shock. "What have you done?"

"It's time that woman's reign of terror came to an end."

I was so proud of my, normally meek and mild, mum at that moment. I went and stood beside her folding my arms to match hers – a united front.

"Penny," I said, "you have a decision to make. Stay with us, or run after your mistress with your tail between your legs."

Penny only hesitated for a second or two as she bit into her bottom lip, a tad too hard. "I'm sorry," she said as she rushed out the door.

I gazed at Mum. "Is there something you want to tell me?"

CHAPTER 13 - SHOP

We weren't interrupted by many customers that day – unfortunately, in fact, we only opened 1 bottle of bubbly, and gave away three cupcakes. I sold two packs of herbs, four greetings cards and a pomander on my first day of trading, a grand total of £37.93 went through the till. It would get better, I was certain. But in between, I listened to Mum's story. It was a bit long-winded, but here are the highlights.

Mum, Jacqui, lived with Gran, Gramps and Aunt Ellie by the sea – of course she did, she's a sea witch. She swam almost every day, even in winter. I thought her spirit guide would be a dolphin – how cool would that be? But no, her spirit guide is a fish – something called a cuckoo wrasse – colourful, by all accounts for our grey, British, east coast waters. Anyway, Gramps died young – I never knew him, and Gran moved the family inland where house prices were lower. At this stage, Mum didn't know she was a witch – *hmm, know that feeling* – all she did know was that she yearned for the sea. But her talent hadn't gone unnoticed. The local coven, led by a rather dodgy male witch called Humbert, *what kind of a name is that?* initiated her into their ranks. She was taken in by promises of power and wealth, and gave herself over to the coven wholeheartedly. Humbert believed she had 'above average' talent, and began grooming her for leadership.

A couple of years later, a new and talented witch joined the coven, Kat. Outwardly jolly and friendly, she turned out to be ambitious and self-serving. *Tell me about it!* Kat was determined she'd be the next leader, so she set about undermining Mum's position, until finally she convinced Humbert that marrying

Mum off to a powerful warlock called Alexander, would yield equally, or more, powerful offspring, that could take the coven to new heights.

Despite her fear of the strange and mysterious warlock, Mum complied, believing she was doing the right thing to benefit the coven. Having got Mum effectively out of the way, Kat took over the coven when Humbert passed away. Kat was quick to grab Penny and initiate her into the coven, convinced she would be 'the one'. Once Penny turned out to be a competent, yet unremarkable witch, Kat bent her thoughts on me. If I had power, she wanted it under her jurisdiction.

Well, that's it in a nutshell, and wow Mum, what a life!

I guess I'm a disappointment to Kat too, as there's nothing special about me either.

I regarded Mum with new eyes now, but I had questions. "So what exactly is a warlock, and how are they different to witches? You know, 'cause I'd always thought witches female and warlocks male equivalents."

"A common misconception. Rather like people think witches are light or dark, when in reality, it's a grey area. Most don't mean any harm, though will follow their own agendas – like anyone else really. And like everyone else, some are more benevolent than others, and some will step on anyone to get what they want. Warlocks, however, are different. They are wizards gone bad."

Wait, wizards?

"They don't have spirit guides as such, and they aren't born with innate power like witches, but they call on the spirits to draw power to them. There are a few good wizards out there, but for the most part, the craft they use inevitably corrupts. Normally witches steer clear of them."

"And they made you marry one?"

"At first your father was a good husband. I didn't love him, but he was kindly, and he provided for us. He knew Kat had manoeuvred us into wedlock, so he kept us all away from her and from the coven. I had mixed feelings about that. I didn't trust Kat, but I'd made a lot of friends, and now I was isolated."

"What about Aunt Ellie?"

"When it turned out Ellie had missed out on the gene, and wasn't a witch at all, he allowed her visits. She knew about everything of course, and I think she was secretly jealous as she had no power, though for my part, I envied her freedom. I'm so proud of you for seeing through Kat so quickly."

"But I've seen Aunt Ellie use power."

"Borrowed power, I'm afraid. Kat showed her how to draw on the spirits, a bit like the warlocks do, only on a much lesser scale. It changed her. In many ways she's the sister I remember, but there's always a thread of steel masking the kindly person she once was."

"Mum, we have to get Penny out of there. And Venus."

"Venus?"

"She got initiated as an eight-year old."

My mum's eyes widened as she gasped.

"She helped me get away. She doesn't think she's even a witch. The only problem is, her Gran's in the coven, and she's her only family."

"Hmm. We need to give it some thought. The whole coven is committed to looking out for each other. They'll resist any attempts to remove their members, and they are powerful."

CHAPTER 14 - PROTECTION

Concern for Penny and Venus niggled constantly at the back of my mind. But I had more immediate things to deal with. Firstly, the business grew beyond anything I could imagine. Mum says it was because I'm a witch. Witches draw good fortune to themselves without even trying. I struggled to believe this, bearing in mind my first witchy act got me banged up for a year – where was my good fortune then? But whatever the reason, keeping up with demand became a major issue. Within six months I had two full time staff, plus I was buying in local crafts to fill the shelves as the stock I was able to produce myself flew out the door. Mum started making up soaps, shampoos and hand creams, and even she ended up getting help to keep up with production.

The second challenge was staving off potential attacks from other witches. Once Kat withdrew her protection, it became a free-for-all. Fortunately, I was able to have a face-to-face with Joy on the computer, and she instructed me in the art of setting up, what she called, a doorstop. It was a kind of protection spell against any witch entering either the house or the shop with ill intentions. I used it on the car too, just to be sure.

That nasty Jo was the first to try her luck. The spell temporarily stripped her of power as soon as she walked in. Actually it was hilarious. She tried to use her magic to flick goods off the shelves. She looked such an idiot waving her arms about, cursing and stomping her feet. Four ladies sitting at the tables turned to stare at her in amazement. When I started laughing, so did they. Jo ran out the door swearing. I glanced across at the ladies drinking their tisanes. "Crazy woman, right?" I said. They nodded sadly. I was just grateful it never occurred to the silly cow to use her waving arms to physically knock everything off. Well, let's face it, she's not the sharpest tool in the box.

One day Amber came by for a 'chat'. "Good afternoon Kitha."

"Amber, what a pleasant surprise. Can I interest you in one of my herb collections, or a bar of rose-scented hand cream perhaps?"

"Funny. You should know you've made quite an enemy of Jo. Your ward won't protect you or Jacqueline outside. You know that right?"

I affected my best narrow-eyed glare. "Are you threatening my mother?"

"I'm giving you the opportunity to leave town. None of the covens want a rogue witch in their patch, and the others won't afford you the courtesy of a warning."

"I'm sorry. Your threats are courteous?" I tipped my head to one side and put my forefinger to my chin as if thinking about it. "If only everyone was as pleasant and polite as you eh!"

My sarcasm wasn't lost on Amber. "You are young. You have significant ability, it's true, but you have to understand that you can count over forty witches in the three local covens – and these are just in the town. There are a couple in nearby villages too. How long do you think it will be before someone catches you unawares?"

I could feel my magic building in my chest, but I took control of it thanks to Joy's training. I checked through the window to make sure no-one was looking our way, then I flicked the door open with a minor hand movement, before turning my gaze to Amber. She nearly fell backwards as I used controlled pressure to push her out the door. Her eyes widened. It was clear she had no idea I could do that.

Once Amber was gone, I let out a breath I hadn't realised I'd been holding. Quickly I shut up shop, putting the 'Back in 30 minutes' sign up, and ran to the back room. I was dripping sweat from the exertion of using my magic, and shaking from the disturbing encounter. My mind raced. *Are we in danger? I need to talk to Joy.*

Jules, one of my staff came back from her lunch break, concern creased her brow. "Kitha? Are you okay? Why's the shop shut? Hey! You look awful. Are you ill?"

"I'll be fine." I glanced at her worried expression. If Jules knew anything about witches and covens, she'd never said anything to me. But she could be trusted with a bit of an explanation. "I've just had a...rival in the shop. She was a bit... threatening."

"Huh! You mean Amber. I saw her leaving. She and all her coven are nothing but trouble."

I did a double-take. "You know about... you know?"

"Of course. It's why I was so keen to work here. I belong to a small coven myself..."

Oh shit, not good. I stared at her in disbelief.

Jules held up her hands as if to stave off an attack. "Don't worry. This whole 'local covens see off rogue witches' nonsense is so not true. The trouble is, they recruit a lot of witches, get too big, then there's always someone with ambition, wanting to take control. There are only four of us in my coven, including Roma, and yes, we look out for each other, but no one leads and no one follows. We try to do good work that benefits, not just ourselves, but the village community too. We consider ourselves white witches – though honestly, the whole white witch, black witch thing is a bit of a cliché. Mostly folk are kind of somewhere in the middle – grey if you like."

I believed her to be genuine – still it made me nervous that she and Roma, my other full-timer, had been working for me all this time and I never knew.

"So, how did you know about me?"

"Are you kidding? You've been the talk of the town ever

since you arrived. And besides, an empath-witch, that's what I am by the way, can sense your aura a mile away."

I wracked through my memory from my early days at Joy's. I don't believe she ever mentioned empath-witches, but she definitely talked about auras.

"I have an aura?"

Julia looked at me in amazement. "Everyone has an aura. Yours has a potent purple feel about it."

I was confused. "So you can see it?"

"Not really. It's more of an impression. You have a lot of talent Kitha, so think about it. When you meet someone with magic, don't you associate them with a colour?"

I gazed long and hard at Jules. Then, just as I was beginning to think she was a bit off her rocker, it hit me. "You're blue! No green – well a kind of bluey-green."

She grinned. "There you go. Now, think about Jacqui – and anyone else you know."

I was on a roll now. "Mum is a deep blue – like the sea – of course, she's a sea-witch. And Joy – she's purple, like me. Penny's blue too, but paler." My thoughts turned reluctantly to Kat. It'd been a long while since I'd seen her, yet still, I could see her colours in my mind now. "Not so sure about Kat – she seems all over the place. A deep russet sometimes, but also dark green."

Jules shuddered at the mention of the coven leader. "I met her once. I didn't like her. We hear from her from time to time. She sends instructions to us – which we ignore, of course. She told us to steer clear of you – it's partly why I came for the job." Her sly wink made me chuckle. "As I understand it, she's lifted the ban now. Hence Amber's visit."

"I don't know what to do. I'm going to try and get hold of Joy tonight. But what do you think?"

"Honestly, it's not good. I sense the ward you've put on, but you still have to go outside, and then there's Jacqui too."

I had to go out later that day to pick up some stock, and do a bit of grocery shopping. It was so weird. Suddenly I could sense everyone's aura. In most people this was just a pallid hint of colour, yet now I could spot a witch whenever I saw one. It gave me an edge I suppose, but it was a bit disturbing at first. *How is it I'd not noticed this before?*

While selecting this week's coffee blend – I know, I know, all these healthy teas and tisanes, but I still liked coffee – strong and fully caffeinated – I looked to the right, and there was a witch with a red-orange aura standing at the end of the supermarket aisle, making no bones about the fact she was watching me. Not wanting a confrontation, I turned the other way. At the other end of the aisle was another witch, her stance the same. Her aura was yellow, paler.

Shit. Don't panic Kitha.

I opted to head towards the witch with the weaker aura. She said nothing, just edged enough in my direction to knock my shoulder as I passed and headed for the checkout.

"Intimidation tactics," said Joy when I described the encounter to her later.

I gazed at her visage on the screen. She looked a little peaky, and her face carried lines that I didn't remember seeing there before, but that may just be the light from the computer enhancing her features. "What should I do?"

"Your options are limited I'm afraid. You could just stick to your guns and not let them get to you. Though quite honestly, you'll always be looking over your shoulder – and then there's Jacqui to think about. This was the option I took, and they eventually got bored with bothering me after they saw I was no threat and had my magic well under control. You could join the coven your two staff are in. They'll probably leave you alone if they no longer consider you rogue. Or you could expand your business. Set up elsewhere, and leave Julia and Roma to run the shop in town."

"That sounds a lovely idea, but, though the business is doing well, I'm not really in a position financially to take on another property."

Joy's smug grin made me frown in confusion.

"Actually you are. I've made the decision to stay in New Zealand with my family. I've drawn up the paperwork to sign the house over to you. You just need to go along to Gilbert and Blackfords in town – it's next to the optician – to collect the deeds. I suggest you sell the house and head for the coast."

A shiver ran down my spine as a whole set of conflicting emotions pretty much floored me. The main thing I took from it at that moment, was Joy wasn't coming home. I was shaking, and tears welled as I stared at her wonderful face on the screen.

"But..."

"No 'buts'. It's done."

"Will I ever see you again?" I could hear my own pathetic whimper as my voice shook.

"Well. Never say never." She sighed then. "Look, you're clearly a bit overwhelmed. Have a chat with your mum about all this, then we'll have another call together in a few days."

Bottom line, that call-back never happened. Well actually I did call, and I got Joy's son, Tom. He explained how the brain tumour took his mum quite suddenly. I'll remember that call, in all its detail, to the end of my days. Tom and I wept together as he told me how she hadn't had to suffer for long. How she thought of me as a daughter, and that he was happy for me, his adopted sister, to have the house. I got an open invitation to visit – something I have yet to take up – but maybe one day. Joy's grandkids waved and blew kisses, which made me cry even more. Now, back to the story.

CHAPTER 15 – WHAT TO DO ABOUT VENUS

Packing up Joy's house was a sad task. Not so much the furnishing and kitchenware etc, but it was filled with all those little bits and pieces that people collect over their lives. Each piece would have a story attached to it, but I didn't know what most of those stories were. I kept a few, gave a lot to charity, and sent a few bits over to Tom.

My relationship with Mum had grown, and we decided to move to the coast together. My dad was still in prison, and would likely be there for quite some time, having been convicted of attempted murder, at least we hoped that would be the case. Mum had no intention of ever allowing him back into her life. She sold the house, put half into an account in his name – only fair, she said, as he bought it in the first place, and she didn't want any complications on that front when he finally got out – and she invested her half in the new shop on the sea-front. It's quite a popular tourist spot, so good customer footfall. I used the proceeds from selling Joy's house to buy a property close to a little, lesser-known beach a few miles up the road.

Julia and Roma were absolute bricks, keeping the shop in town running for me. I gave them each a pay rise, and free reign to employ more help. In the end, all four members of their coven had a hand in the business, and added some new stock – and I was happy for them to continue this way. After another year or so I decided to take a fixed income from it, and trusted them to run everything as they saw fit.

Taking on staff in the new shop too, gave me and Mum a bit of freedom to work on how we were going to get Penny and Venus away from Kat's malevolent clutches. It was a difficult proposition. At this stage, I had no doubt if Penny knew where we were, she'd tell Kat. I trusted Venus more. So I made a decision to contact her first.

Venus was probably about a year younger than me, so she must be eighteen at least, if not nineteen by now, so she'd be considered adult. I wasn't sure how that would affect her status in Kat and Darbie's coven. I mention Darbie again, as her siren influence may be the harder barrier to penetrate when getting through to Venus. There was a time, albeit briefly, when I'd have done anything to please Darbie – until I broke her spell.

Roma, like Joy, was up on shields and wards. She cast a spell that would hide my aura from other witches for several days, and I headed back to my home town to see if I could find a way to get Venus on her own and talk to her.

I stayed in a B&B just up the road from Kat and Darbie's cottage, and went about staking the place out – *damn forgot the dark glasses and Columbo raincoat.* I liked my hair in the dark colour Darbie had chosen for me, but I added some deep auburn low-lights, and I wore it long now. So I pinned my curls back tight into a bun, and wore a hoodie. With no aura showing, and looking rather plain, I hoped no one would recognise me if they saw me hanging about. I tried to be subtle, of course, sitting on a bench with a book or a newspaper, walking up and down the road with a conscripted stray dog on a piece of rope, who was happy to provide his services in exchange for sausages, and so on. In the end it wasn't until the third day I saw Venus head out the door on her own. She didn't live there, and so must have arrived before I got there in the morning.

As Venus walked along, I checked around once more, then headed over the road, caught up with her, keeping pace alongside.

She didn't recognise me at first. "Hey, what's your...

Kitha?" She quickly scanned around to see if anyone was looking our way, then took hold of my arm, dragging me against a hedge, and out of sight of the house. "What are you doing here?"

"I wanted to see you. How's it going?"

"Much the same. I still live with my gran, I still haven't 'manifested'. I'm still regarded as a hanger-on. How about you?"

"Things are pretty good. I have a house and a business, and my mum lives with me."

"Seriously? You'd think from listening to Kat and Darbie that you're just a rogue witch with nowhere safe to go. 'A warning to us all' apparently."

"Well, as you can see, they're wrong. I just wanted to check on you. You helped me get away, and I'm so grateful. I'd have come before, but I didn't want to get caught."

"But now?"

"But now my aura's masked. Venus, I want you to know there's a home for you with me and my mum if you want to get away too."

Venus stared at me a moment, a conflict clear on her lovely features. "I can't. You know – Gran."

"I understand. I thought that would be the case, but if you change your mind, or..." I was almost reluctant to say it, "...or when your gran passes. The offer will always be open. I want you to memorise my email address. Contact me any time, and I'll come and get you. Not a word to the others mind."

"Of course."

"How's my sister?"

"Penny? She's okay I suppose. But she totally buys in to the coven. I don't think there's much hope of you getting her to leave them, if that's what you had in mind."

I trusted Venus's instincts. Still, I had to find a way, as much for Mum's sake as for hers – and mine.

Just then there was a call from behind. "Venus. Wait up. I'll come with you."

I recognised Penny's voice.

Venus turned to me, wide-eyed. "Go."

I quickly headed back across the road. Keeping my hood up. I could just about make out Penny asking Venus whom she'd been talking to. I didn't catch the answer, but I knew Venus wouldn't betray me. I was just glad it wasn't Darbie. I still didn't know if she held Venus in thrall, as she could so easily do.

It was only a couple of days later I got my first email from Venus. It was late at night, and she told me to only email back after midnight to ensure she could delete my messages before anyone else saw them. Apparently they didn't trust her, and monitored her social media. They knew she'd helped me.

Careful as she tried to be, the following month Penny was at my door.

CHAPTER 16 – FOREVER LOST?

I peered around Penny to see if Kat, or Darbie, or Aunt Ellie – or anyone else I didn't want to see, was lurking in the background. But she was alone. The little yellow VW Beetle she always drove parked on the road in front of the house.

"May I come in?"

I bit my lip wondering at the outcome of this visit. I stepped aside to allow her entry, and she slipped quickly past me and headed down the hall towards the kitchen diner. I followed, grabbed the kettle and went to the sink to fill it.

"Hmm," she said, "the silent treatment? Do you have nothing to say to me?"

"I was waiting to hear what you have to say. You came to me after all, not the other way around."

"Not quite true though is it? You came and spoke to Venus."

I turned briskly on my heel. "So what, you came to warn me off?"

"Of course not. I just don't understand why you wouldn't have wanted to talk to me. I AM your sister. I WAS the one who rescued you from that awful lab."

"Yes, then threw me to the sharks!"

"Oh, come on. Kat and Darbie, and the rest of the crew only wanted the best for you. Have I come to any harm? No. Quite the contrary."

"They were giving me no choice. Join or be dammed it

seemed to me."

Penny sat on a stall at the breakfast bar in front of the tea I'd put there for her. I got biscuits out – Joy's influence was plain. Like tea and bickies could resolve any problem. I snorted at the thought.

"Something funny?"

"Not really, just a private thought. In my world you can have those by the way."

Penny stared at me. "Is that what you think? That we are THAT controlled?"

"Well aren't you? Between Kat and Darbie, they seem to have everyone dancing to their tune."

She changed tack. "I'm sorry that you felt railroaded into joining the coven. But look at it from my viewpoint. It took me almost a year to find out where you were. I had to break you out and avoid the authorities. I was determined, as were we all, that they wouldn't come and haul you off back to that place. Getting you under our protection as quickly as possible seemed the most efficient way of keeping you safe. And of course it wasn't just them. Dad went ape when he knew you'd escaped. He wanted to tap into your magic himself, but ever the sciency-type, he wanted to find out what makes a powerful witch tick first. You, as a minor and under his jurisdiction was the only one he could have experimented on. Still, he got his comeuppance."

"At what cost? Some of the scientists were seriously injured."

"What do you care after what they did to you?"

I think that was probably the moment I knew I'd lost her. That she could be so callous was a shock to me. Sure, I had no love for the staff at the Institute, and yes, I wanted out, but they never actually harmed me. They gave me everything I needed – apart from my freedom, and they probably thought they were doing the world a service by keeping a dangerous kid locked away. I guess I'm more like Mum than I ever thought, but maybe Penny had a dose too many of Dad's dark genes.

"So are you going to tell me what you came here for?"

"Kat doesn't want you coming by again. She thinks you'll be a bad influence on Venus."

Finally I sat. I stared at my brainwashed sister in incredulity. "Is that what you think too? Earlier you said you HADN'T come to warn me off."

"If you'd have just come to the house instead of sneaking around to get Venus on her own, then it would be fine. Why would you do that if you didn't have ideas about taking her away from the coven?"

I couldn't really argue against that. It was exactly what I wanted to do.

"Like me, she wasn't given any choice in the matter."

"And yet, she's unharmed, happy and safe."

"But what about free will?"

"Like anyone really has that."

"I do."

"Yes, I suppose you do."

"And, by the way, have you asked Venus if she's happy?"

"Goodbye Kitha."

With that, Penny got up, handed me her cup and left, asking me to give Mum her love as she headed out the door. Odd she didn't stick around long enough to see her.

Mum had been at the shop that morning. When she came home I told her about Penny's visit. She too understood Penny was lost to us. She wept her poor heart out.

"Come on, let's go for a swim."

If there was anything that calmed both our nerves it was being in the sea.

CHAPTER 17 – FOUND

Life continued to bear its gifts. Both shops did well, and Mum and I made lots of friends in our new home village. We swam almost every day, enjoyed good health, and revelled in our bountiful garden. Life was perfect. Well almost. We still suffered the loss of Penny. I still missed Joy, and I continued to worry about Venus, though we still emailed regularly. Somehow she got that past the others, I guess because she lived with her Gran who had no concept of social media. She seemed okay, but I always felt there was a sorrowful edge to her accounts of life in the coven. I was still determined to get her away from them, but I knew I could do nothing all the while her Gran lived.

Other than this, yes, everything was perfect, until one day, when Mum and I exited the sea after a swim and shook ourselves instantly dry – yes I learned that trick pretty damn quick after a few winter swims – we spotted a man heading towards us along the beach. Mum froze. Her face bore the terror of years of suppression. I couldn't make out his face yet, as he was still some distance away, but I knew it could only be my dad. Who else would engender such a reaction?

I slung my arm over her shoulder. "It's okay Mum. There's two of us what can he do?"

Eyes wide, she tore her gaze from the fast approaching form and stared up at me. "He's a warlock!" As if that answered everything.

I could feel Mum's tremors, and manoeuvred myself slightly in front, and to the side of her. He was suddenly there, like the distance between us had shrunk. He certainly didn't seem to be walking that fast, it was just too weird.

"You're not taking Mum back. She lives with me now, and you're not welcome here," I could hear the uncertainty in my own voice, and cursed myself as Mum's nervousness translated directly to me.

"I'm not interested in her. It's you I've come for."

His words simply didn't compute. He'd taken no interest in me throughout my whole life – apart from destroying the Institute after my escape, if that counts. Why would he want me?

Mum finally found her voice. "Alexander, NO!"

Dad glanced briefly at her then turned back to me. "I know what you're capable of Kitha, probably more so than any of these ineffectual witches you've been involved with. Sure, I have an agenda, I'm not going to try and hide that from you. Not like your mother. All she wanted was to get back to the sea, and she's manipulated you into bring her here."

"No. That was my decision. I love the sea. I'm sure I'm a sea witch like her." *Damn, why am I trying to justify myself to him?*

"Don't be ridiculous. You're a witch-prime, and a powerful one at that. Only I have the skills and knowledge to teach you how to use your craft. Don't try to resist me child. I will take you by force if necessary."

Fear curled in the pit of my stomach as I tried to imagine how he could carry out his threat. Yet suddenly I was filled with warmth. Mum's warmth, like when we're in the ocean. She was lending me her power to add to my own, and now I had to find some way to use it. Once again I thought back to how I felt when my old school friend Matthew was bullied. And there it was, my witchy power – like a ball of energy growing in my chest. I felt like it took an age to build up, but was probably just seconds, and when I couldn't stand to hold it in any longer, I let rip. Dad went flying back along the beach, landing in a heap a good fifty metres away. Wow!

Mum and I made a break for it and headed back into the water, around the headland and up onto a beach out of sight the other side. Shaking ourselves dry, we ran hand in hand up to the far end of the next village and to a friend's house.

CHAPTER 18 – FAIRY OR FAE

"Whatever's happened?" asked Carolyn as we bolted through her front door.

I glanced at Mum, but she was in no position to explain. "My dad's found us." We'd never told Carolyn about him, or what train of events had brought us to live in the area, but it was enough for her to get the picture, especially with Mum as white as a sheet.

"You can stay here as long as you need to. Is there someone I can call?"

I thought about that for a while, but couldn't think of anyone. "Thank you, but no. There's no one that can help. We had no idea he was out of prison or we'd have put something in place. We're going to have to arrange a restraining order or something."

Carolyn put the kettle on.

Mum slumped on the kitchen stool shaking her head. "It won't work. He'll always find a way."

She was right. I bit my bottom lip as I tried to figure out a plan. I knew very little about warlocks except that they were wizards gone bad as they couldn't resist the power on tap from malevolent spirits. I glanced at Carolyn. She had a very faint pinky-lilac aura, not enough to mark her as a witch, so Mum and I needed to talk alone. Carolyn would never understand, but Mum must have forgotten that in her despair.

"We need help Kitha. There's a wizard I know of, back in

the town, and he'll know others too. You'll have to contact the coven your staff at the other shop are in, they must have some power, and..."

My heart skipped a beat, and Carolyn was staring at Mum. *Shit!* I had to shut her up somehow.

"Mum, calm down, you're...talking nonsense." I turned back to Carolyn. "I'm sorry. I think she's gone over the edge a bit – you know, the shock."

"It's okay. I always had my suspicions about the two of you, and now Jacqui's confirmed it. You're witches right?"

I stared at her, and within moments, her aura deepened to a rich magenta. Though it seemed to have an odd, grainy feel about it. "You too? How do you supress your aura like that?"

Carolyn finished making the tea and poured three cups, seating herself at the breakfast bar opposite us. "I'm not a witch. I'm fairy – fae if you like. Hiding ourselves is one of our survival talents. It serves us well. The down side is that in doing so, we are unable to see the auras of others. That's why I've not seen yours."

My mind skipped back to the conversation at Joy's when Mum first came back into my life – when she'd shown up at the door with Aunt Ellie.

'Next you'll be telling me there are vampires and fairies.'

'Don't be silly, Kitha, of course there are no such things as vampires,' said Aunt Ellie. I'd meant to pursue that with Joy, but events took over, and it slipped my mind.

"You're a fairy?" Despite the current situation, I couldn't help immersing myself in wonder. She always looked, well ordinary I suppose, now though, she changed right before my eyes. Her chestnut hair, thickened, lengthened and shone. Her eyes became wider. Her ears developed pointed tips that curled sideways a bit, her clothes were hanging off her as her whole body slimmed to a perfect ten, *whoops, the Beautiful South song suddenly intruded in my brain,* quite frankly she became a whole different species. I couldn't stop staring, but when I finally turned to check on Mum's reaction, she didn't look at all surprised. "You knew?"

"Of course. Why do you think I led us here?"

We'd discuss that later. For now I shifted my gaze back to Carolyn. I had so many questions, but she held her hands up anticipating my interrogation.

"First things first. We need to get you both to safety."

"We?"

"I've called the others."

"When, How?"

"Never mind that now. We have a safe house. The wards on it should be strong enough to hide you even from a warlock. At least I hope so."

Two hours later we were ensconced in a log cabin in the woods. There must have been twenty fae there. I didn't know if I'd met any of them before as they were unrecognisable. I couldn't even see the Carolyn I knew in the face of the fae she'd become.

By the way, I'm going to call them fae, hope that's okay by you, because fairy doesn't work for me. In my head, it conjures up images of tiny people with wings, pretty skirts, and wands. I just couldn't reconcile the doll on top of the Christmas tree with these human-sized, if beautiful, creatures.

All this was great, but it was just a temporary fix. Somehow, we were going to have to resolve the problem – That is, I would have to resolve it. Mum had no resistance against my dad. I said as much to the people...beings... whatever they were.

One of them approached. "I'm Bethany. I'm a solicitor. I can help with getting a restraining order put in place, though I fear your mother is correct. It will not be enough."

Confused, I scanned Bethany up and down. I'd been kind of rendered speechless, but I really had to deal right now.

"Solicitor?" I must have sounded like a moron.

"In my human form, yes. You've probably seen me around, and I've been in your shop a couple of times for soap and candles."

I stared at her like an idiot as she continued.

"Now, you have to understand, we can't hold the wards on this place for long, and besides, we all have lives to live, as indeed do you and your mother. Kitha, I believe you are going to have to confront him. You have power, and we can lend you a little of ours too, and that of a few friendly witches we know, but it may not be enough. This warlock is not known to us, and as they draw their power from an outside source, who knows what they can tap into. You are going to have to appeal to him as his daughter, and only call up your power if there's no other way."

The butterflies in my stomach were making me feel a little sick. My breathing came hard, and I went weak at the knees – *funny, I'd always thought that was just an expression, but it actually happened.* I was glad I was already sitting as I think I'd have fallen otherwise.

"How can I possibly be anything like a match for him?"

Mum finally found her voice. "With only a little help from me, you sent him scooting across the beach. It was quite impressive."

"I took him by surprise, that's all. He'll be ready for me next time."

"Nevertheless, confront him you must. Otherwise you'll never be free of him," said Bethany.

CHAPTER 19 – IMBUING POWER

The next morning, the fae gathered round me. Each in turn laid a hand on my head and muttered something I couldn't make out. Their voices were right there next to me, yet somehow so far in the distance, I simply couldn't make out what they were saying however hard I strained to do so. As each fae touched me, a little fizzle of energy eased its way from my head and down my body. Two witches I'd never met before came in from the kitchen. Each took one of my hands. Warmth crept up my arms, then across my chest. Mum came up then and kissed my forehead. I once again felt her heat penetrate through me. I was buzzing with life energy.

"Go now before the given magic starts to dissipate," said Bethany.

I could do this, infused with energy as I was. Dad won't be ready for me, not like this. I glanced around the room, and felt an unexpected tear dampen my cheek. "Thank you." It seemed so inadequate.

Mum nodded encouragingly and I headed out the door.

Hmm. Where does a disgruntled warlock hang out? I went to the pub first, but it wasn't open yet, so I headed to the beach where I'd floored him before. No sign there. *How did he find us? He must have used magic. Can I do that?* I reached out with my mind. Thoughts of the living sea rushed into my mind. The current, the motion of the seaweeds, the shoals of fish feeding, and the delicious coolness against my skin. The urge to strip off and swim was almost overwhelming. Why? Then another thought filtered through to me. 'Don't get distracted Kitha. He's nearby. He knows you carry strong magic, and he wants to weaken you. Pull your mind back out of the sea, quickly now'. Mum's urgency penetrated past my desire to immerse myself in the surf. After one last longing glance, I turned my back on the ocean to find my dad standing about ten metres away, near the pathway. It jolted me back to the moment.

"What exactly is it you want from me Dad?"

He took a few steps towards me, and I backed up a step. He narrowed his eyes. "I'm your father. Why do you fear me?"

Good question. I don't remember any time that he'd done me any harm. In fact I hardly interacted with him at all as a child. I turned it back on him. "You haven't answered my question. What do you want from me?"

"It's more about what you can get from me. I'm your father, and a warlock. Your mother is a witch, not a very powerful witch of course, but a witch nonetheless. You have powerful magic, everyone knows it, that's why everyone wants a piece of you. Can't you see that?"

"But not you of course." The sarcasm seemed harsh, even to me.

"Sure I do. But I'm not hiding it like everyone else. I'm not the simpering mother that all but ignored you all your life until she found you had power, or the coven leader that has your sister duped, and thought to take you the same way, nor am I a fae company with their own agenda – and believe me they have one. I'm simply your Dad. I can teach you how to tap into your magic and use it properly. Yes, I want to benefit from that, and why not? But you'll benefit too, so very much. I mean, just look at you, running a shop and swimming with the fish. You can do so much Kitha. Let me show you how."

Mum's voice cut through then. 'You can't trust him. Don't forget it was him that enrolled you in that Institute. By now almost a third of the energy given freely by fae and witch alike this morning will have been lost. Act quickly while you still can.'

I'd been so distracted by the telepathy, or whatever it was Mum was using, I hadn't seen Dad approaching. He grabbed my arms. I tried to break free, but he was strong.

Mum again, 'use magic.'

I was still fizzing with energy. I gathered it all in and gave one big burst. Dad slid backwards a few metres, but was still on his feet. I tried again, and again, but he worked his way back to me looking for all the world like he was pushing his way through a gale-force wind. But then the wind stopped all of a sudden, and he stumbled forward, straight in to me, knocking me off my feet.

Sitting on the wet sand, wondering how I got there, I looked up to find my Dad holding out his hand. Without thinking I took it, and he pulled me to my feet. As he did so, something tightened around my whole upper body, restricting movement. What the hell! I stared into Dad's piercing purple-blue eyes. I couldn't shift my gaze, much as I wanted to.

The last thing I heard was Mum's cry in my head, 'nooooo.....'. Then blackness.

CHAPTER 20 – DAD'S SIDE OF THE STORY

What's with the Whole Arthurian Thing?

It was about now I came to find out that everything I learned and experienced so far was just a drop in the ocean. Somehow, I was about to get embroiled in a conflict that had raged for fifteen hundred years. The 'other world' of hidden witches gaining basic daily benefits from their little bit of magic – well that was just the tip of the iceberg…

I woke with a start in my old bedroom and sat up. *Dad had brought me home.* But it's not home to me any more. In fact it wasn't his home either as Mum had sold it, so how?… well, who cares? I had more important things on my mind to wonder at the incongruity of being here. I'm not sure this house ever felt like home to me anyway, having known so much better, both at Joy's, and since moving to the coast with Mum. If bringing me here was part of his plan to make me feel more comfortable, he'd totally misfired.

The curtains were open, but the only light coming into the room was from the streetlight across the road. *How long have I been out?* Dad had pulled my shoes off, they were beside the bed, and he'd taken my phone away, *great!*

I slid my shoes back on and headed over to the door wondering if he'd locked me in. The door opened with ease. I tried to creep quietly down the stairs, but had forgotten the

themselves as better that everyone else…"

I remembered something Penny had said at the start of all this: *As witches we consider ourselves to be more than human – better.*

"…warlocks are different. We draw our power from the spirit world. Make no mistake though, most people can't do this. Wizards and warlocks are also born different. Something about our own genetic makeup allows us to perform the rites that infuse us with magic. It's only that we pull the energy in from outside rather than from within. It's why we are so powerful compared to witches. You've already experienced how easily you can bring on a temporary drain in your power."

Something else I remembered. "Mum said a warlock is a wizard gone bad."

"Humph! She would. The difference is simple. Wizards only take what magic they need each time they want to perform some kind of magic. They don't believe it's right to – how can I put it? – *store* magical energy. Warlocks believe differently. We believe that it makes sense to have what you need 'on-tap' so to speak. It's a philosophical argument that's raged for centuries. But whatever anyone may think about that, please understand that all witches, wizards and warlocks are still human. Generally not good or evil, they fit into all the same character types as any other human being."

"Grey."

He nodded absently. "But this brings me on to fairies. Nasty creatures. They can make themselves appear human, and go about living human-style lives, but human they most definitely are not."

I was agog. "So what are they?"

"No one really knows their origin – probably not even the fae themselves. Over the centuries they have become weak. It's not really understood why, but it's because of this they hide in human form. Maybe they've mixed their blood with humans and they're all hybrids – who knows? But it's their belief that there is, at any given time, a finite amount of magical energy in the world, and that wizards and warlocks, who are increasing in numbers all the time by the way, are stealing magic from them, and they consider it theirs by right. They also think if they can destroy us all, the magic will be all theirs once more."

"That's crazy, why would Mum have anything to do with them if that's the case? She told me wizards at least are good."

Dad smiled sadly. "The fae creatures are exceptionally good liars. They don't have an argument with witches, as far as I'm aware, though they do consider witches to be their best bet when it comes to ridding themselves of my kind. Hence, without any regard for what it may do to you, they gave you what they thought was enough power to do their dirty work for them and get rid of me."

Another short spark of anger ran through me. "So you're just telling me all this now."

"You have to understand Kitha, you manifested no power at all until that unfortunate event at school. I would have spared you any knowledge of this had you been born with no magic. Then of course, since I burnt the Institute down, I've been in the nick."

My mind thrashed about trying to find a flaw in Dad's logic. Only one thing came to mind. "Growing up, you seemed to want nothing to do with me," I accused.

He slumped in his chair and put his spoon down.

The ice cream was melting in the tub. I fastened the lid and put it back in the freezer. Then I sat back on my stool and waited for my answer.

Dad bit his lip. "Honestly, I'd hoped for boys when your mother was pregnant."

I could feel my indignation written all over my face.

"Okay, sorry about that, but it's just how it was. I probably wouldn't have been quite so upset had your mother not rubbed the fact of having two daughters in my face – constantly. It drove me mad. She and I didn't get on, not ever. Not once I found out the whole marriage thing between us had been manipulated into existence by Kat – I hate that bloody woman."

Well, we've got that in common anyway.

"I DO have a temper, I'm the first to admit that, and I'd been manoeuvred into a loveless marriage. It was only after quite a lot of years that I found out she'd been as much a victim of Kat's machinations as me. By that time, however, we hated each other. The outfall of all that hate and bitterness reflected down to you. Penny got scooped up by Kat, and you – well you just got ignored and left out. I'm so sorry Kitha."

I had no idea what to say. I almost found myself feeling sympathetic towards him. Then something else occurred to me and I frowned as suspicion began to reassert itself in my mind. "Hang on a minute. When we were on the beach, you admitted to wanting to exploit my talents as a witch."

CHAPTER 21 – WARLOCK'S GRASP

Dad's demeanour changed in an instant. I watched, fascinated, as a range of emotions played across his face. He went from contrite to worried, to thoughtful and finally settled on angry.

"Okay, I'm done explaining myself to you. So here's the bottom line. There's a war going on between the warlocks and the fae. When I came out of prison and found you were content to tinker with low-level magics, and run your little shop, I was happy to leave you alone. But once your mother took over your training and talked you into moving to where there is a known pack of fae, you got noticed by the warlock brotherhood."

There's a brotherhood of them?

"We need powerful witches on our side so that we can destroy them before they destroy us."

"Whoa! Hold on a minute. I'm not destroying anyone. I'm happy with my life. If you've got some kind of war going on, you can leave me out of it. I'll just run my shop and have nothing to do with our local fairies."

"I don't think you understand Kitha. You interact with them all the time. You have done ever since you first manifested your witchcraft. You just don't know how to recognise them. They look completely different in their human form."

Well, that's true of course. Even when I saw Carolyn change right in front of my eyes, I couldn't reconcile the woman I knew with the creature she became.

"I can't see how any of that matters to me."

"Oh, it matters. You've drawn attention to yourself. I can't protect you from the brotherhood if you choose to align yourself with the fae, and you can't simply be 'on the fence' about all this. I would say that you have to make a choice, but actually you don't, because I've made it for you. You're working for me now."

I slid off the stool and leaned across the breakfast bar, squaring up to my father for the first time in my life. "Absolutely not. You can keep your stupid war. Until two days ago, I didn't even know fairies, fae, whatever you want to call them, even existed. I'm not about to do battle with them. So far all they've done is give me and Mum sanctuary from you, and loan me a little of their power. I'm going home."

I wore my indignity like a cloak and prepared to storm out of the house, but my dramatic exit was pulled up short by the seals Dad had put on the doors.

He waited for me to realise I couldn't get out.

Then I strode back into the kitchen. "Open the damn door," I yelled.

Dad's anger had completely dissipated as mine had risen. Now he was a picture of patience and tolerance – it didn't suit him. "You seem to imagine you have a choice. I tried to do this the easy way. I've explained the situation and rather hoped you'd work with the brotherhood voluntarily, but work with us you will, whether you want to or not."

The fear I'd felt when I first went to confront my Dad on the beach, just yesterday, came back – and then some. It was like a bundle of feathers floating down through my body that then settled in the pit of my stomach. I wanted to throw up, externalise the dread, but I couldn't even muster that up.

"You can't do this to me. You can't force me to cooperate," I said.

"That's where you are wrong. Now, I suggest you get some sleep. Tomorrow morning you'll meet the brotherhood."

CHAPTER 22 – THE BROTHERHOOD

I could hardly believe I was thinking this, but where was Penny when I needed her. If only I could get a message to her, perhaps she could bust me out of here, just like she did from the Institute. Maybe Mum will contact her. It was a thin thread of hope, but at least it was something. I knew one thing for certain, I wouldn't be waging a war – not for anyone. All my efforts would be bent on escape.

I was expecting to be taken to some great Hall, where intimidating men would peer down at me from a wide dais while I shivered in fear and shock beneath their gazes. Instead we went to the pub. It had only just opened for the lunchtime session, yet three men and one woman chatted around a table in the corner of the lounge bar. *So what's with the whole 'brotherhood' thing then – here sits a sister!* We joined them and Dad introduced me like it was just any old jolly at the local.

Damien was the oldest, maybe seventy-ish. *Damien – wasn't that the devil child in The Omen film?* Then there was Cassandra, Philippe and Cain. *Are they having a joke with me? Okay, these names, individually, aren't that odd, but altogether, they seemed a bit demony-obvious to me.* These other three were more like my dad's age – perhaps mid-fifties or so. Cassandra had long, thick, grey hair that she wore loose about her shoulders. With that and her high cheek bones, she looked pretty stunning for a woman of her age. Philippe and Cain seemed to be a couple, though I wasn't too sure.

I decided I wasn't going to beat about the bush, so I just came right out with it. "So, you guys are all warlocks and you want me to kill fairies for you – right? Well here's the news – not happening."

They all stared at me.

I folded my arms and stared back, glad to be a in a public place – even one with no other customers.

Finally Cassandra spoke. "Alexander, why don't you go and order Kitha a drink while she and I go for a little walk in the beer-garden?"

I shrugged, turned to my dad and said, "White wine spritzer," I demanded. Then I pushed my chair back and stood. Cassandra linked arms with me, whether in a friendly gesture or to stop me from bolting, I wasn't sure. The pub garden was quite long and had a number of tables and seats arranged on their own little patios all down one side, and a little stream water-feature leading to a pond down the centre, with a bench beside it. She led me there and we sat.

"I understand why you are reluctant to help us Kitha, so I want to tell you my story before you dismiss this whole thing. Would you be open to listening?"

She seemed so reasonable, I could hardly refuse to listen, though I knew whatever she said would not change my mind about engaging in mystical war between the warlocks and the fae. "Sure," was all I said.

Cassandra smiled. "First of all, please call me Cassy."

Ah. The bonding thing. What next? The hard luck story I suppose.

"Okay, Cassy it is. Please continue." I could hear the impatience in my own voice, and Cassy winced just a little.

She sighed, but began her story anyway. "I'm a witch, just like you, well actually not like you. My witch magic is very limited."

I gazed at her. *Didn't see that coming, and why can't I see her aura?*

"Also, just like you, I had no idea until I saw my mum

attacked by local coven members for being a rogue witch. I manifested my first act of magic by making the wood-axe fly across from the shed and bury itself in the leg of one of the witches. There was blood everywhere. I thought I'd killed her, but she survived – though she has a permanent limp. It was such a shock. I thought I was some kind of monster. After that everything changed. Like you, I had a witch for a mother and a wizard for a father. Unlike you, I wasn't packed off to be a lab rat."

I was flabbergasted that this woman's life story was so like my own. Also, it was clear she'd heard my story, and wasn't overly impressed by my dad's role in it.

Cassy continued. "I didn't want to be a witch, not after what I did. I wanted none of it, but my parents convinced me to accept training so I could control my talent and not harm anyone again – unless I wanted to. Of course, I didn't want to. Both my parents were good people. My father was adamant he would remain wizard and not go down the route of the warlocks." Cassy sighed and briefly turned her thoughts inward before resuming her story "It was just as I was really getting to grips with my talent, I encountered a pack of fairies. They befriended me and convinced me they were benevolent creatures. I spent quite a bit of time in their company, and slowly but surely they extracted information about my father and his work, his life, his general comings and goings. They'd convinced me they were secretive by nature, and thus convinced me not to tell anyone about them. Not even my parents."

A tear rolled down her cheek, her shoulders stiffened and her voice hushed almost to the point where I couldn't hear her.

"Then they struck. They attacked my father while he was out for one of his regular walks in the park. He tried to fend them off, but he had no power as wizards only draw their magic from the spirit world when needed and by invoking rites. He couldn't do this in an instant of course, and they killed him. Made it look like a heart attack."

I gasped and stared at Cassy. I could hardly believe what I

was hearing.

"You have to understand Kitha, I'd always trusted that my father's assertion that wizardry was the way, and warlocks were bad was absolute truth. The fact is, if he'd embraced the way of the warlock and stored up a bit of magical energy, he could have fought them off. He'd be alive today. This was when I decided to become a warlock myself. I can use both natural witch magic, and warlock magic. This makes me very dangerous to them, especially as my warlock magic masks my aura."

Oh, well that answers that question anyway.

"They've already tried to attack me twice. Also, fae magic isn't all that powerful. They think this is the fault of the wizards and warlocks, and are determined to kill us all, believing this will increase their own magical powers. It's nonsense of course, but this is what they think. We didn't start this war, Kitha, but if they are going to impose it on us, then we intend to win. Also, just remember, they are not even human. Their time is past. They're not meant to still exist. All we want to do is set things right again."

"What do you mean they shouldn't exist?"

Cassy chewed her bottom lip as she studied my face. She sighed then and stood up. "Come on, let's get back to the others and enjoy our drinks. Damien is probably the best one to explain the nature of fae creatures to you. I'm highly biased when it comes to fairies. You'll get a more balanced account from him."

My mind was in turmoil. My own experiences led me to believe Mum was a victim, not just of Kat, but also Dad, that warlocks were bad – especially Dad, that most witches were basically okay and that fae were harmless, largely benevolent people trying to make their way in the human world. Yet now, after hearing Cassy's story, and taking into account she's a witch turned warlock, I was left totally confused. Was everything I'd come to understand a lie? Would Mum have ignored me and Penny for the love of the sea? Did the fae just give up a small precious amount of their diminished magic so I could vanquish one of their enemies – Dad? As for my parents, both of them were happy to leave me alone in the Institute, for a whole year. Only Penny made the difference and got me out, but was she just doing Kat's bidding? If only Joy were still alive. She'd have the answers for me.

Cassy and I sat back at the table in the lounge bar with Dad and the other the warlocks. A few more customers had come in for drinks and to order early lunches whilst we'd been outside. Two blokes at the bar with pints in front of them, a couple getting all touchy-feely in the inglenook, and a group of four, maybe two couples, at a table in the bay window.

I glanced at Dad. He was studying me closely with a half smile curling his lips. "What?" I asked.

He nodded in satisfaction. "You are already a warrior at heart Kitha. In moments you've clocked all the people in the bar – how many, where they are sitting, and what their relationships are."

"How the hell do you know what I've 'clocked' as you put it?"

"We're family. We're attuned to each other."

"You weren't very tuned in to me when I spent all that time languishing in the Institute." *Did he just wince?* "Anyway, I'm a people-watcher – that doesn't make me a warrior."

I turned to Damien. "Cassy says you'll tell me why the fairies aren't meant to exist any more."

Damien glanced quickly at Cassy, who shrugged in return, then bent his full, disturbing gaze, and somewhat animated eyebrows towards me. "Okay, it's a bit of a lengthy tale, but you deserve to understand where we're coming from in this matter. I'll get another round in, and some nibbles. Same again everyone?"

We all nodded.

Damien settled back into his seat as he began his tale. "I assume you are familiar with the Arthurian Legend?"

I stared at him. *Seriously?* I raised my eyes and blew air out of my purse-lipped mouth.

"If you're not interested..."

I spread my hands in invitation. “No please. And yes, I’ve read a number of versions.”

“None of them are true. The period is commonly known as the Dark Ages. It’s generally considered this because little is known about it. The Romans, as you probably know, brought order to our land – built roads, sturdy fortifications and other buildings, baths, and so on. There was also structured governance. When they left our shores, after the sacking of Rome, the land sank into chaos. Old rivalries reignited, society fractured. The term ‘King’ was taken up rather loosely, and used to describe pretty much any tribal leader of the time.”

“So King Arthur – just a pumped up gang leader?”

“Humph! Hard to know. I don’t think Merlin would have bothered with him if he was a nobody.”

“Merlin? Seriously?”

“This is the whole point Kitha. Merlin was a wizard turned warlock. His fight with Morgan Le Fae precipitated the conflict between the warlocks and the Fae. The so-called Crystal Cave was actually a wall of ice generated by Morgan that was almost Merlin’s undoing. The magic she used in her attempt to bring Merlin down may have triggered the mini ice age that is well recorded at the end of the fifth and beginning of the sixth centuries. The warlocks believe this abuse of magic was the cause of the loss of Fae power, and thus should have been the end of the Fae altogether. However, Morgan’s death was never recorded, and it’s now our belief that she drew on the spirit world, much as we do now, to resurrect Fae magic – a further abuse. No one knows how many of them exist now, their power, or lack thereof, is so watered down we can’t detect them, plus we think they have mated with humans over the centuries, thus diminishing their magic even further.”

I stared at each of the warlocks in turn as I cogitated this story. I finally landed on Dad. “So do you really think an alleged argument between two – may-not-have-existed – legends from fifteen hundred years ago justifies all out war with a group of people that you claim aren’t human, yet may be in part, if, as you say, they *mated* with humans. Are you people all completely crazy?"

Dad sighed and turned his attention to Cassy. "I told you so."

I'd had enough of this. "Okay, this is what I propose. I've heard your side of this story, incredible as it seems to me, now I want to hear theirs. You need to let me go back home so I can talk to Mum and the fae I met before.

They all glanced at each other around the table, then seemed to come to an unspoken agreement.

Finally Dad spoke. "Agreed."

CHAPTER 23 – THE FAE

I must admit, I didn't expect them to agree. I sidled out of my seat, looking sidelong at Dad in case it was a trick of some kind. I backed part way to the door, then turned and bolted.

Mum flung her arms round me. "I was so worried. What happened?" She put me to arms length and scanned me up and down.

What does she expect to see? Have I grown another head or something?

"I'm fine. I need to talk to the fae. Can you arrange that?"

"Well yes. I suppose so, but are you going to tell me what's going on first? How did you escape?"

"They let me go."

"They? Who's they?"

"Dad took me to the pub to meet up with some other warlocks." I went on to describe the whole encounter.

"Hmm. Well, I've met many fae in my life and I've never had cause to think of them as violent in any way. Yes they're angry with the warlocks, but they only have weak magic and are no match for them. That leads me to wonder why they would want to recruit witches to their cause. Warlocks are still powerful enough to prevail if it came to blows."

Mum had a valid point. *If the warlocks are so much stronger, why do they need me?*

We were back at the cabin in the woods. There were now maybe thirty fae gathered. Again I found myself wondering how many I'd met before in their human form. As fae they were so completely different. They appeared a little ludicrous in their human clothes. They were quite a bit smaller as fairies, so their clothes hung loosely about them.

Bethany saw me looking. 'That supercilious smirk doesn't suit you Kitha."

"Sorry. I didn't mean..."

"Never mind that now. You've summoned us here. Please explain."

Bethany's sharp tone surprised me, but not so much as her turn of phrase. "What do you mean 'summoned'?"

"Surely you understand. If a Witch Prime calls, we have to obey."

My legs went weak. My head was shaking involuntarily.

Mum came to the rescue. "It's not certain Kitha's a Witch Prime."

Bethany turned to Mum. "We are drawn to her power in a way that doesn't happen with other witches. Trust me when I tell you – she's a Witch Prime."

I'd stopped even thinking about what kind of witch I am years ago. Life took over, and the witch in me receded – at least I thought it had. Yet for the first time, I knew with absolute certainty that what Bethany was saying was true. Despite that, I still wanted to deny it. "I don't want anyone at my beck and call." Bethany relaxed as the other fae drew closer and listened in. "We are relieved to hear you say this. We thought you were wielding your power over us."

I was utterly horrified. "Absolutely not." Just as I was about to ask them about Cassy's parents, another, more pressing matter intruded my thoughts. "That's it! That's why the warlocks want me on their side. How easy it would be for them if I were to lead you straight to them." I was horrified. All that talk of Merlin, Morgan Le Fae, and Cassy's sob story about her parents, it was all just a ruse. *But then why did they just let me go?* "Oh shit.' My eyes widened in understanding. They must have followed me. I shouted. "Quick, is there a back way? You all have to get out of here."

CHAPTER 24 – THE BATTLE

The mass panic that ensued wasn't helpful. Some of the fae reverted to their human form. Two started hugging each other and crying, some went for the window in the bedroom at the back of the cabin. There wasn't another door apparently, and Mum and Bethany tried to rally everyone into some semblance of order, while I stood looking on like an idiot. It was all to no avail. The cabin was surrounded – and it was my fault.

I went over to the front window and could see Philippe leaning on a tree studying his nails. His seventies-style feather cut hair and his slightly too long double-breasted jacket made him look younger than he was, especially at a distance. A quick scan around, and I reckoned there must be a least sixteen or seventeen of them out there, though I couldn't see exactly how many lurked to the back of the cabin, or amongst the trees. What's more, I couldn't see Dad. Yet there was no way he would be missing this party.

Around about then, I became aware of a kind of humming behind me. The fae had finally calmed down and had formed a circle. Those that had changed to human had reverted back to fairy now. They held hands and leaned forward so that their heads met in the middle. I glanced over at Mum. She was wringing her hands, her eyes wide with terror.

I had no idea what the fae were conjuring, but I decided I was probably best placed to take charge. I strode to the door and yanked it open. Dad was standing right there. I took a step back, more out of surprise than anything, but the ugly grin on his face meant he thought it was out of fear. Pushing him ahead of me, I stepped onto the deck and closed the door behind me.

As was becoming my way, I went straight to the point. "What are you planning on doing here?"

His quick laugh was as ugly as his grin. "Silly girl I told you you'd work for us, and here we all are. You led us straight to them. We can't detect them in human form you see, so we had to manipulate you into summoning them."

"You knew? You knew I would – could, do that?"

"Of course. We just had to stimulate your curiosity so that you'd just have to hear what they have to say for themselves. Then all we had to do was track along behind you. And it worked perfectly. Thank you."

I could feel my dander rising, and the stirrings of power prickling my skin. Dad felt it too.

"Do you think you can do that again? You caught me off guard last time. Witch Prime in the making you might be, but you don't have the knowledge to out-magic me, child."

'Child'? That was it. On top of everything else he'd done, he had the audacity to try to dismiss me because of my youth. The energy built and built. I thought my chest would explode, but still I held it in. When I release it, he would know just how off the mark he was. When I reached the point where I could hold it no longer, I spat the final words I would ever utter to him. "I am no child of yours you bastard." With that I let rip. I just about caught sight of Dad's eyes widening as he realised his mistake – too late. Magic of hurricane-force burst out of me, sweeping him off his feet. He slammed into a large oak trunk a good twenty metres away, and slumped to the ground. Had I killed him? I didn't know or care. I had my own problems to worry about. The sudden exudation of power left me too weak to even stand. I dropped to my knees.

"Kitha!" The door flung open and Mum was beside me in a moment. Very little else penetrated my thoughts apart from the sounds of a battle. The fae chanted, and a few warlocks dropped with strangled cries. Other warlocks, including Philippe and Damien had made it into the cabin. The last thing I saw before losing consciousness was Bethany's dead eyes in her twisted head.

CHAPTER 25 – AFTERMATH

I roused, blinking in a sunbeam through the window of our house.

Mum sat beside me, a haunted expression on her face. "Awake at last."

"What happened?" I took a sharp intake of breath as my memory of the battle came flooding back to me. "Bethany!"

Mum didn't hold any punches. "Dead. Along with seven other fae, and I don't know how many warlocks were lost."

I wasn't sure how I would ever get past this horrible moment in my life. "I led them there – to the cabin."

Mum took my hand. "Yes, you did," she said gently.

I swung my legs round and sat up.

"I'll make some tea," said Mum.

I followed her into the kitchen. I couldn't bear to be alone, not even for a moment. I was taken aback to find three women sitting around the breakfast bar with mugs in their hands. I didn't recognise two of them, and only vaguely thought I'd seen the other, maybe in the shop, but I knew they must be fae in their human form. "I'm so very sorry." It seemed such an inadequate thing to say.

"We don't blame you Kitha. This was all their doing. They just used you. You are as much a victim as our kind."

"I should have realised. When they let me go so easily I was stupid enough to believe they were being reasonable. One of them was even a witch turned warlock."

They all turned to stare. One of the women, hand shaking, put her mug down. "You mean Cassandra," she spat. It was a statement, not a question, but I answered 'yes' anyway.

"I'm sorry, I don't know your names."

"I'm Amanda, this is Mo and Bree."

Each nodded to me in turn.

Ever the one to get straight to the point. "She told me fae killed her father, and that this was what made her become a warlock."

"Kitha!" said Mum.

Amanda touched her arm. "No, it's fine. Kitha's heard their side of things, she needs to understand ours too." She turned to me then. "It's true that we killed him."

My heart skipped a beat at this open confession. "But he was a wizard, not a warlock, why?"

"This is true – sort of."

"Explain please, because I'm at a loss to understand."

"You are aware that both wizards and warlocks call in their power from the spirit world. The only difference is the warlocks take the magic in excess. They kind of store it so that it's immediately to hand when they decide they need it."

I nodded, wondering what was coming next.

She came in from a different angle. "Though we can pass as human, and have had to do so for the last fifteen hundred years, we, the fae are not human. Not at all. The spirit world is our realm. It's where we come from, and where we have endeavoured all this time to return to. As our power diminishes with time, our chances of going home become less and less, and they are responsible for that, by stealing our source of magic."

I was incredulous. "And you believe this justifies killing someone?"

"John, that was Cassandra's father's name, was a leader amongst the wizards – even the warlocks looked up to him. He was an intelligent man, with a strong insight into how the calling and use of power from the spirit world works. Once he realised that, if the fae return home, that power would no longer be available to them, he made it his business to inform all of his kind, and to lead them in a campaign to stop us, by any means."

I was getting angry now. "I repeat, do you think this justifies murder?"

There was murmuring from the other fae behind me. I flashed an irritated glance at them – I'd almost forgotten they were there. I then turned to look at Mum. If she'd been with the fae on this, I don't know what I'd have done, but I was relieved to see her staring at Amanda with the same look of shock and disgust that I knew must be written all over my face. But I still wanted to hear the rest. What Damien had talked about came back to me. I swivelled back on my stool to look at Amanda. "So you said you've had to do this for fifteen hundred years. Does that have something to do with Merlin and Morgan Le Fae?"

Amanda's tight shoulders eased, like she thought she was winning me over to her case – she wasn't.

"Yes, it certainly does. Merlin was the first wizard to turn warlock. When he realised the power he could command by stealing excess magic from the spirit world, Morgan was assigned to stop him. They both tried to ingratiate themselves with King Arthur, though Arthur would have no truck with powerful women, so he favoured Merlin, and benefitted from the power Merlin wielded – our power. Merlin and Morgan battled for many years, and as Merlin became more powerful, and it became clear he would win out, Morgan took extreme measures to nullify him. She couldn't kill him, so she created a prison of ice that held him throughout the rest of Arthur's time. But her work had an unexpected side effect. It thrust the land into a cold darkness that lasted for generations. For her folly, the fae were banished to the human plane of existence, with only minimal magic – enough to force us into human bodies so that we would not be recognised. We have been working ever since to have the banishment lifted."

I struggled to believe any of this, though I had to admit, the versions from both Amanda and Damien did have their similarities. "I have more questions. Who exactly banished the fae from the spirit world? How do you even know that you belong there and what happened to Merlin? Also, Damien told me the fae have interbred with humans. Is that true, if so, do you really have any such claims?"

"Honestly, we don't really know who or what banished the fae. Some kind of higher power we assume. You have to understand Kitha, though we know we belong in the spirit world, we know nothing of it, or how we know it to be our true home. It's been so very long. As for Merlin, we have no idea what happened to him, though there was a theory that John was his reincarnation."

Ridiculous, does she think I'm falling for all this nonsense?

I'll give Amanda her due, she continued to try to address my questions. "It's true, we have mixed our blood with humans. There are very few pure-blooded fae left. I am one, as is Bree. We are not sure how many there are. Our secret lifestyles hide us from each other as much as from other people. But what else do we have to fight for?"

"Have you considered not fighting at all? What's the point? You've integrated into life here, mixed with humans for generations, and you know nothing of your own origins apart from a fifteen hundred year old legend, with no proof if any of it's true. Why not talk to the wizards and warlocks? Come to some kind of cessation of hostilities?"

Mo piped up for the first time. "And let them suck dry our remaining power, I think not. Who are you to tell us what to do?"

"Apparently I'm a Witch Prime."

Mo's face was contorted into something resembling a snarl.

I held up my hands. "Look, I don't even know what that means, and one thing I know about power and magic is that it causes more problems than it resolves. I have no interest in commanding the behaviour of fae, but neither have you said anything to convince me to take your side..."

Amanda sprung to her feet.

My hands went up again. "I'm not about to take theirs

either. If you're willing to discuss a truce, I'll help facilitate that, if not – I'm out. Decide soon, because I'm done with this." I turned again to Mum.

"I'm with Kitha on this," she said.

I let out a breath I hadn't realised I'd been holding. I smiled at her, then turned back and cast around the three fae. "Please come back here in one week and let me know what you decide."

CHAPTER 26 – EXTRICATION

When the meeting between Mum, myself and Amanda was over, and it was clear they would not agree to my proposal, I put on my best Prime Witchy voice and told Amanda that the fae were no longer subject to my authority – *like they ever really had been* – and never to contact me or Mum again.

I was reluctant to go back to see Dad, but I figured if we were to extricate ourselves from this whole ancient war, I needed to make my position clear to the warlocks too.

It took a while to convince Dad that I was not taking sides – that I didn't like or trust the fae any more than the warlocks, but once he realised I was removing myself completely from the battlefield, so to speak, he accepted it, and promptly disavowed and disowned me – well that was okay, I wanted nothing more to do with him either.

Mum and I resumed the life we'd come to love. I did question her regarding Dad's assertion that we'd lived far from the sea so that Mum didn't abandon Penny and me, just to clear the air – I wanted nothing hanging over us.

"I would have spent more time at sea, that much is true, but witches are nothing if not loyal to their kin. No way would I have neglected my girls. In fact, had I been able to take you to the water, I may have identified you as a witch sooner and perhaps been able to save you from the trauma of the Institute," she told me.

I believed her, and all was good.

We never heard from Dad, or any other warlock again, nor from the fae, though we did stop and wonder when we heard about a riot in the city in which a number of people were killed and injured – perhaps that was it. Perhaps the final battle had occurred. I didn't want to know, though I have to admit, I did go back and read Mary Stewart's 'The Crystal Cave' again.

CHAPTER 27 – HOME IS WHERE THE HEART IS

Mum and I had settled comfortably back into the old routines. The shop did well. I didn't abandon magic altogether. I still made a few potions and used some healing and protection spells, but nothing big. I was determined that what magic I had was only minor, and for good reasons from now on. Perhaps the Grey Witch that was Kitha was a shade paler towards White now after all.

Some years later, sitting here in the conservatory, gazing at the sea, I feel blessed in life. I have my Mum, my adopted sister, my cranky dog Bandit, and another family, I'd yet to meet in person, on the other side of the world. I had a lovely home and a thriving business. As I said, I almost never use magic, and often wondered if it really did have any influence on my life – apart from getting me into trouble – yet the routes out of those troubles have indeed led me to this moment.

Anyway, going back to Venus. I hadn't heard from her for the next three years or more. I guess the coven compromised her freedom to keep in touch, even on social media, even though she was an adult. Then one day she arrived at my door with a rucksack. Her gran had passed away, and she'd come home. She became the sister that Penny could never be, and the three of us lived well in our seaside home. Well, four of us if you include Bandit. The scruffy pooch also just turned up on the doorstep one day, and stayed. Oh, I tried to find out if there was an owner somewhere pining for him, but it came to nothing, and he became my constant companion. Mum reckoned the humble beast was my spirit guide – humble? Who was she to talk – her spirit guide was a fish!

EPILOGUE

November 2024:
I'd thought many times about the conversation with Mum and Aunt Ellie that day they came to find me at Joy's. Of course I knew about fairies now, but what about vampires? Joy was cagey on this topic, and somehow I never got to hear any more about them from her. It turned out, however, that they were real after all, that Venus knew of some in Kat and Darbie's neighbourhood. She put me in touch, and we arranged to meet up one evening. I got to the pub first and got myself a drink. A little later, the vampire walked into the bar, and much to my astonishment, he'd brought a friend, well I knew he was bringing someone along, but this was a very large, hairy friend. This would be an interesting evening – I had no doubt.

THE END...

Narrator:

With the three stories all told, and empty glasses littering the table, this most unusual evening came to an end.

The pub was mostly empty, and the bell had wrung for last orders a half hour earlier. The Landlord kept peering at the group of unlikely characters sitting at the table in the middle of the lounge bar of his pub. He'd seen it all before of course. All sorts frequented his establishment, especially witches, though he had to admit, the sasquatch was a first.

Either way, he wasn't going to try to hustle them out the door. Well, would you? One bites, another could probably crush just about anything or anyone with those paws, and the third one could probably turn you into something you really didn't want to be – like a warty toad or something slimy.

WHAT THE HELL!

THE END – no, really, it actually is the end now. Goodnight.

ACKNOWLEDGEMENTS

My husband, Stephen - ever my biggest fan and most supportive reader.

My sister Sonia for her amazing proof reading skills.

All those poor souls from my three literary groups that have to listen to me harping on about my latest bit of writing - those being: Kirkmahoe Writers, Moffat Writer Ink, and Pitch Perfect.

ABOUT THE AUTHOR

Sarah Burchett-Cook

I am an ex-academic on a mission to rediscover my magic. Fantasy has been my passion as a reader since I was a youngster, and now I'm equally passionate about the genre as a writer.

I live in Scotland with my husband and find it's other-worldly landscape and history a constant inspiration when I write. The books I've written are partially set here in Scotland., but also in other parts of Britain. I'm fascinated by the idea of parallel worlds, and go out of my way to derive ways of bringing them to life.

BOOKS BY THIS AUTHOR

Elysian Dream

BOOK 1 of the 'Elysia and Beyond' series. KIM is a kelpie agent from the realm of Elysia tasked to locate a human-fae hybrid with enough latent fae magic in their blood to restore the kelpies to their natural form – an ability snatched away by a vengeful dark fae witch. Her current project, BENJI, may be the unsuspecting donor she's been looking for.

The Book Of Tamonah (Rerurn To Elysia)

BOOK 2 of the 'Elysia and Beyond' series. When Benji starts getting frightening and dreamlike 'sendings', his girlfriend, Kim, seeks Professor's Long's help. His story has been foretold in and ancient book ionce thought lost forever. Can Kim prevent Benji from falling into darkness?

Across The Veil

BOOK 1 in the 'Rosa Chronicles' series. Rosa, a woman of mixed background – her father, a lighthouse keeper from Scotland, her mother a descendent of the long-lost, dark-haired Epiddi tribe. Rosa inherits certain abilities, (that some might call magic), and extreme long life from her mother's side, but her mass of fair locks, inherited from her father, leads a shaman to call her 'the golden-crowned child of two worlds' – a woman with a destiny written long before she was born. These two worlds are separated by a Veil that few can cross, but Rosa leads a double-life on both sides of this invisible barrier.

Printed in Dunstable, United Kingdom

66482686R00160